For Father Tom Ward,
whose *persistent* insistence on God's love
built the framework
for the character of Mother Clare.

Acknowledgements

My deep appreciation to Antonio Aja
for providing an accurate translation for the Spanish in this story.

Heartfelt thanks also to steam engineers Daniel and Marc Pavlik
for verifying the accuracy of information in this book about riverboats
and steam engines.

# *Softly the Silence*

Jean Dixson

PublishAmerica

Baltimore

First printing

ISBN: 1-59129-726-5
PUBLISHED BY PUBLISHAMERICA BOOK PUBLISHERS
www.publishamerica.com
Baltimore

Printed in the United States of America

# Chapter One

The slit in the stone wall was so small. Barely six inches wide and about three feet in height, it was a tiny opening on a circumscribed world. Catherine stood gazing outward, past the meadows to the far range of hills. Occasionally she saw people in her vista and often – as there were today – animals roamed the meadows, but neither the people nor the animals existed in the language areas of her mind.

She had not heard a voice since she was brought here a decade or more past. There were sparse lingual memories in her brain, but they scarcely exceeded words such as "momma" and "no." Had she needed to use those ancient words she would not likely have been able to voice them. Occasionally a faint murmur of sound reached her tiny room, but it was never a meaningful sound and was barely distinguishable from the silence of her life. Her name existed in her mind, but so dimly that she might have recognition memory only, and would not have been able to recall the name-word without assistance.

She had barely been tall enough to see out through the window slit when she was brought here. Long taught not to voice complaint, she had entered the room silently, and only after the heavy door closed did the tears begin to run down her cheeks. She had crumpled then into a ball, braced by the walls of a corner, and sobbed silently until she slept from exhaustion.

In the dim light of the first morning there, she had found a quilt, a chamber pot, a tin of water, a bowl of porridge and another of vegetables and a slab of bread lying near the door. Each morning since then there had been again a clean chamber pot, the water, the bowls – always old, chipped bowls with blue stripes around the rims – and the bread. While the bowl was changed daily, the water tin was only replenished. Sometimes there was a fragment of cheese with the bread. Catherine had never tasted meat.

She had worn this dress for a year or more now. She remembered the colors changing on the hillside trees when it was put on her and the trees were again blossoming into the scarlet and gold of autumn. She felt the beauty of the trees but had no words for their colors, as she could not have identified "brown" as the color of her dress. She remembered when her old brown dress was too small and the caretaker took it off and replaced it with this one, but the transaction had been wordless, and the food was always brought while she slept. The dress bagged shapeless from her shoulders; should it need replacing sometime with a larger size it would be a very long time.

Catherine spent long hours gazing out from the window slit, but her mind was curiously quiet. With no language to remark the sights below her, she stored vague memories of color and movement only. The house, of buff-colored stone, commanded the top of a river bluff. Had Catherine been imprisoned in the front, the opposite side of the house, she would have seen the mighty Ohio, although there would have been little suggestion of the power of the waterway from that distance and height, and she could have seen the burgeoning city mounting the far bank of the river.

But she knew not the existence of the river or the city. Had she been able to see the house itself, she might have been impressed with its massive grace, with its stables and cottages and other outbuildings sprawling around it, but she had no dream of the scope or substance of her environment. Had she been outside looking in she might have noted the generous expanse of windows about the house except for her single, cramped window slit. And except for the person who daily provisioned the room's occupant and one other, those who inhabited and served the house gave little or no thought to the room or its occupant. Indeed, only a few of the staff now here had known of her existence and only the caretaker and that other knew she remained here. The door to the room was kept carefully locked so neither the occupant nor any unauthorized other could cross the boundary.

The world outside the window turned brown, then briefly white, and was brown again and pale green. Catherine had observed the cyclicity of the changes and awaited the deepening of the greens without being able to form word-thoughts about the changing conditions. She did observe that life outside the window was different now. Carriages had been frequenting the lane leading to and from the stone house for three days. Vehicular traffic was usually rare. She was gazing toward the ridge west when the door opened.

Catherine did not react to the sound of the door at first. It took moments to grasp the notion of a sound, and when she had done so in her sensorially-impaired fashion, she turned slowly toward it. She was amazed at the vision of a woman framed in the doorway. Tall and regal, her silver hair was piled atop her head and her simple dress, gathered at the waist, was black, her face framed in a white lace collar. Her eyes were red-rimmed and sunken; the area beneath the eyes discolored darkly.

"Come here, Catherine," the woman commanded. "It's all over now. You're free."

Catherine stood immobile, her face open in shock and more than a little fear. Something stirred deep within her brain at the word "Catherine" but she was unable to absorb or define its meaning.

"Come!" the woman ordered sharply. "He's dead and this nonsense is over now. You are to come with me immediately."

In response to the sharp tone, Catherine shrank against the wall beside her window, eyes wide now in shock and terror. A quiet whimper began as the woman took steps toward her, but the old prohibition against noise quickly silenced it, and Catherine rather simply held her arms around her upper body and ducked her head as shield against the blows her body remembered though her mind did not.

~ ~ ~

James yanked mightily on the towline, hoping to set the boat afloat again from the sandbar. He and the men helping were snapped up short and stumbled as the slack came out of the line without moving the boat. Regaining his feet James plunged back into the shallows beside the boat and grasped the shovel lying on the deck where he'd left it.

He felt the futility of trying to dig the boat off the sandbar even as he shoved the blade of the shovel into the sand under the boat. "Here!" he commanded. "You men shove those bales portside and then come down here with me. If we can't dig it out or pull it off maybe we can tip it enough to get the keel free." The shifting of the heavy bales of cotton and tobacco altered the pitch of the deck by about three degrees, and the men in the shallows starboard put their shoulders to the task.

"Now!" commanded James. The boat rocked slightly but remained grounded. "Again! Harder! Now!" he ordered. Finally, with the increased effort, the boat slid off the sandbar. Stumbling about to get their footing again, the men pulled from the water those few who had lost their balance and tumbled into the deeper water of the river. Grasping the towline, James hauled himself back onto the deck and pulled the others up after him. They'd make New Orleans yet.

*Why do I do that?* he thought. *I know the river is a living thing that changes from day to day, sometimes more often. That's what I love about it. About them.* He felt again the jagged twist within his inner self as he glanced aft and saw the name *Marian Dee* in curly-cued letters across the base of the

7

pilothouse above.

Struggling to keep his face impassive, he climbed to the Texas deck, to his cabin to don dry clothes. He'd known of her death these long years and it still gripped his soul like a vise to think of her. Perhaps he'd visit her grave the next time he passed there. Perhaps that would help him close that joyous, agonizing chapter of his life.

Few pilots navigate all of the three principal rivers of the continental catch basin; most specialized in only one river or a few pilots on two. James was among only a handful who were expert on all three rivers, knowing their underlying structure and with the ability to read them from moment to moment.

Only an experienced and expert pilot could guide a boat safely. And *attentive*, James scolded himself. He had allowed his attention to be diluted by that old memory. They'd make New Orleans if he kept his focus on the river, and didn't allow his mind to stray as he'd done just now, stranding them on a sandbar that a green apprentice would have seen and avoided.

~ ~ ~

Catherine stood, arms still clasping her upper body, in the center of a room cluttered with things. A second woman had joined them, this one of dark face and hands, with a white apron atop her deep blue dress. This second woman, undoing the buttons on the girl's dress, divined Catherine's terror and began to croon to her in a deep rich alto. The words had no meaning for the girl but the quiet rise and fall of the voice with the warm touch of the woman's hands had a soothing effect and Catherine allowed the brown dress to be taken from her.

Having been bathed as best was possible, considering her labile emotional state, Catherine was wrestled into pantaloons, which she had not previously worn, and a white petticoat was slipped over her head. A black dress, much like that of the woman standing in front of her but lacking the white collar, was then put on her and buttoned.

The dark woman rested her hands gently on the girl's shoulders; Catherine felt the warmth and looked into the woman's eyes for the first time, puzzled by the feeling but not alarmed by it.

"That will do," the tall woman in black approved briskly. "She is not to go to the funeral or the burial. She has already eaten. She will sleep here tonight. You are needed in the kitchen as soon as you have her ready for bed," and so saying, the woman left, snapping the door firmly shut behind her.

Having dressed her, the dark one then removed the dress and petticoat and slipped a baggy gown over her head. The dress and petticoat were hung in a tall box near the windows. "Good night, Catherine," she said. Then she was gone also. Catherine – those sounds did rouse something familiar from within her – felt the fabric of the gown. It was soft and fuzzy. The feel was wrong and the look was wrong. Catherine in her longest memories had worn nothing but brown dresses of cheap cotton. This gown was white and made of flannel.

She investigated the dress they'd put on her. It felt and looked different from both the gown she wore and the dress to which she was accustomed. The fabric was fuller, heavier to the touch than the brown dress she remembered. The color was wrong, darker than her custom.

She looked at the window. Curtained now against the coming night, she'd seen the trees and sky through its glasses before the drapes were pulled. She had no memory of being shut in by drapes. Her slit of a window was always uncovered. She'd missed the slash of the dropping sun this evening as it shone briefly through the slit. Perhaps the evening was clouded, preventing the shining. She had words for neither cloud nor shine, but she knew the practical aspects of both.

Walking to the window, she shrugged a drape back, as she'd seen the dark woman tug to close it over the window. It was still dusky light outside, but – the terror rose in her again. She saw trees outside the window, but they were cedar, balsam, elm. Not the towering oaks that she knew. The ground beneath the trees was dotted with gold and bronze spots. There were no flowers on the west side of the house. Her trees and pasture were gone.

As she walked away from the window, leaving the drape askew to light the room, she looked about her at the various furnishings of the room. The bed took a major portion of the space, lofty with posts rising up from the corners and broad with a rose satin spread. She fingered the satin, pleasured with the soft slickness of it. With a hand still on the satin, she half turned, and gasped, drawing both hands into fists tucked up against her chest and shrinking backward.

Facing her was a girl, dressed also in white, with her fists drawn up in front of her. Instinctively, Catherine thrust her left arm out, palm spread, to protect herself. The other girl did likewise. With held breath, Catherine gazed at her. The other girl didn't move or seem to breathe either. Catherine took a tentative step backward, but her leg encountered the baseboard of the bed.

9

Watching the other, she realized there was a bed behind that girl also. Peering closer, the other mimicked her movement. Finally, Catherine crept forward until she could see that there was window-like glass in front of her. Reaching out, her hand was met by that of the other, but she felt only glass. She moved aside and peered behind the glass, but there was only wall there.

She settled then into the corner of the room to the right of that glass and gave way to her exhaustion. Her back was jammed as tightly as possible into the joining of the walls, her knees pulled up to her chest, feet braced to support the knee-up position, and arms about her knees. The fireplace of the room loomed black and empty, and she was chilly in the room now with the warmth of the day gone, but her quilt was not in evidence. She was too frightened to risk pulling the satin comforter off the bed, not remembering the function of a bed.

She made no sound, but tears of despair rolled down her cheeks. Minutes passed and despite her need to stay alert in this strange place, her head began to bob. A clock struck somewhere in the house, but she didn't hear. Her head had dropped to her knees and her legs slumped against the wall to her left. She slept, her sleep haunted with leaping attacks on piles of varicolored leaves, a warm feeling of comfort against a larger body, terror attending the appearance of a tall figure, pain, and utter devastation in an empty room.

The dark woman entered the room a bit past sunrise. She stared in amazement at the sight of Catherine crumpled in the corner, still asleep. "Catherine," she spoke gently.

"It's time to get up now. Why did you sleep on the floor?"

Catherine awoke into terror again. Abruptly sitting up and pushing with her bare feet she forced her body as far back into the corner as it would go, clasping her arms about her upper body as a shield. Again, the whimper started but ended almost in the same moment.

"You're afraid of me, aren't you, honey?" the woman spoke. "It's all right. I can wait a bit for you to get used to it." Her voice began again the melody that had comforted the girl yesterday. She twitched back the drapes and coaxed the fireplace into warmth with her skilled fingers. Seeing the girl still wide-eyed afraid, she settled into the rocker near the fireplace and continued the melody.

Catherine relaxed slightly as the pleasant sounds continued and the woman did not approach her. She watched, looking puzzled, the woman sitting in the chair. There was something calling her about the back-and-forth, back-and-forth of the chair, but her sensory-deprived mind could not assign real feeling nor any function to the action. Her slitted room had contained only the implements for eating and elimination and no furniture. She finally became comfortable enough with the woman in the room to express her curiosity with a gesture toward the other.

"What, baby? Me? I'm Sarah. Sarah," she repeated, placing a hand on her chest. Catherine frowned in bewilderment. "Sarah," the woman iterated. "Can you say it? Oh my goodness. They didn't talk to you up there, did they? And none of us even knew you were there." She rose from the chair and approached the girl, sinking onto her knees beside her. The child tensed but did not draw away.

"Sarah," she said again, patting the flat of her hand against her chest. Catherine made no effort to repeat the name-word after her. "Do you know your own name, baby?" she mused. "Catherine," she said, fingertips to the girl's shoulder. "Catherine."

The girl's eyes widened a bit at her name word and a frown of puzzlement creased her forehead, but she still made no attempt to respond verbally. Sarah considered the possibilities briefly and then gently grasped the girl's hand and held it to her throat.

"Catherine," she repeated. "Catherine."

The girl looked bemused as she felt the vibrations of the other's voice. Sarah then took Catherine's hand and held it gently against her own throat. "Catherine," she spoke. "Catherine."

Sarah repeated the process three times before Catherine attempted to vocalize a sound when her hand was again returned to her own throat.

"Kkhaaa," she voiced tentatively.

"Yes!" Sarah responded with a warm smile. "Caaa-therine."

"Sarah!" The woman's voice rose peremptorily from the hallway as she opened the door. "Whatever are you doing on the floor, Sarah? And why is she," gesturing at

Catherine, "on the floor and still in her nightgown? I see you've already made up her bed."

"No, Miss Emily. I found her on the floor in the corner asleep. She didn't sleep in the bed."

"What kind of savage would sleep on the floor when there's a perfectly good bed in the room!" Miss Emily exclaimed. "I knew she was going to be trouble when we let her out but it's too much bother to take care of her in the attic room. I don't know whatever we will do with her."

"Miss Emily," Sarah rejoined tentatively, "did she have a bed in the attic room?"

"No, of course not. She was being punished."

"I don't think she knows what a bed is for, Miss Emily," said quietly. "She was just a little bit of a girl when she was put in the attic..."

"Perhaps," Miss Emily proclaimed impatiently. "I don't want to be bothered with her at table. Get her dressed and feed her in the kitchen or up here." Miss Emily swirled out the door and was gone as quickly as she had spoken.

"Come here, lovey," Sarah coaxed Catherine, "Let's get you dressed for the day."

Catherine faced again her bewilderment when she looked out the large window of the room she'd been placed in immediately after her removal from the attic. She found the clutter of furniture in the room disquieting, but the view out the window robbed her of the last bit of familiarity from her prior life. Agitated, she tugged at Sarah's sleeve and pointed out the window.

"What is it, child?" Sarah asked. "What do you see?"

Catherine clutched her arms about herself and rocked back and forth. Still gazing out the window, she began to moan quietly but piteously.

"Sweetheart, I don't know what's wrong. I don't know how to fix it if I don't know what the problem is."

Still holding herself with her right arm Catherine freed the other and tapped at the windowpane, still rocking and still moaning. Her agitation did not still, as Sarah put an arm about her shoulders. She continued to tap on the pane and gesture toward the view outside.

"Ah. The attic room is on the west side of the house. This room is on the south. Is that the problem? You can't see what you're used to seeing? Here, lovey. Take Sarah's hand and let's go see. Everybody's downstairs now so we can walk about up here."

Taking the girl's hand gently but firmly, Sarah opened the door and led her out, turning left in the hall. Catherine hung back but Sarah continued to speak to her in soothing tones as she led her toward the window at the end of the hall. "Here, baby. Is this it?"

Catherine's balled up body relaxed slightly as she gazed out of the window toward the meadows and the range of wooded hills. Darting a quick sidelong glance at Sarah she looked back toward the familiar landscape. It was different; trees she looked across from the attic room now blocked part of her view, but where she could see past the trees hinted at the old vision from her life and calmed her anxiety.

"She's your problem," Miss Emily declared. "I'll not put up with her obstinacy and ingratitude. She's to sleep in your cottage until she can be trusted in civilized company. She'll take her meals there or in the kitchen. Had Mr. Durrant listened to me she'd be in an orphanage where she belongs. They wouldn't take her now with this kind of behavior!"

"Damn!" said Samuel when Miss Emily was gone. "They keep this girl locked up alone all these years and now she blame her for bein' what they made her. That woman has to be the coldest excuse for a human being I ever see."

"Hush!" Sarah rejoined. "Somebody might hear you! And besides Miss Emily isn't nearly as cold-hearted as that man they put in the ground this morning. Come on. I'm finished with my work in the big house for today. Let's take this little girl home with us and see if we can settle her in."

Sarah's heart had yearned over the years for a child, but her years of possibility were nearly gone and her womb had borne no fruit. She had come to love Catherine in a matter of minutes when the girl's terror and vulnerability had called to her child-lonely heart. In turn, Catherine had come to relax a bit and lean ever so slightly toward Sarah when the woman put her arms about the girl's shoulders.

They put Catherine's cot under the west window so she could see her familiar landscape and hung a sheet for a curtain to grant some privacy to both the girl and themselves.

The girl looked long at a red scarf on the table and Sarah, observing her reaction, picked up the scarf and handed it to her. "Red," she coached. "Red," said slowly, lips carefully pursed. "Red," she said again, holding Catherine's hand to her throat. She moved Catherine's hand to her own throat while saying the word yet again.

She was rewarded with a faint "rrrh" sound and smiled in reward. As Catherine tentatively offered the scarf back to Sarah the woman smiled and closed the child's hand on the fabric, saying "No, baby. You like that red color, you keep the scarf. I didn't wear it anyway. Too bright for an old black woman like me. It's yours now."

At bedtime, Catherine looked around in bewilderment. Sarah had again helped her into her nightgown, this time with Catherine trying to help, but behind her curtain there was no open place on the floor where she might sleep. When Sarah saw her puzzled look and the beginning of fear again, she sat down on Catherine's cot and patted the bed beside her. "Here, sweetie.

This is your bed. Come sit beside me and let me brush your hair for you."

The child's strawberry-blond hair had been such a tangled snarl when she was liberated from the attic that Sarah had finally cut it short. It didn't require much brushing, but Sarah judged that the child certainly needed nurturing, and brushing hair gave a reason to be close and touching. She needed also to help the girl begin to learn how to care for it herself. Catherine came near Sarah and, taking her hand, the woman drew her to a seated position beside her.

The girl wiggled her bottom tentatively on the soft surface and looked at Sarah in surprise. Her mouth jerked up slightly on the left side, as if in a tic, in response to Sarah's smile. Sarah smiled more broadly and smoothed the girl's cheek to coax the tentative smile but it didn't make it out into open expression.

After the hair brushing – brief because of the closely clipped hair – Sarah rose to her feet. As Catherine got up also Sarah said, "Here, baby. Say your prayers so you can go to bed," kneeling at bedside and resting her elbows on the bed. Looking baffled, Catherine knelt beside her, looking at Sarah with raised eyebrows as if to say "Like this?"

"Yes. Fold your hands like this..." and Sarah steepled the girl's hands, then her own. "Dear Lord Jesus," Sarah prayed, closing her eyes. "Bless this child of yours, Catherine. And bless us and help us take care of her. Amen.

"Now, honey. You lie down right here on your bed and go to sleep."

Catherine looked at her with a little frown of concentration, trying to fathom the woman's direction.

"Here." The woman pulled down the bedclothes and patted the bed for Catherine to sit. The child complied, looking at Sarah tentatively. Sarah reached down and lifted the girl's feet, pivoting her so her feet were resting on the bed. She gently pushed down on Catherine's shoulders, saying "Lie back, child. Just lie easy and let the Lord Jesus comfort you to sleep." As Catherine complied, Sarah tucked her in and bent down, leaving a lightly brushed kiss on her forehead. "Dear Lord Jesus," Sarah murmured, "I know she's only lent to us, but for however long, thank you for this child."

## Chapter Two

"Yes, Miz Emmaline. I'se laid the fire in the parlor and yo' lap quilt is folded on the arm of yo' chair. Tessie will finish the clearin' up from dinner and he'p you up to bed. Sleep well, Miz Emmaline."

Miz Emmaline merely nodded. She owed no conversation to any slave.

Martha carried the boy securely bound up in a cloth tied about her neck and shoulder. She needed to have him bound to her so her own body was free to run, to hunker down, to climb or wade. She needed him where she could easily reach him should he need anything. She'd carefully taught him not to cry aloud from the time he was born.

Mr. Jensen had sold Jimmy before the boy was born. In a rage at the loss of his prized chestnut stallion, Jensen cast about for someone to charge with responsibility. Jimmy, at about seventeen years, was the stable boy and though the laming had taken place in the south pasture, Jensen decided it must have been the boy's fault. Had he walked the pasture before he turned the horses out he might have found the mole tunnel the horse had fallen into, breaking his near front leg.

"Chain that nigger t'a the..." he hesitated. He would take great satisfaction in tearing the whip across his back. He *needed* to lash his rage out with the whip. But...but if he did that, he'd get less for him. A lot less. Even if the lash marks healed before he took him and sold him, the scars would scream that he was a problem nigger and he'd get a lot less for him. He wouldn't be able to tolerate him on the place long enough for lash marks to heal anyway. 'A course, he'd get a lot of satisfaction from whipping him dead – but... Well, hell. That just wasn't practical. "Chain 'im to the wagon," he finally ordered, flicking the whip toward the buck's face, smiling grimly when he cringed away.

The corn bags were loaded into the freight wagon, going to market in Johnson's Ferry, and Jimmy was piled atop the load and carefully chained to the heavy wagon. There were always a few slave traders wandering through, or he could be held in the jail until one did come by. The chestnut had been the best horse he'd ever had, and Tom Jensen wanted full retribution for loss

15

of the horse.

All he really required was for that young buck to be sent South, where he'd never have to look at him or deal with him again. The driver had just picked up the reins and Jensen was mounted on the bay when that house nigger came tearing out of the kitchen door, across the yard and threw herself at the wagon, clasping the ankle – all she could reach – of the buck who'd killed his chestnut.

Jensen was amazed. "Git away from that wagon," he yelled. "Git down!" The wench just clung to the buck, sobbing and slobbering, trying to scrabble up beside him. "Here! Gimme that whip back," he motioned to the overseer, who was moving to grab the wench. "I'll take care of this myself," he said in a harsh voice.

The whip slashed out. Her shirt didn't tear, but a weal of blood rose up through the fabric, tracing the path of the whip. She only clung tighter, and the whip rose and fell again, and then twice more. Now the shirt was torn and hanging in ragged pieces about her back. Her right hand faltered and lost its grip on Jimmy's sweat-slicked ankle. The buck tried to move to protect the wench but his chains prevented him. Once more the whip snaked out and found her back, again tearing both shirt and skin. The whip was pulled back, poised for yet another strike, when she finally crumpled into a heap beside the wagon. The buck atop the load was slobbering now also, screaming out curses at Jensen, tugging at his chains.

Jensen lashed toward the buck again, the popper on the end of the whip snapping just inches from the boy's face. When the whip was cocked back again he laid it then toward the off horse of the team hitched to the wagon, cracking it just above the horse's back. The big draft horse startled as Jensen yelled "Git that wagon out of here!" and the driver finally recollected himself and slapped the reins to get the near horse moving also.

The wench was crumpled on the ground, senseless, in a heap of torn cloth and blood. That should teach her to mind her own business! "Git her out of there," he ordered an older nigger. "If she dies the whip'll find you next!" He spurred the bay as he laid the reins across the right side of its neck, turning it away from the barnyard scene and sending it prancing and high-stepping after the wagon.

The night was moonless, a factor that Martha had considered in choosing it. She clutched her shawl about her shoulders, letting her feet find their own way on the well-packed trail she would follow to the river, praying that a loose dog not interfere with her passage nor raise an alarm, praying that there'd been no rain upstream to make the river too deep to walk across, praying for a tomorrow for the precious bundle she carried strapped to her chest.

She gained the river without problem and waded carefully across. When nearly to the other side she turned and waded upstream two miles or more, hoping to discourage any dog that might be set on her trail. She waded out of the water once on the south bank, then after another half mile or so struggled up onto the north bank, walking for a hundred yards or so each time and returning to the river by the same path she'd left it. Others had escaped the Jensen place, only to be caught and returned. She had listened not only to the runaways themselves – those who survived the lash or weren't immediately sold – but as she waited on table in the Jensen house, she listened to Jensen relate to his son the tricks of catching runaways. She forgot nothing of what she heard from either source.

When the river narrowed so it became too deep to continue she left the river, and continued in a general northward direction. Pausing in a wooded area a couple of miles from the river she gave breast to the boy, who had begun to wiggle but who made no noise that might draw pursuit to them.

She walked northward, or north by northeast, until the stars told her it was near dawn. She had no conception of the distance she had come, but she knew for a fact that it was already the longest journey of her lifetime for she had never before been off the Jensen place. Whether from the chill of the near dawn or simply from her fear, she shivered. She ate a piece of bread from the compact bundle she carried, and spread the shawl over herself and the child. By daybreak, she was sleeping lightly, fearful of any alarm, dug deep into a patch of gooseberry bushes well off any path. Day one of freedom was half past when she awakened, roused by the movements of the boy.

"Please, can you help me?" Martha begged of the older black woman at the clothesline. "We'se come so far and I'se had no food for two days now. If my milk dries up I won't be able to feed the baby."

Rebecca looked long and carefully at the young woman. "Where you from?" she queried. "An' where you go?"

"I'se from south of here, about 11 days' walk. And I'se going to freedom, wherever that is."

"Umm." Rebecca looked around, seeing no one to notice the young woman. "There's some's free here," she offered. "But most's not. Pro'ly be better for you to get across the Ohio. It be safer there."

"How can I do that?" Martha asked. "Can I wade across like I did the river by Massa's place?"

"No, but they's ways." Making her decision, Rebecca gestured toward the small weathered house. "Come'n here."

Rebecca set out a bowl of beans still warm from her own lunch and a slab of cornbread. "Here. You feeds yo'se'f and I goes to see 'bout the river."

Martha passed through three more houses, where she was held in seclusion in cellars or attics, before reaching the guide who would take her across the final river between her and freedom.

They crossed on a cloudy, moonless night in a small rowboat. Martha clutched Samuel tight against her, terrified of the powerful current they rode. As the boat gained the still waters on the northern bank, the man, whose name had not been told, rowed a bit further downstream. The oarlocks were muffled with old rags and the rower dug the oars deep, carefully avoiding splashing.

At a landmark not obvious to Martha, the man grounded the boat, still in silence. The man helped her out of the boat and gestured to a clump of bushes. Martha was astonished when her guide swept away a curtain of bushes with his hand and motioned for her to enter the dark hole in the earth thus revealed.

Another pair of hands reached for her as her boatman melted away in the darkness. She stumbled and found herself caught without a fall. "Here, Miz. Put your hand on my shoulder and follow me," a quiet bass voice said. When they had turned a corner, her guide opened the slides on his lantern, revealing the tunnel before them. They walked quickly a hundred yards, two, finally emerging into a small room hacked out and carefully shored, as the tunnel had been also. "This is the Baptist church," her guide said quietly, gesturing toward a doorway. "It should be safe here but I need to check for sure that no one is out this late."

He returned and picked up the lantern, saying "They ain't nobody around. I'll take you to a house where you can stay and be safe while you decides what you wants to do."

"What do you mean, 'what I wants to do'?" she queried. "I wants to be free. I wants my boy to be free! They done sold his daddy; I ain't studyin' on lettin' they have his son."

"You free now, honey," the older man said with a quiet smile. "But you gots to have a way to earn your way now that you free. *Livin'* ain't free when you'se free. You hast to have a way to earn you livin' when you'se free. Miz

Eva Mary she h'ep you think about it and finds a way to live."

And so it was that Martha came to live in the shantytown near the northern bank of the Ohio, taking in laundry and ironing to pay her keep. And Samuel grew and flourished under the protective gaze of his mother.

~ ~ ~

Samuel had smiled warmly at the child each time he'd been near her and reached out once with gentle fingertips to brush the top of her head, but she'd sensed his difference and shied away from him. Sarah stayed with the child Sunday morning and evening, allowing Samuel to go to church without her. It looked like it would be some time before Catherine was ready to see more than two or three people at the same time.

As Samuel returned Sunday evening, he tucked the bundle he carried carefully under his arm and walked quietly into the cottage. Catherine sat on a chair near Sarah at the kitchen table while Sarah relaxed with her tatting. She'd thought about how children learn to talk and so chatted about the cottage, herself and Samuel, how Catherine would learn to talk and be an ordinary girl, or anything else that came to mind.

When she remembered that she was missing church and the girl had never been, she began to talk about Jesus to the child. She was just finishing the story of Jesus feeding the multitudes when Samuel entered.

A small nose poked out of the cradle of Samuel's arms. Sarah's face lighted and she said "Yes! That might be a good idea. It's easier to trust puppies than people."

Samuel walked carefully toward Catherine, allowing the pup's head to emerge and watching Catherine's reactions.

Catherine oo'd her mouth, eyes wide. Samuel held the pup in one large hand and petted it with his other. The girl raised a hand toward the pup and looked at Samuel. He smiled and nodded, saying "This is your puppy. Go ahead and touch him." After a cautious wait, she allowed her fingertips to brush the pup's head, jerking her hand back at the soft feel of the pup's coat. Glancing again up at Samuel, smiling at her surprise, she reached forward again. That time she stroked the pup's head as Samuel had done. The pup rewarded her with an enthusiastic licking of her fingers.

~ ~ ~

Marian walked along the riverfront, looking curiously at the steamboats queued up to shoot the falls. "Why are there so many of them tied up here?" she asked Anson.

"They're waiting their turns to go through the locks. I imagine they're grateful to have the locks now, so they don't have to shoot the Falls. They used to have to allow plenty of time between them in case one of them hit the rocks and capsized," her brother responded. "They could pass by here only when the water was high. Most of them got over the Falls without an accident, but it was still dangerous. It's much better since they get the locks built. It's safer and they can navigate through here at any time, not just when the river is up."

"He's right, Miss," said the youthful redheaded man standing near them. "We could carry tons of shipping over the Falls when the water was high but we couldn't navigate the Ohio when the water level is low. More than one boat was torn up trying, when the river was almost high enough but not quite. It took an experienced pilot to be able to tell when it's safe. And then it took a little luck," he added quietly.

"Do you work the boats, then?" queried Anson.

"I do. James Mason, apprentice pilot on the *Daisy Lee*. That's us there, the second from last boat in the queue. We won't get through until tomorrow since so many are ahead of us."

"Have you worked long on the river?" asked Marian.

"Yes, about three years, Miss. I've worked the river since I was thirteen and my father died. I have seven younger brothers and sisters, so I send Ma most of my pay to support them every month. Some of the time, we work the Mississippi out of New Orleans or the Missouri out of St. Louis. May I ask your name?"

"I'm Anson Durrant. This is my sister Marian. We live here, up on the bluff. You can't see the house from here for the trees but we can see the river from there."

"We don't know the river at all as you do but we love the sight of it from our house," Marian offered.

"You're fortunate to be able to share her. Without the cold in the winters and the heat in the summers," he added with a grin.

"Do you come through here often?" asked Anson.

"We get through here once or twice a year, at least. If there's not much snow up in Pennsylvania or a bad drought upstream, we might not make it more often. This is my fifteenth trip through here and it looks like we should easily be able to make it again if we aren't delayed. This load only goes to St. Louis; we expect the water to be up yet so we can turn around. We've already got a full load contracted if the river holds for us."

"I'd like to make a trip with you," Anson stated. "Do you think I could get on as a hand on your boat?"

"Likely. We've been running short-handed all season. Would you like to talk to our captain?"

"Yes. Father said I needed to get some experience in work before I go away to college so I'd appreciate college more. I've always loved the river and I'd really like to learn more about her. I'm strong and I'm willing to work hard. Do you really think I might have a chance?"

"I do. If you're really a hard worker and willing to learn, I think Captain Marat might be very glad to see you. Shall we go now? I know the captain planned to stay on board during this queue-up."

"I'd like to... Do you think it would be all right for Marian to walk down with us and stay near the boat while I see the captain?"

"Of course. I'll be delighted to keep her company while you're on board."

Anson hesitated at the words "keep her company"; he certainly was not offering his sister to this stranger, but quick reflection assured him that he would not be gone from her long and there were numerous people busy on the waterfront; Marian would not be left alone with this man.

"Do you come down to the riverfront often?" James asked with a smile.

"No, not really," she replied. "Anson was restless today and we could see all the boats from the bluff so he decided to come down. He invited me to come for the ride with him."

"Has Anson chosen a trade yet?" queried James.

"No. He just finished preparatory school this spring and Father has been teaching him a bit about business. He's to go off to college in the fall. He'll likely come back into the business with Father when he's finished college."

"Ah. Your father is a business man then."

"Yes. He owns the company he and his brother started when they were young. My Uncle Aaron died several years ago."

"And what do you do with your time, Miss Marian?"

"I study with my tutor. Father didn't want me going out to school as Anson did. He said it wasn't safe for a young lady. Mother wants me to go to Stevens Finishing School for Young Ladies in Missouri next year but Father thinks I'm too young to be alone like that."

"Your father must be quite wealthy to provide you with a tutor," James

21

remarked.

"Oh, we're comfortable," Marian responded. "I don't think we're really rich, but I don't know a lot of people so I guess I can't judge that very well."

James was somewhat put off by the notion that the girl he faced was likely rich and with a father protective enough to have her tutored at home, but he was drawn to this young woman with the soft blond hair falling in curls about her shoulders. He would be gone on the morrow; he might as well enjoy this moment to its fullest potential.

"Would you like to learn more about river life from your safe and comfortable home?" James offered with a grin.

"Yes..." she responded cautiously. "What do you mean?"

"Would you like to exchange letters with me? I can tell you a lot about the river and you can tell me about your dreams."

Marian thought a bit. "I think I would like that but I don't think Father will allow me to correspond with a man. I'm not quite sixteen and he's very stern about what I do."

James experienced a sense of loss not proportional to the acquaintance with this soft-spoken young woman. Before he could respond, however, Anson came up the stage of the Daisy Lee, grinning broadly and almost dancing his high good spirits.

"I'm on!" he announced. "I'm to be a deckhand. I report this evening at eight o'clock in case the Daisy Lee can get through to the locks earlier than anticipated."

"Don't you think you should ask Father first?" Marian said tentatively.

Anson refused to allow his spirit to be dampened. "How can he object? He wants me to get some experience and learn how to work hard before I go to college. I expect the work on the *Daisy Lee* will be hard quite a bit of the time and think of all the country I'll get to see! I'll be much better for the experience, I'm sure."

Edward Durrant did object. His notion of summer work for his son was in the office of one or another of the businesses owned by his acquaintances or friends. His son was certainly not meant for common labor.

"You will send a message to this Captain Marat that you have changed your mind, Anson," he ordered. "I will not tolerate you dallying about the country on some river boat! You will inherit Durrant Furniture Works one day. You must prepare for that by learning management. Any slug can do physical labor."

"Father. I signed a contract to work the *Daisy Lee*. I gave my word of honor that I would report this evening at eight o'clock to begin learning my duties. I'm not afraid of hard work, Father. I've always loved the river from the time I was big enough to climb up on a chair to look out the window at it. And I really want to see this country we live in.

"I'm a man of the nineteenth century, Father. You've given me every advantage any young man could hope for. But you can't give me strength of character. I have to earn that for myself. That's why I need to make my own way now. I want to become a man like you are, Father, and I know no one gave your character to you. You worked hard and earned it. I'll come home in the fall and go to college as you wish, but I need to go now and find myself and my own life."

In the end, Edward was undone by his son's sense of honor and his courage, and the boy, not yet eighteen years of age, was allowed to follow the river to seek his manhood.

Marian was delighted when she received a letter from Anson to find an enclosure from James also. In her responses to her brother she included missives for James, and a warm friendship developed between the two who had spent scarcely an hour in each other's company.

Anson composed the letter carefully. He knew the expectations of his father for him, and while it was difficult to chose not to meet those expectations, it was easier to announce such a decision by letter than in person. In any case, it was not possible to go home for such a meeting. The Ohio had been down for a month or more, reflecting the summer drought of the lands above the Falls of the Ohio; the river was not navigable.

Edward Durrant almost cut off Marian's correspondence with her brother – and unknowingly, with James – in his pique at Anson's decision. In the end, he did not, and his daughter's friendship with James flourished into affection. It was far easier to share one's real self by mail than in person and the young couple held many values and interests in common.

A season passed and two, and finally the *Daisy Lee* was again lashed to the sturdy posts of the Indiana riverfront below and a bit upstream from the Durrant house. The young men had sent a letter by messenger for Marian and her parents on the journey upriver, when there was no time to stop. It had been easy to persuade Samuel, the Durrant groom and driver, to watch for her brother's boat to make its way back downstream. Mr. Durrant was away from home and Emily, his wife, abed with a fever when the arrival of the

*Daisy Lee* was announced.

Samuel thought only briefly, when Marian asked him to drive her to the docking area. It was shameful that the father had essentially disowned his son; it was reasonable to help the sister maintain her relationship with her brother.

Samuel, remembering the boy in his growing years, gazed at the man coming off the boat's stage. His shoulders were square and his stride firm. Surely, his father would be proud of him if he would only see him. But Edward had left for Chicago unexpectedly, only hours after the brief letter from Anson announcing his likely visit. Samuel shook his head regretfully.

The young redhead disembarking with Anson was a likely young man also. Tall and slender, he wore his red crown easily and laughed good-naturedly with Anson as they crossed to the Durrant carriage. Samuel was amazed when the young man unaffectedly offered his hand to shake when Anson introduced him to James. He readily gave consent for Marian to accompany the men as they showed James about. Anson would keep the family carriage to deliver his sister home safely while Samuel was sent home in a hired hack.

"Elizabeth!" Anson exclaimed, unexpectedly encountering an attractive young woman as they rounded a corner in the business district. "How are you? It's been a long time since I've seen you!" A few dates, carefully chaperoned by her family, were their history. As Anson had attended a prep school for young men, she had been sheltered at home as was Marian. "I'm just in off the *Daisy Lee*; I'll be here until tomorrow. May I take you walking?"

Anson had known James, now the assistant pilot on the *Daisy Lee*, for two seasons of shared work and dreams and had no compunction about leaving his sister in James' care. Nor did James or Marian object. "Mother will expect her home by nine o'clock or so..." he called to the couple as he and Elizabeth set out together.

James and Marian had shared heart-deep thoughts and feelings with each other. It took little time for them to become as comfortable with each other in person as in correspondence. They walked about for two or three hours and then enjoyed a light dinner at a riverside cafe, where they continued the process of growing affection.

The evening had clouded over and it was nearly twilight within the cover of the woods as James drove Marian home that evening. The pair was alone as Anson remained absent, apparently catching up on young local life with Elizabeth. Turning into a rutted logging road James secured the reins about the brake lever and turned to his warm young companion.

~ ~ ~

Sarah wistfully prepared an absorbent pad for her monthly flow. Another month gone and no baby started. Sarah's upbringing had been joyful with her minister father and a warmly affectionate mother. They'd lived well, comparatively speaking. The reverend received the use of a rambling big house and assorted produce from the gardens and back yards of his congregation as part of his salary, and the weekly collection, while always small, was adequate for the upkeep of that parsonage and the church, and for the other needs of Reverend Montenard's family.

Sarah's mother, Ruth, had taught the colored grammar school in the tiny Indiana town where she grew up and Sarah's father, a native of France, was a distinguished graduate of the Boston Free Seminary. Philipe had come to the United States as a youth.

After his education in Boston, he came west as a missionary to the congregations of free blacks that were developing there.

They were one of the few free black families in the area and the reverend, while supported by his free congregation, considered it his lifework to carry the Word to those trapped in slavery and he took all opportunities to reach them. He was a natural leader and in an era where few white men and almost no colored graduated high school, his education was a rare treasure for the children of his family. His graduation certificates hung proudly beside his citizenship certificate on the dining room wall.

Sarah, the oldest save one, a brother, lovingly helped with the care of her younger siblings and was privileged to have lessons from both of her parents. She had a nimble and tenacious mind, and she grew rich in the words of Shakespeare and the Bible, her parents' most common texts for the children past the primer stages of reading. The family owned a shelf of books, carefully and reverently tended. From an algebra text and an old Euclidian geometry, Sarah and her siblings learned the beginnings of mathematics, and the favorite evening entertainment of the family was to parcel out the roles and sit around the evening fire reading the works of Shakespeare. Life in the Montenard family was rich.

~ ~ ~

Samuel'd held scant hope for his pursuit of the reverend's oldest daughter. He knew well that she had surpassed his second or third grade educational level while still a young child and she could now, as a young woman, hold her own in any conversation with her comfortably correct standard English and her wide background of knowledge. He had no way of knowing that she was as fluent in French, German and Spanish as in English, gifts of her European father.

But in honesty, Samuel had to admit that no man surpassed his willingness to work and the strength of his character. He was known to smile and say occasionally that he was "raised by hand" to be an honest man. He could handle any horse and drive a pair or four-in-hand with consummate skill. He was neat – also the result of his upbringing – and he looked forward each morning to the possibilities of that day.

He was a strong and healthy twenty years old and he was in church every Sunday morning and evening and sometimes – especially since he'd been smitten with the reverend's daughter – for Wednesday night prayer meetings also. He had a fine bass voice and a love for music, which allowed him to share the choir pews with Sarah, who sang a rich, deep alto. He made it a point to always thank the reverend for the message of his sermon and he continued to smile at Sarah, hopefully.

~ ~ ~

Marian didn't miss her monthly flow that first month, and only questioned it in a desultory fashion the second month, unaware that Sarah was waiting in vain for that which never happened. Shortly after the second flow should have occurred Marian found herself nauseated in the mornings.

"Who is it, Miss Marian?" asked Sarah, cooling the young woman's brow with a damp cloth.

"Who is who?" Marian rejoined.

Sarah gazed steadily at her for a moment and realized the girl might not be aware. "Do you know that you are with child?" she asked.

"What??" Marian sank down on the side of her bed in shock. "I'm in the family way?"

"You've missed two monthly flows now, child, and you're sick in the mornings. There's not much question but that you're pregnant."

"Oh my! A baby!" Marian was unable to continue. Her eyes darted about the room as if an answer might lie there somewhere. "A baby! Oh, my! Mother and Father will be so angry! Oh my gracious!"

"Can you tell me who's child it is?" Sarah quizzed. "Do you know how women get pregnant?"

"Um... I think so. I'm not sure..."

Sarah explained briefly and simply. Marian's face flushed and she looked away when Sarah spoke of the sexual intimacy that engendered pregnancy. "Do you know who it was, baby?" she asked again. "Might it be more than just one man?"

"No!" Marian rejoined sharply. "No. There is only one man. You have to help me get to him, Sarah! Please! Please help me!"

"Who is it, honey? Whose baby is this?"

"It's James's. Anson's friend, James. He's the assistant pilot on the river boat *Daisy Lee*. Please help me get to him," Marian pleaded.

"Oh, honey. You don't even know where he is if he's on a riverboat! You have to tell your parents about this. They love you and I'm sure they'll help, won't they?"

Mrs. Durrant's attitudes about servants assured a careful boundary between herself and any help, especially one so recently come as Sarah – and one so likely to get above her station with that careful, prissy mouth of hers – but Sarah could not believe that a parent would do anything less than the most loving thing possible with a child. Sarah had been here nearly two years now, since she and Samuel were married and she moved into the cottage Samuel occupied as the Durrant family head groom and driver.

"Do you want me to help you speak to your mother?" Sarah offered.

"No, Sarah. Thank you for asking," Marian responded despondently. "You're sure I'm pregnant?"

"Yes, honey, I'm sure."

Neither Marian nor Sarah could have prophesied the rage of her parents. While Edward raged hot, Emily withdrew into frigid silence after her first shocked words. "Who let you traffic with a man?" Emily demanded. "Was it Sarah? Or was it one of the others who are supposed to take care of you and obviously did not!"

"No, Mother," Marian said timidly. "I did it myself, when I was on the riverfront in the summer with Anson. It was while you were in Chicago, Father, and you were sick," gesturing at her mother. "I knew that Anson was to be here that day and I went to meet him. I've been writing his friend,

27

James, for two years. James Mason. I met him one day when his boat was queued up to go through the locks. We became good friends and ..."

"You've been writing him *how?*" demanded Edward. "How pray tell has be been writing to you?"

"He puts his letters in with Anson's, Father" Marian replied hesitatingly. "He will be delighted and proud when he finds out we're to have a child..."

"There will be no 'finding out' for him to do!" roared Edward. "No one will be proud and certainly, no one will be delighted with this disaster. You will remain in your room for the duration and you will never communicate with that man again! I'll own no grandchild sprung from the loins of a boatman! My God! How could you let such a person..." His voice trailed off, too overcome with disgust – or perhaps an ironic remnant of protectiveness for his daughter – to complete the statement.

So it was that Anson's future letters came they did not reach Marian, and when the letter from James Mason came, telling of the death of Anson in a boating accident, Edward simply tossed it in with the pile of others previously confiscated, in the bottom, locked, drawer of his desk. Emily grieved for the loss of her son but she believed he'd simply chosen to stay away from the family after receiving Edward's raging missive about his complicity in the pregnancy of his sister. And when James came to the front door, neatly turned out, asking for a audience with Mr. Durrant, the front maid, coached by Emily, told him Marian had died and was buried long since and he was not wanted in the Durrant household.

~ ~ ~

Catherine could now say several words, the result of Sarah's patient tutelage. Sarah was amazed to hear the child greet her as "Momma" when she came in from her work in the big house one evening. They had reached a comfortable plan of daily living, with Catherine staying in the cottage by day – she'd encountered Miss Emily again one afternoon in the big house and Emily was appalled at both the girl's obvious fear and her harsh, guttural effort to speak. Either Sarah or Samuel was not far from the child and they looked in frequently to assure her of their care.

Catherine had lived in a vacuum of life before being set free at Edward's death. She was now comfortably at home in the cottage and had no fear of being left alone during the days, especially with Sandy to keep her company. Sarah and Samuel had suggested names for the dog for days until Catherine finally smiled at the suggestion of naming him Sandy. "Seems we had a dog here named Sandy once," Sam mused, "I think..."

"Do you remember your momma?" asked Sarah. "Your momma was a beautiful young woman. She was always pleasant to be around and everyone loved her. I wish she could be here now so you could see her."

"Momma?" Catherine's face showed her struggle to assimilate the concept "Momma."

"No, baby, I'm not your momma, but I'd be proud to be."

"Momma," said again, this time without the rising inflection of a question.

"All right, honey. You may call me Momma Sarah if you like, but only while we're here. You must not call me Momma in the big house. Do you understand?" Sarah was unsure how much the child understood of their conversations but it was apparent that she was bright and that her receptive language skills far surpassed her expressive ones. And it was so evident that this child was a blessing from the Lord.

Chapter Three

Mother Clare sat comfortably erect on the hard wooden chair, gazing at the tearful postulant seated across from her. "I, I'm sorry, Reverend Mother," the young nun stammered. "It's just so hard for me to learn to keep silence and be obedient. My life before I was brought here was so different! I really am trying, Mother."

"Don't fret, child," Clare rejoined. "This life *is* very different and God only asks for our best efforts. It's God you struggle to obey. We sisters are only his tools. You really are making progress, child."

The younger woman's shoulders and clasped fists loosened a bit at the unexpected praise. It was *so* hard. If the Reverend Mother only knew how hard it was. But if the Reverend Mother knew, she would not likely allow her to stay and she must not be cast out of this refuge. She remembered too well the rage that had delivered her here short months ago. She had no other home than this Carmelite monastery. Memory brought fresh tears and she bowed her head.

"I have a special task for you, child," Mother Clare said softly.

"Yes, Mother. I will do the best I can at whatever you give me to do."

"You are to take your Bible with you each morning when you go to Lauds. You are to remain in the chapel after the Eucharist. You will read the 139th Psalm each day and stay in the chapel and reflect on it."

"All right, Mother," the novice responded in a puzzled tone. "But what do you want me to do, then?"

"That is your task, child. As you know, each of us is expected to spend two hours each day in personal prayer and an hour in spiritual reading. This task will fill both of those expectations for a time. There is nothing here more important than your meditation."

Still not fully comprehending, the young nun tried once more. "How long should I do this, Mother? This will make me late for my work in the kitchen each day. And how many days should I continue?"

"You will know when you have grown into this assignment, child. And Sister Mary Elizabeth will do the chores in the kitchen while you are working at this task. You will clean the corridors and the common room during this time. That can be done at whatever time you are finished in the chapel, so you won't feel a need to hurry from your reflections.

"But... Sister Mary Elizabeth can't do my chores in the kitchen! She is the Novice Mistress. She has more important things to do..."

"Nothing is more important than our conversation with God, my dear, and His with us. That's the only reason we're here. Sister Mary Elizabeth is much more experienced at being a Carmelite than you are. She's not better than you are, nor is work in the kitchen less important than any other job here. We all work together to live together so we can pray without concern for our physical needs. Do you see, child?"

The younger nun murmured, "Yes, Mother," with a still-bemused look on her face.

"You may begin this task tomorrow morning. Now see if you have anything you need to do before supper. And smile, child. You are very well loved."

The younger woman's eyes widened in surprise. She bit back a sob and nodded, bowing her head toward the Reverend Mother and left the room. She hadn't yet learned to read the milestones but she would begin the next phase of her life on the morrow.

~ ~ ~

It was a bitter December day when the labor began. "You look like you don't feel too well," Sarah remarked when she came in to help Marian dress. "How do you feel?"

"Oh, I'm all right," Marian responded. "I just have a nagging backache that won't go away. Sometimes it stops but then it always starts again."

"How long has your back been aching?" asked Sarah.

"Since last night," Marian replied. "It woke me up a little while after I went to bed. I heard the hall clock chime midnight. It's been a nuisance off and on since then, and I think it might be getting worse instead of better. Now it feels like the backache spreads around in front and I get a cramp in my middle. I just wish it would go away."

"I think you're probably in labor with that baby," Sarah said. As she spoke another contraction started, and Marian sat on the edge of the bed, holding first her back and then her belly. "Yes, honey. That's labor. There's going to be a new person here before too long. Let me go check with Miss Emily and see what arrangements have been made. I'll be back in a bit. You just make yourself as comfortable as you can while I'm gone."

"She got in the family way without any assistance from us. She can have this evil wretch of a baby without our help too. You may go now, Sarah. I'm sure you have plenty of work to keep you busy."

Sarah held the beautiful morsel in her hands reverently. "Look, Miss Marian. Look at how beautiful your little girl is. Here. Let me wrap her up and you can hold her for a bit." Sarah had slipped in with the midwife shortly after her conversation with Miss Emily. Miz Hester Ann had brought all of the babies in the black community into the world and a number of the white ones also, those who couldn't pay the white doctor.

Miss Emily had not seen the midwife come. Miz Hester Ann knew the Durrant family would not pay her for this. She understood when she saw who was to be delivered why the white doctor was not summoned. Talk among the whites in town was as Edward and Emily Durrant had started, that Marian was living abroad with family in France, taking advantage of a finishing school for young ladies. She was not expected home before the completion of her training.

The babe was washed and swaddled and laid tenderly in her mother's arms. Neither of the elder Durrants had stopped in to visit their first grandchild. "Catherine," Marian spoke softly. "Her name is Catherine. James said that was his mother's name."

Before the end of the infant's first week, she was moved to the back end of the hall, away from the rooms of the Durrants. Her crying in the night disturbed Mr. Edward, it was said. Before long, the advent of the infant was causing noticeable strain in the family relationships. Emily railed bitterly at Marian on the infant's three-week birthday when Marian tentatively broached the subject of the infant's baptism.

"This spawn of evil may not be baptized!" she ranted. "She does not exist. Nor do you exist here anymore. You are in finishing school in France, and I promise you there will be a terrible accident that will take your life before you are to come back here. You will never leave this house again. You are dead and this child does not exist, except in the depraved reaches of your unclean mind. She is a bastard and there is no baptism for her. Do you understand me clearly?"

"She is a beautiful child and I love her. She is mine and I will not allow you to hurt her."

Miss Emily reached down toward the infant in Marian's arms and slapped the babe smartly across its right cheek. The infant jerked away reflexively and tensed up into a sharp cry of pain.

"Shut her up," Emily commanded. "Her life is never going to be anything but pain and I never want to hear her voice again. Do you understand me? Your father – no, my husband – you no longer have a father – my husband will not hear this child again. Not ever, not under any circumstances." Emily spun on her heel and left the room, closing the door smartly behind her.

Marian held the still-crying infant close, trying to fill the tiny mouth with her nipple to quiet the child. Sarah, who had witnessed the whole transaction, came and gently showed Marian how to pinch the child's nose while holding the hand over its mouth. "If you do it so, every time the baby begins to cry, she will learn silence. It's a trick I learned from some of the mothers who have escaped from slavery. They had to teach silence to their babies to protect their lives."

Baby Catherine was nearly three when she and her mother were banished still higher in the massive stone house. Catherine, with the bright inquisitiveness of the normal toddler, had slipped away a few times from the room she and Marian shared, and to which they were confined. Each time one of the elder Durrants caught her and visited her body with sharp punishments.

Marian and the babe were released when her parents went to Europe for a few months "to visit Marian in her school" and do a continental tour. Catherine learned the tantalizing smells of the kitchen in that brief time, especially on baking days when Rosemary, the cook, brought out of the oven loaves of wonderful hot bread and sometimes pies or cakes. With an appreciative toddler in the house Rosemary began making cookies every baking day also.

Catherine ran and laughed freely outside, enjoying especially the huge piles of leaves raked up by the garden boys. She would run from yards away, shrieking with laughter as she leapt and splatted into the piles, which the accommodating boys would restack as she scattered them. She and her mother owned the world and life was joyful.

Catherine was outside with only one of the gardeners while her mother slipped into the outhouse near the stables when the Durrants returned. The child was engrossed in her play and failed to hear the team and carriage climbing the hill. Mr. Durrant stepped out of the carriage, leaving his wife to the driver's assistance, and approached the errant child. She had finally detected his approach and stood rooted to the ground, hands akimbo as if she thought to run but had been arrested mid-flight.

Her bruises were nearly healed when they took her mother away. Neither had dared even peep from the third-floor maids' room in which they'd been confined, but that apparently wasn't helpful.

Marian was taken away late at night, while the household slept. Jenny, the downstairs girl, was roused to come and help Miss Marian pack her things. She'd taken one small suitcase only, with minimal clothes changes, as Jenny had been instructed. She'd be back in a few days, surely. She begged Jenny to care for Catherine, whom she was forced to leave alone.

She wept silently as she was handed into the carriage, with window flaps down, and was amazed to see the old groom at the reins and her father seated before her in the conveyance. When the carriage returned on the second day, Mr. Durrant was alone. Both Jenny and the old groom were dismissed upon his return and the household was informed that Marian and Catherine had been transported to a new situation developed for them by the Durrant parents.

~ ~ ~

Catherine struggled with the silverware. She'd had a large spoon with a loop in the handle during her long confinement, but no other utensil. As her hand outgrew the baby spoon, she had fisted it awkwardly and most often used her hands for eating vegetables. Sarah first gave her a spoon and allowed the girl to become familiar with its feel and acquire some facility in its use. The girl watched Samuel and Sarah closely at meal times and mastered eating with little spillage quickly.

After a few weeks, when the girl had acquired skill in the use of the spoon Sarah added a fork. The fork proved easier to manage that the spoon, except for those few slippery things that sent a piece flying across the table when she pressed with the edge of the fork, trying to cut it to mouth size chunks.

Catherine was comfortable eating morning porridge, vegetables and bread; she enjoyed also the sharp cheddar cheese Samuel favored. Her first introduction to meat was in the form of pot roast. She looked warily at the strange substance on her plate and pushed it around with her spoon, working to free the carrots and potatoes.

"Here, baby. Try it this way." Sarah cut off a small portion of the meat and handed it toward Catherine's mouth with her fork. The girl pushed the meat around with her tongue, trying the unusual substance, sucking the juices from it. "Like this." Sarah demonstrated chewing a piece of meat and

Catherine imitated her. She thereafter consented to be served small portions of meat but never learned to enjoy it in any of its various guises.

Catherine had sat upon a wooden box, borrowed from the stable, since joining the household of Samuel and Sarah. Samuel now labored patiently, using the last of the day's sun falling through the window of the cottage where he worked. He'd earlier shaped the legs and spindles for a chair with the drawknife and hatchet and patiently smoothed the wood by drawing a sharp knife edge down the length of the grain, again and again, until his fingers and hand rubbed across the wood found each piece silky-smooth.

Samuel now finished the frame for the seat and assembled the chair frame. Sitting by the fire while Sarah added stitches to her tatting, he split wood into narrow, thin strips, fastening them together end to end with the barbed tongue he whittled into the far end of one piece fitted into a slit in the near end of the next. He wove the strips carefully over and under the wood bars that constituted the warp of the chair seat, and soon set the finished chair aside, looking at it critically.

"I believe that will do," he remarked.

"Of course it will," Sarah responded. "You always make fine things with your hands. You know though, we could have brought over a chair from the big house; Miss Emily probably would never have noticed and she wouldn't care if she did. She told us to care for this child..."

"Yes. I understand that. It's just that the big house and everyone in it have done so much harm to this child. I know she isn't really ours but right now she seems like she is, and I'd like her to have something made with love, 'specially made for her."

"She is a treasure, isn't she?" looking toward the girl sleeping on her cot. "We tried so hard for so long and couldn't have our own. Maybe that was so we would have the time and energy for this child when she was given to us. Do you think?"

"I don't know what I think about it. I don't know is God that thoughtful of us or not. I just know she's easy to love and I'm sho' grateful she's here!"

"Momma! Momma Sarah!" the girl greeted her mentor. "Momma! Look!"

"Why, Catherine! You've set the table for us for supper. What a fine and thoughtful thing for you to do!"

Catherine smiled, ducking her head with a touch of shyness. "Momma." She said it a dozen times, more dozens of times each day. "Momma." Each time Sarah's heart contracted with an immense love for this borrowed child and with a stab of fear for her future.

"Momma!" The girl's eyes were wide and she gazed behind Sarah.

"What is it, baby?" Sarah quizzed, setting the fresh bread on the table.

Catherine peered about for a few moments more, then "Momma," flatly said and the girl's arms wrapped around her body, her head drooped.

"What is it, Sarah?" asked Samuel in a hushed voice. He came in from the doorway where he'd paused as the child spoke.

"I don't know, Samuel. Maybe something just nudged her memory. I don't see anything different with her."

"I believe I begin to understand why Mr. Durrant had this child locked up all those years. She's the most graceless, ungrateful wretch I've ever seen." Raising a hand toward the girl she became even angrier when Catherine ducked, holding her left arm up, palm outward, to counter the anticipated blow. Emily had struck the girl only twice since her release from the attic room, but those blows were added to the many struck before the child's confinement. Catherine was distinctly afraid of Emily.

In the tiny cottage 30 yards southwest of the big house however, Catherine continued to thrive. In addition to the company of Sandy, Catherine now had daily lessons to complete while Sarah and Samuel were at work. Her speaking vocabulary had passed a few hundred words with Sarah's and Samuel's patient tutelage, and she now could read at an easy primer level. Sarah had no books from which to teach the child, but she wrote down simple stories, painstakingly crafted in manuscript print, using words that Catherine had now learned or relearned.

Sarah was delighted at the girl's progress. She had not before known a child deprived of such a basic living skill as speech, and she had questioned if the child would be able to learn so long past the normal time to acquire language. Catherine learned as rapidly other living skills also. She now dressed herself unassisted. She spread up her own bed and had just learned to set the table. Her beautiful strawberry blond hair was growing out well, and Catherine could brush it herself.

She had been afraid initially of the old wooden tub Samuel brought into the house and Sarah poured first boiling, and then cold water into. Sarah had shown her then by taking her bath first, but the family order now gave the child first use of the warm water, then Sarah and finally Samuel.

Samuel had always made errands to do in the stables on Saturday nights at bath time; he now stayed away a bit longer and always rapped at the door and awaited a reply before entering. When his turn at the tub came Sarah sat with Catherine on the girl's bed tucked behind her sheet-curtain and told Bible stories to her while Samuel splashed. Catherine was then helped with her prayers and tucked into bed.

~ ~ ~

"Look there at the color of the water, son," James admonished. "A difference in color from the rest of the river always tells you something. That's one of the vital things you have to learn."

"Yessir, I see it," Thomas responded. "It's a sandbar, isn't it?"

"Good job. Yes, it is a sandbar. You're coming right along with learning the river. It won't be long and you'll have enough experience to make an assistant pilot. I always enjoy seeing young men like you doing well."

"What are the locks like?" the boy queried. "I've never been in a lock. Is it exciting, like shooting the Falls? Everybody says it was exciting to shoot the Falls." Completed in 1830, the three locks designated as Lock and Dam No. 41, the Ohio was now navigable in all water conditions except extreme drought, with the locks and a canal leading safely around the Falls of the Ohio. Indeed, the Falls no longer really existed, with the wicket dam in place to harness the power of the river.

"Be thankful we don't have to experience that excitement. The Falls was a wicked place. The river drops 25 or so feet in a couple of miles there. I've heard those who shot the Falls talk. A lot of boats survived, of course, or no one would have tried it. But some boats were destroyed and crewmen lost or injured at the falls. It was the worst place on the three rivers I run.

"Some boats would come just to the falls and then put their passengers and cargo onto boats on the other side of the falls. That would cost a lot of time and labor, but if the water was low at the Falls, it was the only way to navigate past them. The locks opened the same year I started working the river. I'm very grateful I never had to shoot them."

"What is it like to go through locks, though?"

"Hang on a bit son, you'll see for yourself."

"Yessir. Will we go up the Missouri this season?"

"Likely. Later in the fall, there'll be plenty of grain to carry down. We'll probably take a train or two of coal first, and then assorted other stuff down the Mississippi: meat, salt, flour, New York butter, whiskey, nails... There's no end to what we carry. We may run some of the coal north, up the Missouri. And we'll likely carry sugar, rice, coffee, and whatever else up both the Missouri and the Ohio. We'll see how the season develops."

A river man for nearly two decades, James loved the river now even more than he had when he became a deckhand at 13 years of age. He'd moved about too much to settle on a woman to wife; in truth, he'd never wanted another woman after Marian's death. She'd been so perfectly fitted to him, pouring out herself in her letters, following with interest his news of the river and disclosures about himself.

He'd never quite finished grieving for her... Her letters remained in his locker where he still sometimes took them out and reread them. So much she'd had to give. So little he could give in return. He was gone most of the year on the *Marian Dee*. He would have been pressed to give her even short weeks from the year or occasional layovers of a day or so.

He wasn't sure if naming his boat for her had helped the grieving process or hindered it, but he kept his crew sharp to keep the boat at her best performance and appearance always, even when loaded to the Texas deck with cotton bales. His men were better paid than average and they worked better than average. He believed Marian deserved some of the credit for that, since it was her honor that the boat represented.

He brought his attention back sharply. "Look smart there at that riffle. There's a log or something snagged there just under the surface."

"Yessir. I'm steering to port to stay away from it."

The *Marian Dee*, the sparkling white boat trimmed in blue, Marian's favorite color, continued its way peacefully up the mighty Ohio.

# Chapter Four

Martha paused at the knock on the door. The tiny black community here – *free* black community, that was – was close knit and trusting of each other. They tended to call from a neighbor's doorway rather than knock upon it. Strangers were actually expected to call from outside the yard, asking permission to approach the house, rather than knock at the door. Martha approached the door cautiously.

The man at the threshold stood poised on the balls of his feet, as if ready to run. His face was a study in fear, with eyes flickering rapidly looking behind her in the house and to his side in the yard. He opened his mouth and formed a word, but no sound escaped his lips. His clothes were damp and dirty.

"What do you want, brother?" Martha queried. "Are you being chased?"

"I-I-I think I lost them at the Ohio," the man stammered, "but I'm not sure."

"Get inside out of sight," Martha rejoined with scarcely a hesitation. Others had risked their lives to keep her Samuel and herself free. She felt obliged to pass freedom on when an opportunity presented itself. She stepped back as she spoke and gestured to the man to come inside.

The man shivered with a chill not entirely of the weather or his wet clothes. "Here. Wrap yo'self in this quilt and gi' me your clothes. I'm doing laundry right now and I get your things done up for you."

"Do you live alone, Miz?" he asked. "Won't somebody see a man's clothes on your line and find me here?"

"I'll dry them on a chair by the fire. I misthink anybody would much notice anyway, I does laundry for others to pay for what we need. The white folks don't come here much. They sends they colored with they laundry."

Samuel entered, stopping in place at sight of the stranger.

"It's all right, son. The man needs a little help, that's all."

Martha placed a bowl of beans, seasoned with side pork, in front of the stranger, with a large slab of cornbread. "Oh, Miz, I don't want to take your food away from you and your boy," he hesitated, obviously hungry as his body strained slightly toward the food while his mouth denied his need.

"We got plenty t' share. I makes enough to feed us and an extra, if need be. Rest yo'self. You with friends now."

The man waited no longer, but began to eat ravenously. Martha hesitated, but decided to follow her usual custom of saying grace before she and Samuel ate. Her hand gently stayed the visitor's hand, and she spoke, "Lord Jesus, look on us kindly. Guard Samuel and raise him up to manhood as you would have him. Bless this man here and bless the food which we eat gratefully. Amen."

They sat by the fire in the chill evening after they had eaten and cleared away the remains of the simple meal. "Does you have a name you prefer?" Martha asked him.

"I'se called Samson," he replied. "My mammy said Massa wanted me to grow up strong so's I'd make more money for him. She say they's a story in the Bible that Samson was a strong man."

"Yes," murmured Martha. "But they's not many here with names like that. *Slave* names. If you be staying here long you might want to change that name some."

"Does you think I might stay here a bit?"

"I don't see why not. We's free on this side of the river. If you acts like you always been here nobody will notice you. *We'll* know, but the white folks won't notice."

"I'd be real grateful to stay a bit, Miz. I been runnin' so long and I be so tired. I just like to rest me some."

"You can make your bed in the loft with Samuel then. An' rest yo'self. Sam. How about if you's Sam? Anybody ask young Samuel here named for you. You be Samuel instead of Samson, but we call you Sam."

"Yes, Miz. I likes that. And I sho' thanks y'all."

"My name's Martha. Just Martha. Sleep well, brother."

~ ~ ~

"Momma." Catherine spun toward the door, eyes seeking eagerly. When she failed to find what she sought, she quieted and tears stood in the child's eyes as Sarah entered the cottage late on a Thursday afternoon. Catherine had set the table for their simple supper, which had been simmering on the fire all afternoon, but her alert look as Sarah entered sagged into downcast eyes and drooping shoulders. She dropped dejectedly onto her chair, head lowered.

"What is it, honey? What are you remembering that makes you so sad?" Sarah asked. There was no response from the child and Sarah stepped on toward the table, setting the fresh bread down so she could caress the girls' head. "Go ahead and cry, lovey. You have plenty of reason to cry."

~ ~ ~

"Papa!" exclaimed Naomi. "That's not fair, Papa! You always help Joseph!"

"Ah," he replied, grinning broadly, "we men have to stick together, you know. And Joseph *is* the youngest. He needs some encouragement from time to time."

"Papa, I already knew the answer to that question. It's John the Baptist. I'm not a *baby*, Papa!"

"Oh my gracious!" Papa laughed. "Now I'm in trouble from both sides!" Still laughing, he retreated to the kitchen where Ruth, his wife, was lifting pies from the brick oven adjacent to the fireplace. "Um, you surely smell good!" he remarked.

"You just get your pie-stealing fingers away from here," she ordered good-naturedly. "These pies are all spoken for. You'll not flatter me out of any!"

"But Ruth, my love, just a small slice? Just a little, tiny piece? Ah, no one in the world makes better pies than you do..."

His voice trailed off as she pushed him back toward the parlor. "Now you're in trouble from *all* sides, Reverend Philipe the Flatterer!"

"Children. Are your lessons all prepared for tomorrow..." as their heads nodded up and down, she continued, "...and your chores finished?"

"Yes, Maman," they chorused.

"Then away with you little ones to your night clothes. Papa will hear your prayers as soon as you're changed. Joseph! March!" pointing toward the boys' room."

"But Maman! I want to stay up with Papa. S'il vous plaît?

"Don't think you can rascal away with me just because you plead in French, young man!" she admonished, controlling her smile with difficulty. "Away!"

"I'll come and hear your prayers directly," Philipe offered. "And if you are very, very good, perhaps I'll have a little story for you."

Joseph scampered off smiling. Papa liked to give him what he wanted, the boy knew with perfect confidence.

~ ~ ~

"And so, how is your young charge doing?" Miss Emily demanded. "Has she learned a civil tongue yet?"

"She has made some progress, Miss Emily," Sarah replied. "She still has trouble saying some words."

"Perhaps I shall see to her later." Miss Emily spoke absently, leading Sarah to pray fervently that she spoke only meaningless words, with no real intent to see the child. Sarah continued her steady pace, working through the chest of silver with her baking soda polish and cloth. She'd take the ironing home with her today, so she could keep Catherine company while she worked and to begin to teach the girl the art of using a sad iron.

"Miss Emily asked again today about Catherine's progress," Sarah said.

"What she gonna do with this child?" Samuel fretted. The evening work was cleared away and Catherine was softly snoring on her bed. "I think she got something planned for Catherine. She not goin' to just leave her here. She gonna do somethin' to her, somethin' to hurt her..." Samuel's talk usually followed the patterns of standard English modeled by his wife, but when upset or anxious he tended to fall back to his childhood speech practices. Sarah understood and shared his anxiety, but was unable to find any assurance to give him.

"I don't know, Samuel. She scares me to death every time she mentions the child. I'm afraid I think the same thing you think. She has something terrible planned for her."

"Maybe we can leave and take her with us. We's free. We can go whenever we want to."

"And live with a white child? Those white-sheet riders would have us in a heartbeat. No, we have to find a way to protect her here. I just don't have any ideas."

Catherine walked beside Sarah on a Saturday afternoon. They'd been visiting in another cottage and now were going home. As Catherine spied one of the lawn boys piling faded leaves high she laughed suddenly and began to run toward the pile. The carriage, returning from town with Samuel at the reins emerged from behind the tall spirea hedge. Catherine's headlong rush toward the leaf pile stayed as suddenly as it had started and a brief, terrible scream arose from the child, who stood frozen in mid-flight.

"Catherine! Catherine! What is it, child? What's wrong? Oh, honey, tell Momma Sarah what it is so I can fix it," she pleaded.

"I think I understand, Sarah. I was the assistant groom then. The Durrants had gone to Europe for a few months and Catherine and her mother were free while they were gone. Old Steven saw them coming in a hired hack when they returned and told me take the wagon down to pick up their luggage. I saw Catherine run and jump into a pile of leaves when I was going to the stable to harness a horse. The carriage drove up then with Miss Emily and Mister Edward. Catherine didn't see the carriage coming. She was just a baby anyway.

"Mr. Durrant got out of the carriage and beat that child 'til she was all bruised and tattered. A few nights later he took her momma away."

"And they said they took the child away too. All those years we thought she was gone away and she was locked up in the attic alone. And then we find out Miss Marian died and they said Miss Emily's sister kept Miss Marian's child.

"It's all right, lovey. Come on home with Momma Sarah. Come on where it's nice and warm and safe."

Samuel stood shocked and motionless as Sarah murmured to the tall, lanky white man with the stovepipe hat. He heard her words clearly but they were utterly devoid of meaning. She had responded to loudly said – also meaningless – words of the stranger.

"*Buenas tardes, señor. ¿Puedo ayudar?*"

"*Gracias, señora, gracias. ¿Usted sabe donde está el Senor George Prentice del periodico* The Times*? ¿Usted lo conoces?*"

"*No, yo no lo conozco, pero el está en el centro de la ciudad de Louisville,*" gesturing across the river. "*El bote está ahí. Se va a las tres.*"

"*Gracias, señora, muchas gracias.*"

"*De nada,*" Sarah responded with a smile.

Turning toward the ferry the man left, pulling a watch out of his pocket as he walked.

"Woman, what was that?" Samuel demanded. "What was that you said?"

"Nothing important, love. He was looking for the editor of the *Louisville Times* newspaper. I told him where to find him and pointed out the ferry. That's all."

"What were you saying?" Samuel demanded again. "I couldn't understand anything you said!"

"I'm sorry! I didn't realize you didn't know. My father was from Europe, remember? He spoke a few languages and taught them to us children. I was speaking Spanish to this man."

"Spanish. And where do they speak Spanish besides in your father's house?"

"Actually, in a lot of places. In Spain, of course, and in Mexico and some countries in South America."

"Where are these places?" Samuel rejoined. "Spain and all the others."

"Spain is in Europe. Mexico is south of here and so is South America. I have maps at home, I'll show you."

"If Mexico is south, then they have slaves there, yes?"

"No, Mexico doesn't have slaves, although the Spanish did try to make slaves out of the Indians when they first came to the New World."

"My mother came from the South. She was a slave and I was born slave, though I don't remember anything from then. I was just a baby when my mother ran away and came here, after my daddy was sold South. Further south, my momma said."

"I've been thinking about starting Catherine on a little history and geography. Her talking is coming along so well and she still understands more than she can say. If you'd like, we can all study together. Father said it was important for us to know where we were and where we'd come from. Father came from France, which is next to Spain in Europe."

"Hmmph," Samuel mumbled. "I guess maybe I need to learn some of this so you won't take a notion and run away with a smarter man!"

"Samuel! I would never run away with any man but you. You may only speak one language, but it's my language and it's my heart that hears it. And you're as smart as any man ever; you just didn't have a chance to get the book learning I did. It will always be only you, Samuel. I fully believe God made us for each other."

Samuel wasn't given to much public display, but he reached around and hugged her fiercely to himself, entirely unaware of the people around them.

Catherine was delighted to have Samuel added to her lessons. He pored over the maps Sarah provided. "This here is water?" he asked, pointing to the blue of the map.

"Yes, that's the Atlantic Ocean. That's what my father crossed to come here."

"It's too big! It's bigger than the land, here, and there's more land than anyone can see at one time!"

"Papa said when he came to America it took weeks in the boat. They didn't see any land for all that time. He went first from a little town here in France – it's too little to be on this big map – across the English Channel. Here. They left from Southampton in the early spring. It was hot by the time he got to America. He stayed in Boston – here, on the map – and finished seminary.

"He wanted to go South and preach to the slaves, but Maman persuaded him not to. She was afraid he'd be taken by a slave catcher and sold into slavery."

"Likely would have. They still do it sometimes. Heard when I was in town last that a man disappeared from just up the road there. Colored man, born free. Hasn't been seen since but they think a slave catcher stole him. Said a strong man's worth $1000 or more."

"Oh my. I hadn't heard of that. That makes me worry a bit about you..." Her voice trailed off, not wanting to voice her fear lest the voice give power to the evil.

"Sarah, my love. I'll always be here for you. Always. I give you my word."

"And I take your word. But this child sits waiting to be taught and we're here chattering like squirrels. Back to work!"

Samuel found the learning of another language difficult and tedious, unlike the child whose brain was still malleable in the language areas. But he was fascinated by the study of geography and the differences in people's culture and language from place to place.

"So that man downtown likely came from Mexico, yes? Or maybe I should say '*si*'?"

"He might have, but his accent sounded like he might have come from Spain, maybe southern Spain. Since Papa grew up there he could make different kinds of accents like those that people spoke in different countries or regions. The man downtown sounded like he was from southern Spain."

"Sarah, I'm glad I didn't know how much you knew when I was courting you! I'd have been afraid of you and run away. Since I didn't know, I was only afraid of your father!"

"Papa was a dear old softie. He knew very well what kind of man you were or he'd have stopped you courting before it really got started. He was most meticulous about the young men who came courting his daughters. I heard him talking to Maman about you when you were still just coming to church and not courting me yet. He told Maman you were a strong, proud man who would be a good husband. Why do you think he had the altos move back by the basses in the choir?" she asked with a mischievous grin.

"No! Do you really mean that?"

"Yes. Papa picked you out for me himself. So Maman just quietly helped out a little, like inviting you to Sunday dinner more often than anyone else got invited."

"My goodness. I knew I honored your father but I didn't realize how much I owed to him."

"Well, of course I helped with getting the courtship going too, you know. Do you remember the time I stumbled by the door of the church so you had to catch me?"

"No! You did that on purpose?"

"Of course. And it worked well, didn't it?"

"Oh my, yes it worked. Do you know I didn't sleep at all that night? All I could do was remember how you felt for that moment in my arms."

"Hmm. Would you like to try it again and see if it still feels the same?"

"Oh yes. No, it doesn't feel the same. It feels much better."

## Chapter Five

Catherine was speaking fluently now and could read simple stories. She had been taken to the big house at times when her grandmother was not present, and had visited in company with Sarah, other cottages on the grounds or nearby. Sarah considered carefully. "Do you think she might be ready to go to church?"

"I don't know, Love. In the first place, which church do you mean? They're Catholic. Don't reckon she'd," gesturing toward the big house, "take kindly to her granddaughter going to the Baptists. Do you?"

"Catherine isn't Catholic. I remember the terrible time when Marian asked to have her baptized. That was when I showed Miss Marian how to keep the baby from making noise when she cried. Miss Emily slapped the baby and then ordered Miss Marian to shut her up and keep her silent. All because Miss Marian asked to have the baby baptized."

"Well, I don't think baptism really had much to do with that, do you? I think she just hated Miss Marian for taking away all her dreams for her future, don't you?"

"Yes, I'm sure you're right, but the fact remains that she wasn't baptized and she isn't Catholic. Miss Emily surely didn't mean for us to lose our religion just because we're taking care of this little girl, did she?"

"I wouldn't put nothin' cruel past that woman. But she doesn't seem to care what we do with Catherine as long as she doesn't have to see her or hear her. Do you think Catherine might be ready to meet a few more folks? All at the same time?"

"I don't know, Samuel. I guess we might try it and see."

"How about if we take her on Sunday evenin' when there's not so many folks there?"

"I think that's a good idea. Shall we try this Sunday?"

And so it was that Samuel stayed with Catherine on Sunday morning while Sarah went to church. When early supper was cleared up that evening, Sarah checked to see if Catherine was presentable.

The girl wore the same black dress she'd been given at the death of her grandfather, but unlike the brown dresses she'd had while locked in the slitted room, this dress was kept washed and pressed. Sarah had used a piece of material she'd been saving and stitched up a presentable dress of the navy blue fabric so she had one to wear and one to wash.

Although Sarah would not let Catherine wear the red scarf, since the mourning period for her grandfather had not yet passed, she did allow the child to carry the scarf so she would have a familiar, favorite thing to hold. Sandy was confined to the woodshed, to the dismay of both the girl and the pup, but Catherine took the hands offered by her foster parents and walked peacefully between them to the old barn on the adjoining property where the little church met.

Samuel and Sarah arrived early, to give some time to the girl to adjust to the new setting before others came. Both were in the choir on Sunday mornings, but the evening service was more spontaneous and everyone sat together in the congregation. Samuel had helped make the benches on which they were seated, and he looked proudly at his wife and Catherine as they followed his gesture to be seated on one of the smooth benches. Poplar wood. Difficult to work but the benches would last for a lifetime and more.

Sarah started with Catherine as she'd been taught from young childhood. "This is Jesus' house, Baby. Do you remember when you say your prayers at night you talk to Jesus?"

The young brow furrowed briefly in concentration. "Yes," she said, steepling her hands as Sarah had taught her.

"Yes! That's right, Catherine. You say your prayers with just us at home but in church, other people come to pray too. We'll wait and watch; others should start to come soon. And we'll sing songs together and pray."

Catherine watched with a certain wariness as others began to enter the church. All those who came, however, were black, and Catherine relaxed somewhat as the little church filled. She had never been hurt by any black person and had been loved warmly by Sarah and Samuel. Giving one last look over her shoulder as the preacher stepped up to start the service she saw no one to fear.

As the minister lined out *Beulah Land* and the congregation began to sing Catherine caught her breath and looked up at Sarah wonderingly. Sarah just nodded and smiled as she continued to sing. Catherine reached over and felt the vibrations of Sarah's throat as the woman had done in teaching her to begin to speak. She then tried to sing with the others, stumbling over some of the words but seeming to catch on easily to the task of singing itself.

Sarah noted that while the girl's voice was still sometimes harsh from her years of silence she seemed to have a good sense of pitch and rhythm. She would add some singing to the daily lessons. It would give her something that she looked like she was going to enjoy and – as Sarah knew from her father tutoring her in European languages – was a good way to learn vocabulary.

Everyone in the little church – pastored by a man who'd been trained by the Reverend Philipe – was aware of the identity of the girl. After the last Amen was said, they filed outside and waited patiently for Samuel and Sarah to come out with their charge.

"Reverend Abram, please meet Catherine Durrant. She's staying with us for a while."

"Evenin', Miss Catherine," the reverend said. "We're glad to have you with us. Maybe you'd like to come to the morning service also next week. We'd be proud to have you."

Sarah had carefully coached Catherine to respond to introductions. "Thank you, sir. I'm glad to meet you."

A few among the congregation reached out gently as Sam and Sarah passed, touching the child with their blessings. Catherine showed no anxiety, having spent the past hour and a half with these folk, openly enjoying the singing and tolerating the lengthy sermon with only several wiggles. Sarah, without consciously noticing, relaxed a large part of the tension in her body. The child had made the transition into her first social situation successfully.

~ ~ ~

Mother Clare lingered at her morning prayers, struck by the pain and effort spent by young Sister Mary Joseph. How long it had been! A change was beginning to come forth in the young nun. She was meeting the eye contact of others now, while before starting her meditations on the psalm she'd habitually kept her eyes down, looking up only when spoken to during recreation at dinner or supper, or in meeting with Mother Clare.

Sister Mary Joseph was more relaxed now, striding freely through the corridors to and from the places of her day in the convent. Previously she had huddled near the walls when she had to move from place to place. She had begun participating in the conversations during the mealtime recreation periods and even laughed occasionally when the group spirits were high. She seemed more focused and centered and less in pain.

Mother Clare waited patiently in the back of the small chapel until Sister

Mary Joseph rose and genuflected. As she turned toward the chapel door, Mother Clare signed that she wanted the young sister to come to her office.

"Are you ready to continue your journey as a novice?" Mother Clare queried.

"Yes, Mother. I seem to be becoming a part of this place and I do wish to stay."

"You know your dowry is available to you should you choose to leave."

"Yes, Mother. I do want to stay. There's no place for me on the outside, even if I had my dowry. And I'm pretty sure this is where I want to stay for the rest of my life."

"I'll talk to Father O'Maine after Mass in the morning and see when he can schedule a bit of extra time for us. We'll celebrate your growth toward God then."

"Thank you, Mother. Thank you for everything you've done for me."

~ ~ ~

"Ease it up now," James coached. "Watch the flow of the current. You need to slip the boat clear over to the portside bank so the barge train will flow into the lock. If your barges aren't lined up with the current the lead barge will slam into the gate or the middle of the barge train will scrape the gate going in. Yes! You've got it just right. Give it just a nudge more power now."

"This is weird! It feels like being in a trap, with the walls so high!"

"You'll get used to it. It sure beats holding your breath while you shoot the falls. They never knew if they were going to survive that or not. We're almost low enough now. The lower river gate will open pretty soon. Yes. There it is. Hold her steady now and watch for the current coming in from starboard, around Sand Island there. Good job."

James studied the shoreline as wood was being loaded. Off to the northwest he could see a high stone wall that looked substantial from this distance. Beyond the wall, a roof could be seen. "What's that place up there?" he queried of the farmer whose wood had been purchased and was being loaded. "The place with the wall around it."

"That's some kind of nunnery," the man replied. "A man comes in the mornings for a half hour or so, a priest, I guess. The nuns never come out and hardly anybody else ever goes in. I've heard that the nuns in there don't talk, but I don't know about that. I don't really want to know anything about Papist stuff."

"It seems so peaceful off that way," James said softly.

"Yeah, I'll admit that. It is real peaceful hereabouts. I misjudge if those women have anything to do with that, though.

"Well, these men should be about finished loading now, shouldn't they? How many slaves have you got on your boats?" observing Will, a tall, wiry black man. "Do you find them reliable? I've never thought I'd be able to turn my back on one. Ya' hear so much about slave uprisings..." The wood seller's voice trailed off as he turned to watch the men finish loading.

"I have only one boat; that's all I can manage personally and I guess I've seen enough boats ruined or sunk by hired hands to not want more than I can take care of myself. And I own no slaves, nor do I believe anyone could ever really own another person. I think it's an evil system and when it comes to an end – which I think may not be too long now – I think those who have relied on slave labor will be ruined, utterly."

"Well, I suppose you might know more about such things than I do, seein' as how you go clear to New Orleans all the time. I just never took to having any slaves. Bad enough to have to feed the farm animals whether they're working or not. Don't need any more open mouths. Well, I thank you kindly for your business. You know I try to keep 60 or 80 cords at least cut and seasoned and ready to load; hope you'll stop by on your next trip. Gettin' a bit chilly out here, guess I'll get on out of your way and get finished up so I can get me out of the cold and get around some good, hot food. Thank'ee again!"

James stood, hands spread over the warming barrel. "Gonna be a cold one on the river tonight," he remarked. "Give us a day or two and we'll be far enough south to get away from the winter weather. I will say it's good to be able to run until the ice sets in, though. Not like the old times when we just ran a load upstream in high water and hoped for a load at the other end, and hoped for the water to stay high enough for us to get back downstream again. And hoped not to hit any of the trees or logs or other trash coming downstream in high water. This contract hauling tobacco pretty much makes our expenses for the whole season. Haven't been up to Sioux City for so long I reckon they may have forgotten what we look like since we've been running the Ohio so steady."

"James, suh..."

"I'm just James, Will. Nobody special and not old enough for you to have to say sir. What's on your mind?"

"I, I...would you teach me to pilot? I've been a deckhand for two years, Mr. James, and if you won't teach me to pilot I'll stay a deckhand because I love the river and the *Marian Dee*, but I'd really like to learn the river as a pilot..."

James contemplated the man with whom he shared the burning barrel on this cold night. "You've been on the *Marian Dee* for two years, eh? How old are you, Will?"

"Almost 18, suh."

"James."

"James, suh..." Will broke off and both men grinned.

'Everything shipshape for the night on the barges?"

"Yes, James," still with a grin.

"Let's think this out, Will. I've got Thomas on as an assistant pilot now. I haven't had an apprentice since he was ready to jump from apprentice to assistant. It's nice to have someone I can trust so I can get a good night's sleep."

James continued in a musing tone, "Tell you what, Will. We're in good shape for wood for a while and there's not a lot to do on the barges as long as they're secure. I've never had to tell you how to do anything twice and I've never had to follow behind you. Your work is always done and always done well. You report to the pilothouse in the morning when I come on. As long as we can spare you as a deckhand, you'll work the pilothouse.

"If we need you to load or whatever you can switch jobs back until we get to New Orleans or maybe St. Louis. We'll take on an extra deckhand when we can find a good one. It's been a good season; we can afford it. So you're now the new apprentice pilot. You'll learn the river. And the boat...the Marian Dee. She's a special lady, Will."

"Thank you! Thank you! I didn't really think you'd let me learn to pilot. And I've loved the *Marian Dee* since I first saw her at the wharf in New Orleans. Yeah, she is a special lady..."

James looked back up river with an expression Will couldn't read. He was sad, or brooding, or wounded... "Good night, Will. See you in the morning," he said in a quiet voice, turning toward his cabin. "By the way," he added, turning back to the other man, "apprentice wages are something higher than deckhand wages. We'll figure that out tomorrow. Night, son."

~ ~ ~

The small community of free blacks in the area completed the church building they'd been planning for months. Over a period of several months, they cut and shaped the wood needed and traded here and there for other materials. The shingles in particular were a community effort: each man of the community – and a few of the women – had set hands on the drawknife and the other women and the children had proudly carried the shingles to the clearing where the church was planned.

They gathered on a sunny day and, working together, quickly framed it up. The women folk had brought generous parcels of food and as the men were roofing, they were summoned to eat.

The building was finished by late afternoon, and after the last peg was driven one of the women with a rich soprano started the *Doxology*. One by one, the others in the group joined the hymn, filling the air with rich harmony. As the 'Amen' died away another started *Amazing Grace*.

The Reverend Abram then raised his hands, praying, "Glorious Father, look down on us, your *needy children*. Bless this house we have raised in *your name*, Lord. Keep it safe in *all weathers*. As Jesus drove the *moneychangers* from your temple, Lord, we declare this to be the *house of the Lord* and a sacred place of worship. Let all who come here *honor the Lord* and his house. Keep us safe from *all* harm and as you promised Isaac, the prophet of the Lord, hold us *safe* in the palm of your hand. We give you *all praise* and *all honor.* In *Jesus'* holy name, we ask this. Amen." As he rallied the congregation with the rhythmic rise and fall of his voice, they joined the prayer of the reverend with murmurs of "Yes, Lord," "Amen," and "All right, Lord!"

As the last "Amen" faded away, a reverent silence ensued, as the workers took stock of the fruits of their work. Gazing inside and out, they admired their handiwork, successful by the blessing of the Lord. It didn't have a steeple or a bell yet but likely those things would come later. The benches would be brought from their previous meeting place. The Lord was good to them. He truly held them in the palm of His hand.

"Miz Martha," Sam asked quietly, "will you marry with me? "You been knowin' me now for all this time. Remember how little Samuel was when I first got here? Hit's been a long time and I'd favor marryin' with you if you willin'."

"Sam. You been good to Samuel and me. You been the onliest father he's ever had...I know he likes you and so do I. Maybe it's more than likin' that I feels for you. Yes. I believes it is..."

She hesitated, lost in thought. She would never see Jimmy again. It had been a very long time alone, but she'd worked hard and she and Samuel lacked nothing they needed. Except...maybe a husband and father? She did care about Sam, even though it was different from the fiery passion she and Jimmy had shared.

It would be right nice to have Sam around all the time. After his first night in Martha's loft, he'd moved to another lodging, saying, "Hit's not right to have people talk about you having a man staying in yo' house."

His visits to Martha and Samuel had at first been only every week or two, but he gradually shifted the frequency of his calls until he now found it necessary to explain if something hindered his coming on any evening. He'd worked hard and earned the respect of the small community of free blacks. He taught young Samuel as if he were his true father, taking him fishing, teaching him how to fix things, teaching him to begin to recognize his beliefs and responsibilities. "Yes, Sam, I'd be proud to marry with you."

Sam's grin lit up the room and he reached out and snatched Martha in a giant hug. .

"Hey! You smashin' me!" she protested, but her smile was larger than her protest and Sam gentled his hold on her and reached for her lips with his. The kiss began softly but became demanding, with a passion she'd not known she still owned.

Neither of them noticed Samuel as he quietly came in the back door and saw the two of them standing in the kitchen, so involved with each other that they were oblivious to all else. With a broad grin, he silently slipped back outside. His boy's heart treasured the company of the man and he rightly deduced that the kiss meant Sam would be around a lot more now.

The Reverend Abram presided in the first wedding in the little clapboard church.

The entire community came, giving their blessing to the couple all liked and respected. Samuel played an important role in the service: he walked up the aisle beside his mother and, reaching the front of the congregation, linked Martha's hand with Sam's. He was clearly delighted with the turn of events.

The only pause in the celebration was when Sam's full name was asked. He hesitated, knowing the name of the white master he'd been born to but averse to taking it, somewhat because of the lingering potential of falling to the slave catchers but mostly because he wanted to be his own man, heading up his own family with his own name.

"Freeman," he declared. "My whole name be Sam Freeman." And so they became Mr. and Miz Freeman.

"Ma'am," Samuel asked for his mother's attention. "Do I be Samuel Freeman now?"

"Samuel," she responded, holding tight to the hand of her new husband, "your father was a man named Jimmy. He knowed you were comin'. He was glad that we have a baby but scairt 'cause you'd be slave. Massa solt him down South because he horse broke its leg and Massa shot it, so he hadda be mad at somebody. He sol' your daddy and we never sees him again. That be why we come here. Your first daddy want you to be free and so do I.

"We'll never see you first daddy again. Mr. Sam Freeman be yo' real daddy for a long time now. If he don't mind I think yo' daddy Jimmy would be right proud for you to be Samuel Freeman."

And so it was that the boy proudly became Samuel Freeman, to grow to a man's stature under the lovingly firm hand of a man who treasured both the boy and his mother.

## Chapter Six

"Bring the girl here," Miss Emily commanded. "I shall see how well you've done with your obstreperous charge."

"If it's all the same to you, Miss Emily, the girl is still very anxious. I believe coming here might remind her of being shut up and make her afraid of being punished more."

"If I want another opinion, I won't ask it from a *nigger*!" Emily spat the word out, enraged at having her judgment questioned by so obvious an inferior. "Bring her here *now!*"

Sarah nodded, lips compressed, and turned to walk toward the kitchen door.

"I didn't hear your response, *nigger!*" Emily flashed. "I won't tolerate disrespect!"

"Yes, ma'am," Sarah said, flat-voiced. "I will bring the child."

Catherine hung back, toe-scuffing, as they approached the kitchen door. "Please, Momma Sarah, don't make me go in there. Please..."

"We have to do this, child. I'm with you; it will be all right. Come, Catherine."

Angel, the cook, looked up sympathetically as the pair walked through the kitchen. All the servants were cognizant of the plight of the girl, denied family status by her grandmother, the only remaining member of her family.

It was well-known that the child's mother had died, and no one questioned this long after his leaving that her mother's brother, Anson, must be dead also. None had known her father, who obviously had not known or had not cared about the girl's conception, so the child was left with the grandmother who hated her, openly and menacingly.

The knock on the door sounded as Sarah entered the front hall with Catherine. "Leave her here!" was the peremptory order from Miss Emily. "See who is at the door and send them away. I am not available for company at this time. I have a family matter to settle."

Sarah reluctantly dropped Catherine's hand, leaving the girl trembling alone in the hall. "Come here!" snapped Emily. "You have caused nothing but trouble since your conception. I believe we can settle the matter satisfactorily today of a *bastard* child."

"Miss Emily!" a man's voice spoke heartily. "I was in the neighborhood and thought to drop by on my way past. I've seen little of you since Edward's death. How are you?" as he walked around Sarah and approached Emily. "Ah. This lovely young lady is the child I've heard about. What a wonderful gift for you. I'm sure she assuages some of your loneliness!" The priest's voice was hearty but his eyes were wary. He had indeed heard of this child and her exile, first in the attic room and now with servants.

"Father O'Malley. How do you do. This is an unexpected pleasure." Like the father, Emily's eyes told a different story than her mouth. She'd never been taken much with priests and in the last two or three decades had gone out of her way to avoid them when possible, since one had told her after the birth of Marian that it was sinful to occupy an empty bed rather than that of her husband. Indeed. Perhaps he would like to produce the next infant for Edward's lineage. She would certainly never be taken abed in childbirth again.

And now, *this* priest. Come a-meddling again, no doubt. "Take that girl back upstairs, to her old room," Emily ordered Sarah.

"Ma'am?" Sarah responded in shock. "To the bedroom she stayed in after..." Sarah's voice trailed off.

"No," Emily said, decisively, "to the room she had before that one. She must be trained to her station in life."

"Miss Emily. You cannot lock this child away alone again. She suffered enough years for many lifetimes already. You must not inflict more harm on her."

Sarah's maternal instinct, always ready to fly to the defense of Catherine, left her standing, shocked into her response and personally vulnerable to the growing rage of Emily. "You will do as you are..."

The priest's voice overrode Emily's. "Perhaps I can be useful to you in this little problem," he offered. "You do have a beautiful grandchild, Miss Emily."

"This spawn of Satan is no grandchild of mine!" Emily retorted. "I'll not have her sullying the family reputation. She obviously is doing so, since you knew all about her."

"Miss Emily, I think you assign blame where it cannot lie. This child," gesturing toward Catherine, "is as innocent as any angel. Others made the decision of her birth. She had no voice."

"She literally *has* no voice," Emily shot back. "She's a retard who can't even talk. She's not of my family and I want no part of her."

"Miss Emily. Can we not sit down and quietly make some plans for this child? She is a beautiful girl and I should think she would be a credit to any family. Why do you say she can't talk? She certainly does not appear to be retarded. She seems to understand everything we say. Is that true?" he queried Catherine.

She looked to Sarah for guidance, as Sarah hovered near the door of the room. Sarah nodded slightly, more a movement of the eyes than of the head. The child then looked at the Father and nodded her head, yes, she did understand his words. The kindly priest reached out a hand to touch the girl's arm but Catherine shrieked and raised both arms to protect her face.

"I'm sorry, Reverend. You're only the second white man she's seen and..." after a brief hesitation she decided that telling the exact truth would only cause more harm to the girl, "she's afraid of you."

Father O'Malley looked cannily at Sarah's downcast eyes and posture. "I think that's part of the story, yes?" he said softly.

Sarah's eyes flicked up to meet his briefly, then dropped again. Emily interrupted, angered still more by the bypass the conversation had taken around her. "Perhaps the two of you would like to just settle this without me! Perhaps there's been enough meddling in Durrant family business already."

"Perhaps you'd like to pray," stabbing a finger at Father O'Malley, "and *you* would like to return to your proper work. Or perhaps," she said, her icy blue eyes flaring, "you'd like to take that *nigger* husband of yours and just get out. Out of my house, out of *my* cottage, off of *my* land, and away from *my* business! Get out! Get out!" she nearly screamed in rage. "And take this brazen slut with you," delivering a backhand blow to Catherine that knocked the child off balance; she would have fallen had Father O'Malley not caught her. "Get her out of here! Now!"

"Miss Emily," Sarah spoke quietly, "no one means to be disrespectful of you. "This is a tragic situation and we mean you no harm. We just speak to care for the child."

"Please come and sit, Miss Emily," the priest murmured. "How can I help you in this difficulty? I know it must be terrible to loose one's spouse after so many years together. Then to have this burden added to the weight of your sorrow. How can I lighten the load for you?"

Sarah remained standing by the door, knowing Emily's mind was utterly closed to her but hoping not to be sent away bodily also. Father O'Malley, aware of the servant's importance in this situation, was careful to look only at Miss Emily, so as not to draw the woman's attention back to Sarah. He had chosen a chair for Emily that faced away from the door, hoping that Sarah would recognize the opportunity to remain available to the discussion.

"Have you had any word of the child's mother?" he asked.

"What do you mean? That fallen woman has been gone a decade and more. She's dead. And the opportunistic devil who sired this bastard has never set face here. This child has no place here. She's to go to the orphanage. She certainly isn't wanted here!"

Sarah's face contorted in agony at Emily's words, but she was careful not to move nor make any sound.

"How old is the girl?" the Father asked.

"She's thirteen. Much too old to be staying here."

"Miss Emily, the orphanage won't take her. They're overcrowded and she's too old."

"You are not serious! Whatever am I to do with her if the orphanage won't take her? Edward's been gone since October, and it's June now, and there's nothing I can do for her. She can't stay here! Maybe she can go and work for some family somewhere else. Up north, maybe. They don't seem to be choosy up there about who they let run around free."

"Miss Catherine," the father spoke gently to the girl, standing alone, afraid to move to the comfort of Sarah's proximity. "Do you have any ideas about what you would like to do?"

"Please," the girl begged, "please, let me stay with Sarah. Please." Too frightened to look directly at Miss Emily, Catherine focused her plea – and her hope – on the priest. He mused silently for several seconds.

"Might it not be possible for Catherine to remain with Sarah for a time? She appears to be adequately cared for and she's out of your way while she's living with them. I can understand the pain her presence must bring you."

"Get her out of here. Send her home with that *nigger.* I don't care. Just get her ugly, evil being away from me."

"How terrible it would be to cast off one's child!" Father O'Malley mused as he visited briefly in Samuel and Sarah's home before leaving. "I should think the pain would be unbearable."

"She's a beautiful child with an exceptional mind in spite of the way she's been treated," Sarah asserted. "She must not come to more harm."

"Perhaps when she's older I may have something she'd appreciate," the priest said with a bemused look on his face. "She's a bit young now, and she needs all of the nurture you can provide her. I can't believe I didn't know she was here all those years..."

"None of us knew. It seems that the Durrants fired almost everyone who knew about Catherine as soon as they got rid of Miss Marian. The ones they didn't fire they lied to. They said Catherine had gone with her mother. No one knew better. Miss Emily herself was going up there every night to leave food and water for her. We just didn't know until she brought her downstairs, and by then she was terrified of anything and everything and she'd forgotten how to talk. It didn't take her long to catch up, though, at least in her speech. I'm not sure her *feelings* will ever catch up."

"It would have been terrible to suddenly learn there was a child locked up away from everyone for years. It was a terrible shock when *I* heard the rumor and a worse shock today when I finally learned the rumor was true. A terrible thing...

"Well. It seems to be taken care of for the moment. By the by...would you perhaps be interested in teaching other children?" he queried of Sarah. "There are almost no qualified teachers here and it appears that you might be better than average qualified."

"My mother was a teacher. My father was a multilingual immigrant from France. Yes, I am well qualified to teach except for one problem. Well, two problems. First, no one would allow a black woman to teach white children, and even though we're technically in a free state, whites are very unforgiving of blacks who are better-educated than they. I teach *my* child..." Sarah's voice dropped off as she realized what she had said, and to a white man.

"Bless you, Sarah. God bless and keep you and yours. Feel free to contact me any time you need help with Catherine. As do you, I feel like she's somehow partly my child." Making the sign of the cross over them, he left, shutting the door quietly behind him.

~ ~ ~

"Set dinner back and clean up and get out of here!" Emily ordered in a harsh voice.

"Miss Emily, do you not intend to eat...?"

Emily spun and stared out the window toward the activity near the river far below. A barge train moved with massive dignity downstream. Another followed half a mile behind the first. Men, made tiny by the distance, moved about the wharfs on both sides of the river. All was happening. Nothing was happening.

The servant, perceiving the rigidly held back and shoulders to be a response to her question, silently pulled the door to and walked away. Her children relied on her alone to keep them fed and housed. Their father had vanished one night on the way home from his work down in the small town growing up from the river. In her continuing terror, she knew unquestioningly he'd been stolen and sold South. But there was no time to grieve in her world. There were only the children to be sheltered from the hands of the slave-catchers and those who hated them for their skin. The children would eat well tonight.

They would partake of the bounty refused by Miss Emily.

~ ~ ~

Emily gazed over the distant scene, unseeing. Her shoulders hurt from their tension and her insides were a cold hard knot. A painful, cold, hard knot. As she recognized the discomfort of her body, a sweat appeared on her brow and it was necessary to swallow repeatedly to quell her rising gorge.

*Momma, I have to throw up. Momma...*

*There, there darling. It will be better now. Momma will sit with you 'til you go to sleep. Hush-a-bye, my darling. Hush-a-bye. Momma's here and you will feel better in the morning...*

*Momma! Where did you go? Please, Momma. Please come back. Please hold me and tell me it will be all right...* Emily broke off mid-thought as she realized she was pleading with the dead to comfort her.

*All dead. Everyone dead. Edward! You left without me, Edward! Please, Edward. Please tell me what to do...*

*Edward is dead. Marian is gone and maybe dead. Anson is gone and likely dead. Or he wants to be dead to me. After what he did to his sister, he'll wish he were dead if he isn't.*

*This child! What to do with this child! My god, she doesn't belong here!*

*You've wished her away and dead every day for a dozen years, Emily. Face up to it.*

*I took care of her! Every single night for all those years, I took care of her. She always had food and water...*

*You hated her, Emily. She took Marian away from you and you hated her.*

*That's preposterous.*

*Marian was a dream child, Emily. She was going to be all the things you wanted to be and couldn't achieve. And she got herself in the family way with a complete stranger. She'd rather have him than you, Emily! And his child...*

*No! Tell me, no, no, no, no! The denials wrenched from her very heart. Better she should have gone with her mother. She couldn't do that... Better to have left her at the orphanage then. She'd have been taken by some family who wanted her...*

*No! She can't stay here! I don't want her! I want Marian. My own beautiful girl... Catherine looks like Marian... When I saw her out in the yard yesterday, I thought for an instant it was Marian. Please! I want my own girl. Why did he take her away! Is she still there? Where is she?*

*A part of her is here, Emily. A lovely part of her...*

*No! No red head ever came from here...*

*It's strawberry blond hair, Emily. Not red. It was a gift from her father. From her father to her and to you. It's really lovely hair, Emily.*

*No. My God! That man from the boat that day had red hair. And he came right to the front door. Is he...?*

*He might have been... He probably was... Did he know about the child? Marian wrote him, she said. In Anson's letters. Anson... Where is Anson?*

*Look, Edward. Your firstborn. A son. Isn't he lovely, Edward? See how strong his little fist is. See how he tries to hold his head up? He favors you, I think. Don't you think so?*

*Where is my son? My firstborn. Oh my god! Where is Anson? Where is my little man?*

*You sent him away, remember?*

*No! No... That was Edward who sent him away...*

*And what did you say to your son, your firstborn, when Edward sent off that raging letter disinheriting him? Eh? What did you send to your 'little man'? Ah, yes. You sent him silence. Did you not? You must have loved him very well indeed. And Marian. Did you contend for her?*

*No! No... I didn't know until the next day!*

*Now is that really true? You knew the whispers going around the house. You knew Edward had ordered the carriage. You knew... You really knew. You just wanted to pretend it wasn't happening. Maybe if you pretended it really wouldn't happen. But it did.*

*No! I didn't know... Yes, I knew. Damme! I knew, I did know. But I didn't know it was forever! And he died and I don't know where he took her. I don't know if she's alive. I don't know about my own children...*

Emily rushed to the front door, where she vomited into the tea rose beside the door until there was only bile and spittle left.

~ ~ ~

Will was doing very well learning the river. He'd watched every moment of his two years on deck when he didn't have to be attending some chore of his own. He'd learned to read the river by associating the actions of the actual pilot with any changes in the river. He'd learned to detect the shadows beyond reach of the mirrored lantern on the bow when they ran at night. At first, he missed the subtleties, but over two years he'd learned each clue telegraphed by the river, and he now transferred that knowledge into the action of his hands on the wheel.

"This is going to be a quick apprenticeship, I see," James offered. "You've already learned much of what the river demands. A few more trips and you'll definitely be a pilot I can leave in charge so I can catch a night's sleep. You'll move up to assistant pilot after this trip.

"Thomas won't be coming back upriver with us. He's a competent pilot now and he plans to get a boat of his own. He's saved most of his wages and his uncle is helping him, he says. So the timing was very good for you to move in and learn the river's magic." He grinned at Will, pleased with his fortune in having a good man available when an opening occurred.

Will smiled at the good humor of James and at his own great luck.

Will had been a hard worker since he was only a stripling of a boy. He was about seven when he realized his mother wasn't hungry some evenings simply because there wasn't enough food for both her and the children.

Will went the very next day, knocking at the kitchen doors of all the big houses for a couple of miles around. He was a dark-skinned boy in a city that rated *octoroons* or *high yallas* or *bright skinned* above darker-skinned persons, often even within a family. As young as seven he knew he had no future here – or maybe no future anyplace – but he knew his momma went hungry and if he worked hard he might be able to keep her fed.

He went to the market, at first in the company of the cooks, and carried back heavy loads of food for those who lived in the big houses. When he had learned to tell good from poor and then excellent from only good, and as the cooks learned they could trust his judgment so they needn't go with him, the jobs and his earnings rose. Occasionally he was used to carry messages from one of the whites in the big houses to another white somewhere else, and they also learned that Will Isaacs was trustworthy.

Will was on the docks one day buying fish for one of the cooks he served, when he saw James asking about for a deckhand. "Please, suh. Please let me work for you. I'm strong and I'm reliable and I love the river. Please give me a chance to show you how well I can work."

"You're a bit young, aren't you?" James asked. "Why do you think you can do a deckhand's work?"

"Please, suh. I work for many of the cooks here, buying what they need from the markets and delivering it fresh to their kitchen doors. I comes here to buy fish often and I always watch the men working the boats. I carry heavy loads a long way every day. I can do what your men are doing," pointing at the sweating crew scrambling to off load the heavy bales of cotton. "I've always wanted to work the boats, suh. Will you give me a chance?"

James looked musingly at the boy. He looked to be a bit older than James himself had been when he hired out as a deckhand. He'd loved the river as a boy also. "How old are you, son?"

"I'se 15, suh." Will's excitement caused a lapse from the standard English his mother required – during the brief moments she was able to share with her children – to the idiom of the streets where he worked long hours daily

"You're kind of puny for 15, aren't you?" James queried.

"But I'm very strong, suh. I works to help my momma feed my little brothers and my sister. I've been working for years, suh."

"Yeah, not many years I don't expect," James responded with a grin. "If you hire out on a boat, what will your mother do while you're gone? How will she get along without you? Will one of your brothers help her out?"

Will's face fell. "No, suh," he replied despondently, stubbing his bare toes against the dirt. "I didn't think about that. I guess I can't go, after all. My next biggest brother is only eight years old. The younger ones, they got a different daddy. Daniel, he has to stay home with the little ones so my mother can go and work. I don't know how they'd get along without me. 'Course," his face lifted, "I wouldn't be eating there; Momma would save that much... No, I guess I better stay," he said. "Momma needs me."

"What's your name, son?" James asked.

"Will, suh. Will Isaacs."

"How much do you usually make to give your mother, Will?"

"It depends, suh. Some days I makes six or eight cents and once in a while even a dime. Some days I only makes a penny or two."

"I'll tell you what, Will Isaacs. I'll take you on if your mother agrees. And

I'll pay you half your wages for the first trip so you can give your mother the money she needs to take care of the children. A deckhand earns $2 a week. We're headed for Cincinnati this trip; we'll be out two or three months, depending on the loads and the rivers. I'll give you $8 advance on your wages so you can give some to your mother.

"You come back here tomorrow morning by five o'clock. That will give you time to finish the work you've promised for today and to talk to your mother.

"We'll leave out about eight or nine o'clock in the morning. You can help load wood for the upstream trip so you'll get broke in right away. Deal? Remember, you have to tell your mother and get her permission. Will you do that? Here. Here's your advance," digging into his pocket and counting out eight silver dollars to the astonished boy. "See you in the morning?"

"Yes! yes, suh! Five o'clock sharp suh!" Will spun and raced off, stopping at the fish market and hopping on one leg while his purchase was wrapped and placed in his basket. James watched him thoughtfully. He was pleased that the boy stopped to buy his fish. If he kept his word to old employers, he would likely be reliable on the *Marian Dee* also.

Chapter Seven

Catherine paused in her stitchery. Sarah had set her to sewing strips of rags together, end to end, to later braid into rugs. The work was tedious but Catherine had learned to take pride in it; she always took fine stitches. Samuel had made a quilt frame for Sarah and this winter she would set a quilt on the frame in the cottage. Catherine had always admired quilts and was eager to become proficient enough with her needle to help quilt one.

*What will they do with me?* she pondered. She was nearly a woman grown now; she couldn't stay here much longer. It was a wonder that the men in white sheets had not already come for Samuel and Sarah, having a white child – a white woman, really – living with them. Catherine suspected that those men, so bold they had to hide under sheets, were afraid of Miss Emily. She herself certainly was!

Father O'Malley had happened into another problem episode with Miss Emily – if one believed in chance in such occurrences, which Catherine did not – nearly two years after the first such intervention. The unwilling grandmother had again heard whispers about the hidden child and was again attempting to take vengeance on the child. The good Father happened in as the anguished rage began to boil over.

"Miss Emily. My dear Miss Emily. How can we ease this problem for you? I understand that this represents a terrible loss to you..."

Emily soared into full rage. "Get her out of here. Take her away! *Take her away from here!*"

Catherine held her arms close about her body and shuddered. "Father! Please help me! *Bitte, Vater, bitte.*"

The astonished priest looked at Catherine, jaw dropped. "How did you learn German?" he queried. "Can you speak more German?"

*"Ja, mein Herr. Ich sprechen..."* the girl faltered as Emily turned to glare at her and at Sarah, who had come into the foyer behind Catherine.

"I warned you about being an uppity nigger," Emily flashed. "Decent white folk don't speak all those heathen languages. Well-bred folk speak English."

"Miss Emily, my Irish father and German mother – who were both white and decent and bilingual – would be rather surprised at that judgment. The ability to use other languages well is a rare gift and nearly always limited to those who can afford a fine education or those who have just immigrated from another land. And it's usually the children of those folk who can speak both English and the native language of their parents."

Purple with rage but abashed by the priestly reprimand, Emily spun and stormed up the wide stair, leaving the other adults to settle the girl's terror. Some weeks later, with Father O'Malley finding Miss Emily at peace under the rear arbor, she was persuaded to give the child an opportunity to find a place in life, with the assurance of all possible help from the good Father.

Miss Emily – she was carefully warned by that lady herself to never presume on her good fortune by calling her 'Grandmother' or any other family title – Miss Emily had finally bent enough toward acknowledgement of the girl to begin to require her to lunch with her once weekly. One couldn't trust the colored help to train a white girl, even an unwanted white girl.

Sarah carefully coached Catherine before her first luncheon with her grandmother. "Use your forks and spoons from the outside in, baby. Don't change silver except when the type of food changes. Watch Miss Emily and do exactly as she does. You are the guest and she the hostess. The guest should always wait and follow the example of the hostess."

"Surely we won't have all this silver for a luncheon, will we?"

"I wouldn't depend on that. If Miss Emily wants to believe it's all right to exile you again and again as she has done for almost all of your life, all she needs is to find you clumsy and without proper manners. No, your napkin first, like this..." Sarah pinched the napkin between thumb and forefinger and *swish*ed it open with a gentle flick of the wrist.

"Yes! You do that very well.

"How about the art of conversation, now? How will you spend the time you share with Miss Emily?"

"I think I mustn't talk about family nor encourage her to talk about herself. What do you suggest?"

The first luncheon was terrifying but surprisingly successful. Miss Emily did indeed have full place settings of silver and glassware and Catherine was profoundly grateful that Sarah had bullied her to learn how to use her utensils comfortably and appropriately. Conversation proved more challenging. The neutral topics suggested by Sarah fell flat and silence lay disquietly between them.

Finally, Catherine happened to ask the history of the house they occupied. Miss Emily brightened immediately and soon forgot herself, talking about Mr. Durrant having the house built for them. She shared the excitement of the planning, in which her husband had relied on her sense of proportion and design, and the trips up from the hotel below, where they took up residence during the long months of raising of the house, to see what had been accomplished in the interim.

At the close of the luncheon Catherine thanked Miss Emily formally and was summoned for a second lunch on the following Tuesday.

~ ~ ~

I'm amazed, Emily thought. That girl was entirely competent both in what she did and in what she said. Hmmph. I didn't think Sarah could do a thing with her. No, I didn't think Sarah knew enough to teach her. Why? Why must I make all the decisions and bear all the burdens? Damme you, Edward! You've left everything in a perfect mishmash.

The sound of the doorknocker roused Emily from her painful meditations. She heard the voices of the downstairs girl and of a man. The door closed and the girl appeared in the dining room, where Emily lingered.

"Miss Emily, ma'am, it's Mr. Jarod from the bank. He says he needs to see you."

"Show him into the drawing room. I'll be with him directly."

"Mr. Jarod. To what do I owe the pleasure of your visit?" Emily murmured politely, seating him on the brocade sofa..

"Mrs. Durrant, I'm afraid I bring terrible news. As you know, there was some confusion with Mr. Durrant's will and his estate. We spoke of that shortly after your husband's death. You authorized us at that time to have the bank's attorneys straighten everything out and in the interim, your household allowance remained unchanged from the amount Mr. Durrant authorized some years ago. The attorneys and investigators have finally been able to clear away most of the puzzle, but the news is not good."

"I see. May I offer you a cup of tea?" Emily responded, holding to the forms of courtesy and pushing back the moment of revelation a bit.

"No, ma'am. No thank you. The will was a real challenge, since Mr. Durrant left equal shares to you and to your children. We sent men to investigate the whereabouts of your son, Anson, and I'm afraid I have bad news about him." Jarod hesitated, trying to read the expression on Mrs. Durrant's face. It remained bafflingly aloof.

"Anson Wilford Durrant, deckhand on the *Daisy Lee* steamboat, was killed in an accident on July 17, 1837, in New Orleans, Louisiana. The boat captain, a John Marat, said young Durrant was a friend of the boat's pilot, James Mason. The captain said Mason wrote Anson Durrant's family, notifying you of young Durrant's death." Eyebrows raised, Mr. Jared peered at Emily, noting with some alarm a sudden pallor and tightening of the woman's eyes.

"Indeed, he did not! We had no knowledge of our son's death from any source. After a time we did assume something had happened to him; Anson would never go for an extended period without making contact with us."

"I was surprised to learn he'd been working as a deckhand on a boat..." Jarod murmured. "It's hardly the sort of work I'd expected Mr. Durrant's son – and your son, also, of course – it's hardly the line of work in which I'd have thought your son would engage."

"Oh. Yes, that was some foolishness between Mr. Durrant and our son. Edward told him he expected him to work the summer after his graduation from preparatory school, to get some experience before leaving for college that fall. The intention, of course, was that Anson employ himself in the service of one businessman or another, here in our own community. Our son, however, met a man from that steamboat one day on the wharf and was enamored of work on the river. He signed a contract on the spot and then came and informed his father.

"There was a terrible row and Anson left without taking his leave from me or from his sister. He wrote to his sister regularly, but he allowed... Well, that's neither here nor there. Mr. Durrant thought his contact with his sister was not wise and he stopped it. We've heard nothing since then. I beg your pardon, *I've* heard nothing since until this news you bring. She was silent for long moments, eyes squeezed shut. "Where is my son buried?" she inquired presently. She would mourn her son but not publicly.

"He was interred in New Orleans, Mrs. Durrant, where the accident occurred. I understand that he was interred in the captain's vault there. I'm afraid there have been two or three deaths in that family since then and so your so..." Shaking his head, he stopped mid-sentence.

"Perhaps I need to explain. Some say New Orleans has above-ground tombs because it has ground water almost up to the surface, while others say it's a custom they started because it was fashionable in Europe. For whatever reason, they don't bury underground. Instead, they have aboveground vaults.

"The body is carried to the burial vault in a casket and set inside the vault. The vault is reclosed, and when another death occurs the vault is opened and the 'old' body – usually just bones by then – is put into a bag and laid behind or to the side of the new casket, or some of the tombs have what is called an 'ossuary' underneath. The old casket is discarded.

"After a few generations – and most of the vaults in New Orleans are a few generations old – the bags rot out and so the bones of the deceased might mix together. In the instance of your son it might not be too difficult to retrieve his body to bring it home for burial, but there would be a delay, as there was a death in the captain's family only three or four months ago. They have a firm tradition of not opening a tomb for a year and a day after the last interment – if a family death occurs within that period they actually build a new tomb for that interment."

"I don't understand..." Emily faltered.

"Mrs. Durrant... I don't know how to say this delicately enough for a lady to hear, but a body smells after it's been dead for a little while. That's why we have funerals usually two days after someone dies, so..."

"So the smell doesn't disturb the mourners. Yes. I understand. Perhaps at a later time we might consider trying to have his body extricated and returned here for burial."

"Yes, ma'am.

"Is there more disturbing news?"

"I'm afraid there is, Mrs. Durrant. We've been unable to trace the whereabouts of your daughter, Miss Marian Durrant. Do you have information that might be of any help?"

"Is there no end to this evil?" she exclaimed. "If she still lives I have no notion of the whereabouts of that evil seed. None!"

"I'm afraid that brings me to more bad news, ma'am," the banker said. "The portion of your late husband's inheritance marked for your son will revert to you. I'm afraid that is a small amount. And that's assuming he had no other heirs. Is that correct?"

"As far as I know, he had no heirs. He went to such lengths to separate himself from his family the Lord above only knows for sure."

"We interviewed the captain of the riverboat where young Anson worked and lived. He had no knowledge of any connection between your son and any other person except for the pilot of the boat. Unfortunately, that pilot now owns and operates his own steamboat and we were unable to find him."

"Yes. I cannot help with that, certainly. So tell me about his sister's portion of my husband's estate."

"Miss Marian Durrant could not be located by our investigator. An old black man down in colored town says he drove Mr. Durrant and his daughter somewhere, but he's old and forgetful and he was unable to remember where he took them. He did remember coming back with only Mr. Durrant."

"As far as I'm concerned, my daughter also is dead. We gave her every advantage and she utterly rejected the privilege of being a member of this family. If she still lives I know nothing of her whereabouts nor do I want to know."

"We believe that Miss Marian is alive somewhere but we've been unable to locate any information except for the story told by the old driver and a second hand tale purported to be from another former servant."

"And what pray tell might that be?"

"Someone who knew the cook who used to work here said the cook told her there was a child here. She says she used to bake cookies especially for that child – oatmeal cookies. She says the child, a little girl, loved cookies and hot bread, just out of the oven. She said that you and Mr. Durrant were in Europe and when you returned she was suddenly let go, with extra wages and a good reference, but without giving any reason for terminating her employment here." Mr. Jarod again raised his eyebrows in inquiry.

"Piffle. It should be obvious that such a tale is merely that: a tale with no foundation. I clearly remember Edward firing that cook after we returned from the grand tour. And visiting our daughter in finishing school in France. Yes. We visited Marian and completed the tour and returned home to find the cook was stealing us blind. The help didn't know when we were returning. Edward caught her red-handed. She left the place the same day."

"She left with a good reference..."

"She obviously wrote that herself."

"Mrs. Durrant, she couldn't read or write. She didn't know what the reference said until she showed it to her next employer. She couldn't have written it."

"Likely. Dishonest people have all sorts of resources for such things. You'd be surprised. So tell me about this second portion of Mr. Durrant's will."

"Mrs. Durrant, our investigator was unable to locate any information about the current whereabouts of your daughter. Nor could he find evidence of her death. The information we did receive leads us to believe that your daughter had a baby, a little girl..."

"I beg your pardon!" Emily interjected. "I'll have no talk of such trash in my house!"

"I'm sorry, Mrs. Durrant," Jarod said. He was now obviously uncomfortable, with face red and perspiration clinging to his forehead. "You must understand that Mr. Durrant was a customer of our bank and we are ethically obliged to fulfill his wishes. To do so for a customer we sometimes have to investigate unknowns, so all can be set in order. I assure you that our attorneys and our investigators are men of absolute honor, who never disclose any information they turn up for the bank about our customers. You may rely on our absolute discretion."

"I rely on nothing! Finish stating your business and get out. You've wasted entirely too much of my time already."

"Mrs. Durrant, the portion of your husband's estate earmarked for your daughter must be held in escrow for a period of seven years. If after that time you choose to have her declared legally dead her portion of the inheritance is freed up for her heir or heirs. I believe she had been absent from your family for a longer period than that already; you can likely have such a declaration made immediately if you so desire.

"If you do so choose, however, the bank's attorneys will not be available to assist you, as that would constitute a conflict of interest. We can, of course, refer you to other competent attorneys who can provide able representation for you.

"A second complication arises in your daughter's estate, however. Forgive me, ma'am, but we believe that your daughter bore a daughter herself. That belief is based on the formal statement from the former cook here, Rosemary Sims, and further, on the statement of one Absolom Tanner, whom I believe is a former groom here.

"This Absolom Tanner states that he saw your daughter, Miss Marian, outside playing with her child frequently while your and Mr. Durrant were in Europe. He states that he had just come out of the stable one afternoon when the hack arrived bearing you and Mr. Durrant. He states that the child was playing in the leaf piles raked up by some of the boys.

"He states that the child was looking away from the drive and unaware of your return until Mr. Durrant stepped out of the carriage. He states that Mr. Durrant picked the child up and beat her severely. He states that Miss Marian was in the outhouse when that event occurred, and that she tried to stop your husband when she saw him striking the child.

"Given such a belief as this we must retain in escrow your daughter's portion of the estate until her death is confirmed if she has died, and her child can be located, if such a person truly exists. If you can assist in that task the process can be speeded considerably." He stopped, now perspiring freely, and mopped his brow and cheeks with a white handkerchief.

"I believe you said there was still another matter after this? As for this, I have no information whatever. Anything that might have occurred at that time was family business only. I'm not accustomed to strangers involving themselves in family affairs."

"Yes ma'am, Mrs. Durrant. I do beg your indulgence a bit. I realize that I am a stranger to you but I ask you to accept that Mr. Durrant knew me well and transacted all of his bank business through me. I had the privilege of serving him – and you, of course, through him – since I was hired by the bank a number of years ago. I do beg your forgiveness for the things that I must say, but in my task of being the bank, as it were, serving your husband and you, his wife, there are certain things I must relate, and I am truly regretful of the pain I know this causes you."

"Indeed. I'm afraid you know little of my husband and nothing about me. I am intensely irritated that strangers have been gossiping about our family and that you have taken their words as if they were the gospel itself. As for any inheritance for my daughter, I have no concern. I believe she is finally and irrevocably dead and I am her sole heir. I care nothing about the money, however, so it is a matter of utter indifference what you do with the portion of Mr. Durrant's estate that he so foolishly scattered about."

"Ma'am, this will was drawn up in 1818, leaving equal portions of the estate to you and to your son after the birth of your son. A codicil was added in 1819, subsequent to the birth of your daughter. The bank, as named executor of the estate, has held the single copy of the will since it was drawn. Except for the 1819 codicil, it remains unchanged.

"The house and grounds are left to you for your lifetime and are to be shared by your children at your death. He stated a preference that the home be kept in the family but allowed for its sale if necessary, with the proceeds to be equally divided. The same provision is made for Durrant Furniture Works. All other assets are to be divided equally among the three of you. The final difficulty, Mrs. Durrant..." he paused, looking pained.

"Yes. Indeed you must finish," she interposed. "Pray continue."

"Mrs. Durrant, there isn't any money. There are almost no assets. The sale of the business will barely pay the debt Mr. Durrant incurred. Mr. Durrant had great faith in the investments he made, and frankly, some of them were disastrous.

"The furniture works must be sold to satisfy the debts, else the bank will foreclose on the business, which would likely realize a still smaller return. We have stalled foreclosure as long as possible but we are simply at the end of that road. The debts must be paid and the least disadvantageous way to do so is to sell. That, of course, will preclude any further income for you.

"Forgive me for being the bearer of such evil news, but I have been unable to devise a way for you to keep the living portion of the estate – this house and land – unbroken. There is certainly no way for you to continue living as you have been. How many servants do you have, Mrs. Durrant?"

"You'll find the household accounts in order, entirely. We have lived comfortably on the amount set aside for household expenses. In fact, there is a bit of a surplus."

"Ma'am. Please. What I'm telling you is that we cannot continue the household allowance to which you are accustomed. I'm afraid the servants will have to be let go, or almost all of them. There's no way you can keep this large house without servants, and even if you could manage it without servants, I'm unable to absolutely assure you that the house can be disencumbered from Mr. Durrant's debt. Mrs. Durrant, I'm afraid you'll have to retire to a much more modest dwelling... We can continue for the balance of this year and perhaps a portion of the next, but it cannot be delayed past midyear next year at most. There simply is no money to continue as you have been living.

"Allow me to add, Mrs. Durrant, that the holding of your daughter's portion of the estate would not in any way affect your ability to hold the estate – the house and grounds – intact."

"So I am truly reduced to poverty. Very well. You'll excuse me now, Mr. Jarod. I have things to which I need attend as I'm sure you do also. I shall notify you of my decisions at the appropriate time. In the meantime, you are to continue the household allowance as it has been." So saying, she ushered him to the door and closed it firmly behind him.

*My god, Edward! The final evil. You squandered everything and left me destitute. My god. How you must have hated me! How can you have done this to me? Damme you! Damme you to eternal torment in hell! I trusted you and you have betrayed me so that the whole community now talks of Durrant family business and we'll soon have to move into some shanty somewhere. Perhaps we'll find one in nigger town, Edward. Is that what you wished for us?*

Emily shut herself in her room for the balance of the day, barking sharp orders to cease to each person who rapped on her door, concerned about her welfare.

"Miz Emily in right bad trouble, the downstairs girl confided to Angel, the cook. We in worser trouble. We all fixin' to get fired off 'cause Miz Emily ain't got no money for to pay us."

"Go'on," scoffed Angel. "Miz Emily got 'nuff' money to buy and sell us all..."

Angel stopped suddenly as she realized what she'd said. "Oh good Lawd Jesus! He'p us'n in 'dis evil time. Miz Emily sell us all, 'den she got no money troubles no more. Good Lawd Jesus. What we gonna do?"

"D'on rec'lect nuthin' bout what *you* does, but I know what *I* does. I gets mysel' outta here 'afore she rec'lect can she sell me Sout'h. Lawd Jesus! My mammy tells me how it be down Sout'h when she be slave d'ere. Her massa my pappy! I'se not even borned yet when she got on 'de Un'ergroun' Railroad and comes up here. I don't never want to find out for mysel' what it like down d'ere!

The whispers reached Sarah and Samuel soon after the kitchen was alerted. "What will we do?" Sarah asked. "We've lived here all of our adult lives. We have no place to go. And we have Catherine to care for."

"It isn't going to happen today or tomorrow," Samuel reassured her. "When I heard it in the kitchen I slipped away and talked to Esther. She be the one heard the bank man with Miss Emily. He tell her she got enough money to live like this – making a circular gesture encompassing the big house and grounds – for this year and into next year. So we got some time to plan. Res' yo'self," he comforted her, arms gently and firmly encompassing her. "Res' yo'self."

## Chapter Eight

Life continued as previously in the great sandstone house and its outbuildings and fields except that one by one the servants slipped away to new occupations as opportunities were presented. Esther, the downstairs girl, and both of the upstairs girls were gone before the snow fell. The housekeeper was hard put to keep the house in trim without those key workers. Sarah, whose work was usually as personal attendant to Miss Emily and her wardrobe and belongings, was pressed into service both upstairs and down, as Miss Emily chose not to replace the absent servants.

Christmas came and the great house remained dark and undecorated. Miss Emily, when her children were young, had taken great pains to greet the holiday with wreaths and ribbon and garlands, up and down the staircase and around the crowns of drawing room and parlor, and always with a huge candle-lit tree near the front door in the large central hall. As the children grew the trimmings lessened, but still the wreath was on the front door and the great tree stood in splendor to welcome any and all callers. This year there was neither wreath nor tree, nor any visitor.

Samuel, like Sarah, found himself with extra work when all but one of the stable and yard hands left. He was grateful that the loft was filled with hay and bins of corn and oats were laid by to bring the animals through the winter. He rose earlier now, long before dawn, to care for the animals and worked past his usual time to leave the stable and come home to the snug cottage he shared with Sarah and Catherine.

"Momma Sarah," Catherine said. "Sometimes I'm still so angry when I think about Miss Emily and what she did to me. Sometimes I just want to go and face her down and yell and tell her how evil she was to treat me that way. Sometimes I still go out in the woods and beat on logs with a stick the way you suggested when I was still a child. It helps, but sometimes I still get angry..."

Sarah heard her without interruption, knowing that Catherine must own her feelings so she could eventually work through them. She was unprepared for Catherine's next remark, however.

"Sometimes, Sarah, I think about Miss Emily being in that big house alone. Do you suppose she's lonely? I know I was lonely when I was alone, even though I didn't know then what loneliness was. Sometimes I just ached and ached and didn't even know to cry to let some of it out so it wouldn't hurt so bad."

"You were taught not to cry, baby," Sarah responded. "I showed your momma how to teach you to be silent so no one would think to hurt you. For Miss Emily, I don't know if she's lonely. Mr. Durrant is gone; she let her children go without a murmur and she has chosen to deny you. If she's lonely she's not about to make life any easier for herself."

"Momma Sarah, I still have luncheons with her every Tuesday. Do you think I might make something special for her? Do you think something like that might make her feel better?"

"I don't know, lovey, but you're blessed to think of it."

"She is blessed, and you are the source of the blessing," Samuel said quietly to Sarah.

"Oh no! The Lord Jesus is the source of her blessing and we're just instruments of the Lord. You are every bit as much as I am."

"I know I love you both, fiercely and forever," he replied in a gruff tone.

"And I you," quietly spoken. "What do you think Miss Emily might like?" she queried Catherine.

"I don't know, Momma Sarah. She is partial to fresh bread. Do you think I might bake some bread for her?"

"Of course you can. I'll help you. And it will be a gift for Angel too. She won't have to bake as much this week."

Catherine went to the kitchen early the following morning to get supplies for her baking. Angel nodded her approval and began to gather together the flour, the starter, and the other ingredients for bread.

"If you like, Miss Catherine, you's can make the bread here, since Sarah said it's all right for you to bake. I be glad to he'p you. That be easier than baking it myself...my feets hurts right bad sometimes. If'n you bakes here you can make a big batch like I do, in the big oven. Miss Emily don't hardly ever come in here and if she do she just think you sitting here keepin' me company."

The bread rising, Angel decided to mix up a batch of cookies, her contribution to the holiday of those still there. "Fetch me 'da box of oatmeal, will you, honey?" to Catherine. She started to tell her where to find it but was surprised to see the young woman move confidently to the pantry shelves and unerringly pick up the oatmeal box.

"How you know where 'dat be?" she quizzed. "Ain't nobody tell you where 'dat be. How you know like 'dat?"

"It's where it's always been, Rosemary," Catherine murmured. "I always get it for you..." Her voice broke off as she realized what she was saying. "I always get the oatmeal for the oatmeal cookies on baking day..." She looked at Angel in amazement. "But you're not Rosemary. You're Angel..."

"De ol' cook be Rosemary. Dey fire her way back when dey taken Miss Marian away. Dey say she get into what not her bidsness and dey fire her right off. I be the cook helper den. Yeah, Rosemary know you partial to oatmeal cookies. You just a little bit of a thing den."

"Yes. I remember. Rosemary always made oatmeal cookies for me on baking days, when my mother and I were here together. I remember my mother, here in the kitchen with me, watching Rosemary bake my cookies. That's what she always said, they were *my* cookies.

"I remember her! I really do! And that's why I'm so sad when Sarah brings home fresh, hot bread. I expect to see my momma and she's not here anymore. Angel, do you know what they did with her?" Her tone was pleading, as she looked at Angel.

"No, Miss Cath'rine. I don't 'spect anybody know 'dat now. I knows Mr. Edward, he taken out the carriage in 'de night and he make her go wi'd him. She cry, Miss Marian, Jenny say. She ask Jenny t'take care a' you, she say. But he fire her, too. He fire 'de cook and 'de groom and 'de downstairs girl. He sayin' they right bizybodies, meddlin' in his affairs. And nobody know what he do wid' you. He been a hard man, dat Mr. Edward. A hard man."

Sarah had entered the kitchen quietly and stood by the door, listening to the conversation between Angel and Catherine. Good, she thought. She has another piece of the puzzle of her life now. And she remembers her mother. My gracious, how could anyone ever do such a thing to another human being! Surely even being sold South wouldn't be as bad as this, because whoever is left behind is still walking about, with others to talk to and work to do. Not shut up in an attic with only a slit of a window to connect her with the world.

The bread for her gift was successful, with Angel's able tutelage. Catherine now proudly brought a new loaf to Miss Emily for their weekly luncheon. "Angel taught me to do it," she explained. "I wanted to give you something for Christmas and I didn't know what else you might like. I hope you're pleased with my work."

Emily averted her face toward the window, eyes bright. When she had regained control, she turned back toward her tablemate. "It was very kind of you to think of me, Catherine. I'm afraid I don't understand your thoughtfulness. I've given you nothing but pain... But I do appreciate your gift."

"Miss Emily, we've... you've given me everything I need. You gave me Sarah and Samuel to love me, and a comfortable bed to sleep in. I have two dresses and a pair of boots. I always have plenty of good food. The Lord Jesus has been good to me, and he's worked through you to give me such abundance. I'm very grateful to you Miss Emily."

The older woman stood, her face rigidly controlled. "I'm afraid I shan't be able to lunch with you today, Catherine. I have one of my sudden headaches. We'll meet next week as usual." Turning swiftly, she was gone.

*Momma, I brought you this bouquet of flowers, Momma. See how pink and pretty they are? I got stuck by the rosebush, but I brought you the pretty flowers.*

*Emily, will you never learn? You must not pull off the flowers. The gardener works hard to make them nice so everyone can see them.*

*But Momma! I got them for you... She wiped a spot of blood from a rose- thorn stick on her pinafore. Please, Momma. Aren't they pretty? Shall I put them in water for you, Momma? Shall I have cook get me a vase?*

*Child, just throw them away. They're ruined now; you took them off of the rose bush. Your father will be displeased. That tea rose was his favorite.*

*But Momma...*

*The tears slid down the child's face. The roses drooped forlornly from her small fist. A flower fell and lay unnoticed. Emily did not bring her mother flowers again.*

The Lord Jesus. I suppose Sarah's got her jumping with that nigger church of hers. Oh well. I guess the Catholics didn't want her... No, I guess *I* wouldn't let the Catholics have her...

What am I to do, Edward? You got me into this; tell me how to get out of it. You lost our children. Yes! *We* lost our children. Our son is dead. Perhaps our daughter is too. We'll never know, will we? Or at least I won't know. If there truly is an afterlife perhaps you do know...

Is there an afterlife? Are there truly gold-paved streets? Or eternal fires? And where are you, my fair lover? In heaven? Or in hell?

Some of the servants are already gone, Edward. They heard the evil rumors and slipped away when they could find jobs elsewhere. It's nearly finished here, isn't it, Edward? Most of the stable boys are gone. The upstairs and downstairs girls are gone. I can see dust where it never lay before, Edward. You'd have had a fit if the house had been as slovenly kept as it is now when you were here, Edward.

What am I to do now, Edward? I cannot stay here as the house is gradually reduced to filth and neglect. I have no place to go. I have no one...

What should I do with this Catherine, Edward? Is she truly flesh of our flesh? This child of a flaming-haired boatman... Her eyes look like your eyes, Edward. Like her mother's eyes..."

*Oh Edward. Look! She has your eyes! See the little crinkle at the side of her eyes? It looks like the crinkle by your eyes when you smile. I don't suppose she is really smiling at us, is she? It certainly looks like it though, doesn't it. I'm glad she looks so like you. I'll have this little face to remind me of yours when you're gone at work every day. Isn't she wonderful? How proud you must be, Edward.*

Marian. Flesh of my flesh. Heart of my heart... Catherine. Also of my flesh... of my... Is she? If she is, what's to be done? I know she is... I just don't know what to do with her... How can I ever make it up to her? I know she doesn't want to live in this house. She's made that clear enough since she's been here. Oh my lord. Since she's been free from the attic prison where Edward put her and I kept her. Great God forgive me! Had she been a stranger hell fire and damnation would have taken me. But my own flesh...

~ ~ ~

"James? Are you awake? You're about to nest on a sandbar there."

When James didn't respond immediately Will reached over and spun the wheel hard aport, holding the spoke down until the shallow had been passed safely. "Sorry," James mumbled. "I was woolgathering. Here. You take it for a bit, will you, while I visit the head and get a cup of coffee. It wouldn't have been the first time I set on a sandbar because I wasn't paying attention. Oh well, I guess we great ones all have to have some weakness, yes?" He laughed and ducked as Will threw his hat at him.

"So, how is your mother and your brothers?" James asked, returning with a cup of coffee for both of them. Catching a quick sideways look from Will he pounced. "Aha. The man has a secret! Might that be a young woman secret?"

It was fortunate that Will was dark-skinned enough to conceal the blush he certainly had, or James would have teased him still more. He did grin and acknowledge, "Yes, there is a young woman. There should be letters waiting for me at St. Louis. I'm going to ask her to marry me the next time we get home. Do you think I might take some time off to sort of get better acquainted with her when we get married?" he asked.

"And what is this young lovely's name, Mr. Will?"

"Genevieve, Mr. James. Genevieve St. Martens Lecroix."

"Ah. Some French flavor, monsieur."

"Yes. She's Creole and speaks French and English. She's a wonderful cook."

"What does your mother think of her?"

"Momma thinks she's fine. She's very pleased for me."

The men stood in silence for the better part of a mile, Will still at the helm. "If you're about to become a married man you need to be looking for your future, so you can take care of your family the way you'd like to do it. What would you think of buying a boat for yourself?"

"No, suh. I can't do that. Almost all the money I've earned has gone to Momma so she could stay home and take care of the babies. So I don't have any money to buy a boat. But the children are all still in school," he added proudly. "And my momma doesn't have to spend summers in New Orleans, with the cholera and yellow fever around. She's so grateful to be able to get my brothers out of the city during the fever season. She still grieves over little Jean Paul, who was only two years old when he died."

"And you couldn't go to school because you were working to provide for them and your mother." James was aware of Will's yearning for education. He'd learned enough reading and writing to keep the boat's log and read signs and maps; he could cipher well enough to keep accounts with those whose loads were hauled by the *Marian Dee* and the farmers along the rivers from whom they bought wood for the voracious boilers. He bought a book or two on most trips, and had accumulated several, which he had patiently teased out a word or two at a time, but reading each more fluently than the last.

"I happen to know there's a sidewheeler going to be for sale about the time we get back to New Orleans," James said. "Perhaps I might think about buying it and putting you in charge. Do you think you could manage a crew?"

"If the crew is real river men I can manage it easily enough. If it's crackers and rednecks it'll take a little more time and effort."

James laughed quietly with him. The latest apprentice on the *Marian Dee* had fancied himself above the black man.

"What'cha jammerin' about, nigger?" had been the exact words of the boy of sixteen. James was on the Texas deck and heard the remark. Knowing Will could handle the problem he stood down out of sight of the wheelhouse. He winced when he saw where the barge train was headed but he knew the boy had to learn a lesson and would have to learn it the hard way.

The apprentice continued to refuse to take direction from Will as the lead barge continued to head for shore. When the apprentice finally realized the trouble he was in he first yelled for James, and when James did not appear, finally yelled "Nigger, come and get this wheel before..." Will didn't move and the lead barge rammed aground so hard it burst the starboard cable holding it to the next barge. James stayed away; supervision of the apprentice was Will's responsibility.

Will left the helm lashed and the sidewheels idling and walked the barges with the boy until he reached the broken off barge, now whipping loose its portside line also, as the current shoved against it. Will jumped successfully to the loose barge but the boy was less fit and landed in the river between barges, screaming for help. "I can't swim! Get me out of here!" Looking up at Will lounging on the barge roof at the stern of the barge he finally screamed, "Please! Please get me out of here! I can't swim."

Had he had his wits about him he could have grabbed onto the second barge and hauled himself out but he was too panic stricken. With his "please" Will finally moseyed a few steps up the port side and picked up a coil of lightweight line kept there for just such an event. The boy caught it on the second toss and was hauled out of the water.

"All right. You've made a right mess of things here. How do you plan to fix it?"

The boy looked about him, baffled. "I don't know how to fix it," he whined.

"Oh. I see. You don't know how to fix the mess of your making. You do have some real problems, don't you son?"

The boy walked up the starboard side of the barge as if to find an answer to his plight there, but returned empty-handed, with still no notion of what to do. Seeing James at the helm in the idling steamboat, he shouted to him for help. James merely shook his head and pointed at Will.

"Why should I have to take orders from a nigger?" he complained loudly.

"Everybody knows niggers don't know nothin'. That's why white folks is in charge." He looked as if to abandon the disconnected barge, which the current was beginning to work free of the clayey bank into which it had stuck.

Will simply sat back on the barge roof and awaited the coming of wisdom to his young companion. The boy sniveled a bit, looking sideways at Will while wiping his nose-run on his sleeve.

"Why won't James help me?" he demanded of Will.

"Because I'm your supervisor. He'll never interfere in another man's territory," Will responded simply.

"But yer a nigger..." the boy protested. "I'm white. I can't take orders off a nigger."

"Suit yourself. But if you don't get this barge back where it belongs, lashed properly, and get this train moving pretty quickly you're going to spend a lot of years working for James to pay for the barge and its load. Wouldn't really wish that kind of bad luck onto anybody, my own self." Will still spoke quietly and remained at rest on the barge roof. The sun, which had been low, reached the horizon.

"Mighty hard to lash up a barge in the dark," Will mused. "Course, I guess you bein' an expert on such things, it wouldn't be so hard for you. Call me if you need anything. Last night was pretty short and I reckon I can catch up on some of that lost sleep now, since there's nothing for me to do here." He began to stretch full length on the barge roof.

"All right! Please! I don't know how to do this. Please help me. I don't know..." His voice tapered off to a mumble.

"Ah. A bit of enlightenment in the sunset. All right. Get that line I fished you out with and coil it properly there. No, the other way. It has to be free to move immediately if it's needed."

"Like this?"

"Yes. You've got it now. Feel the line itself. You'll be able to tell if it's being properly coiled or not. It resists you if it isn't laying up smoothly. There. Feel that?"

"Yes. Now what do I do?"

"You need a spare coil of cable from the locker on the boiler deck of the *Marian Dee*."

"But I can't jump that far! I'll fall in again," he protested.

"How do you think you might accomplish getting to the boat without swimming?" Will asked.

"I dunno. If the boat would push closer I could jump to the second barge..."

"You might try that then. If you'll notice, Mr. James in is the wheel house where he's been taking care of our business for the last twenty minutes or so while we've played at being sailors over here. No, don't yell at him," seeing the boy puff up to bellow at James. "Signal like this," holding one arm forward and pulling backward while the other hand stayed straight, little finger parallel to the barge deck, stuck out chest high.

The boy did as he was told and the sidewheels began to gently spin faster.

"Use your hands and arms to tell him which way to go. He knows himself because he's been a pilot for so long but you need to learn how to signal accurately. A boat or a barge or somebody's life might depend on it sometime. And even a top-rate pilot like Mr. James appreciates a little help in the dusk like this."

"Yeah. Signal him a bit more to your left. Yes. Now, hold your hands apart as far apart as the barges are, and bring them closer together as the train moves toward us so he'll know how far he needs to move yet to connect with this barge. Good job. Now go fetch a spare coil of line so you can get this lashed up properly again."

The barge safely relashed, the boy was fined the cost of the broken line. "Did you learn anything, son?" James asked.

"Yessir. I learned how to signal and lash and take orders... I guess I learned it doesn't matter what color your skin is. What matters is the know-how in your head."

"Then I think you had a successful day, son. You're relieved until morning. There's food left in the galley."

"Yessir. Thank you, Mr. James."

"Nice work, Mr. Isaacs. I notice he's even polite to *me* now," James smilingly remarked to Will when the boy had gone below toward the galley. "I thought there was potential in him when I took him on, but I'll admit I was beginning to wonder. Glad to have my good judgment confirmed."

"I'm thinking a partnership might profit the both of us," James remarked, coming abruptly back to the present. "I do have the money to buy a boat because I have no family left to need anything from me. My brothers and sisters are all grown and independent and my mother passed on several years ago. I never need to buy anything for myself except new trousers and boots from time to time. I'm thinking if we buy the boat in partnership, you can gradually repay me for it while you're still making a good living for your family. As a partner running a boat you should be able to make plenty enough to keep your mother at home, your brothers and sister in school, and your wife happy. What do you think?"

"James! I never even dreamed of owning my own boat. I would like that more than anything in the world. Well, except my family, of course. And you. Definitely you. I'd still be hustling odd jobs on the waterfront if you hadn't helped me.

"You'd have found another opportunity, my friend. You've given me years of your excellent work, and if I hadn't had the luck to snatch you off the wharf some other enterprising businessman would have.

"The boat that's for sale. She's a sidewheeler, 171 feet long, 222-ton capacity. She was built in the Pringle Boatyards in Brownsville, Pennsylvania. Has an oak hull, 28 foot diameter paddlewheels..."

"Whew!" Will interjected. "Those should move her right along!"

"Yeah. She makes 6-7 knots up the Missouri..."

"Which is running about 7 knots downstream...Burns what, 30-35 cords a day?"

"Yeah, 30-32 they said..."

"You were giving some serious thought to this boat, James. You know too much about her to have just heard in passing."

"Oh, you know how boatmen are," James replied with a quick grin. "Yes, I was giving it some serious thought. You have a born-to-the-river gift of handling a boat. It should be your own boat that you're handling. So hearing about Miss Genevieve was coincidental. She has several cabins for passengers but she's essentially a freighter. She's called the Wildwood. She's been running the Missouri mostly..."

The men chatted on in the growing dusk of the Mississippi evening, laying plans for Will's proprietorship and – one day, perhaps – for James' retirement. He vacillated when he thought of retiring from the river. The rivers had provided his livelihood from the age of thirteen, and he wasn't sure he could sleep without the rocking of a boat under him. But if he should choose to leave the river, the income from the boats would keep him. He would have the profits from the *Marian Dee* for as long as she remained under good management, and would reap some profit from the second boat until Will was able to repay him the loan for her purchase.

~ ~ ~

Catherine lay on her bed behind the curtain, staring at the ceiling above her. Whatever is going to happen to us? We're almost certainly going to be split up. I lost my mother once and I never knew my father. When the estate is closed down or sold, we'll have to leave here and I can't go with Sarah and Samuel because I'm white. Why do people have to be different colors, anyway? It shouldn't make any difference. Dear God. I need you right now. We need you...

As the thought of divine intercession entered her head, she quietly slipped out of bed and onto her knees. Dear Heavenly Father. We know you love us and don't want to see us hurt. Please help us so we can stay together. Please. In Jesus name, Amen.

She rose and got in bed again, thinking of her guardian angel, whom Sarah had told her was always with her, helping and protecting her. It was too hard to think of God sometimes. She had sometimes likened him to Samuel, the only father she'd known, but when she told Samuel one day that she thought God was just like him he told her gently that she shouldn't think so. "God is more than we can think or imagine, child. God is everything."

So she sometimes thought of her guardian angel instead of trying to think about God. She knew very well what her angel looked like. He was a few inches taller than she was – as was Samuel – and had beautiful mahogany-colored skin, and soft white-feathered wings attached to his back. She'd not told Samuel what her angel looked like in her mind; she didn't want to be told again that she mustn't think so.

As her angel hovered lovingly, Catherine relaxed and fell contentedly asleep.

## Chapter Nine

"Do you know, sometimes I'm still angry with Miss Emily and sometimes I just feel sorry for her," Catherine remarked to Sarah as she pushed a sad iron into a gather in the waist of one of Miss Emily's dresses. "I think it would be very difficult to live alone in that great house without anyone to care about her. And it has to be worse now, when she doesn't have enough money to even continue to live there."

"I suspect she would not be pleased if she knew you pitied her," Samuel remarked. "Or anyone else for that matter."

"Maybe it's not pity I feel. She *is* my grandmother. I wish she'd let me be her granddaughter, but even when she won't, there's something I feel there. It doesn't seem to me to be pity, but I don't know that it's anything like love. Goodness knows I don't *like* her very well, often as not. And I'm still somewhat afraid of her."

"She can be downright unlikable at times," Sarah remarked. "I think maybe it might be harder sometimes for me, because of her cruelty to you and to your mother. It's always harder to bear the hurt of someone you love than your own. The Lord Jesus knows I've tried to be open-minded about Miss Emily, but it certainly is hard at times."

"What are we going to do when she has to give this place up? Anyone have any notions about that?" Samuel queried. "I don't know as there's a place where we can go and work together," gesturing at Sarah, "and I don't think there's another place on the face of the earth where the *three* of us can stay together. That pains my heart so I can't sleep sometimes."

"Yes," murmured Sarah. "It's a devastating thought."

"It's going to be all right," Catherine assured them. "I prayed about it and it's all going to come out all right."

"Did God give you any notion about how He might work this miracle?" quizzed Samuel.

"I think perhaps..." she faltered, then continued more confidently. She'd not had the idea until after she prayed about it, so maybe this was the way God was going to work it out for all of them. "Momma Sarah," Catherine said, "have you ever taught school to anyone besides me?"

"I helped teach my little brothers and sisters, but no, I've never taught anyone outside of the family."

"I've been wondering. There's no school for girls, here, is there?"

"No, Catherine," Sarah replied thoughtfully.

"Momma Sarah, do you think we might have a school here? A girls' school that their parents would pay for? If we could do that, maybe we wouldn't have to leave. Maybe Miss Emily wouldn't have to leave..."

Sarah was suddenly silent. "Samuel, what do you think about that idea? Do you think we could do it? Do you think Miss Emily might accept such an idea? No, I don't think it would work. No one would let a black woman teach their white daughters, would they?"

"But, Momma Sarah. I can teach languages if you'll show me how." Having been without language for such a long portion of her life, languages – any and all that Sarah could give her – were fascinating to Catherine and speedily mastered. She could have held her own in any of the European languages so lovingly given by the Reverend Phillipe to his daughter Sarah, the light of his life.

"Miss Emily could teach the girls their manners and social graces. You could teach mathematics..."

"You know, it might work, Sarah," Samuel remarked. "My momma always told me to aim high and work like the devil himself was after me. If it isn't hard to achieve it may not be worth trying for."

"Let's think about it for a few days. If we decide it might work, you can mention it to Miss Emily at your luncheon on Tuesday. It's your idea and you should bring it up and get full credit for it."

"I don't care about credit, Momma Sarah. I just want us to be able to stay together, and I think you're right that if we have to leave here we won't be able to do that. I've heard Angel and others talking about the Klan when they didn't know I could hear them. I'd be terribly afraid of them if we had to leave here."

The idea stood the test of a few days time, and on Monday evening, Sarah and Samuel and Catherine worked on a bit more detail before Catherine would present it to Miss Emily the following day.

"The girls from town here might come and go each day if their parents send a carriage for them. Girls from further away might take rooms on the second or third floor of the big house. No one is using them, since the servants who used them have gone," Catherine offered. "Well, maybe except the room with the slit window. I don't think I could bear to see anyone else have to live in there. Perhaps they could store their luggage in that room.

"And if we have a school we'd need some of the servants replaced. The ones here now couldn't possibly keep up the work if there were more people to keep house for. We'd need some of the upstairs rooms for them, then."

"Or perhaps some of them might prefer cottages. There are several empty ones now."

"Of course, someone needs to sleep in the big house to supervise the girls at night. I seem to remember that young ladies sometimes get into mischief if they're unsupervised," Sarah contributed.

"Aha! Now I know what you were like before your parents made me take you..." Samuel ducked as he spoke, and the dishtowel snapped in his direction by Sarah found only air.

"Made you take me indeed!" pursuing him around the table.

"My goodness!" Catherine exclaimed. "Whatever are you doing?"

Sarah stopped, giggling. "We're just having fun, baby. My. I feel like a schoolgirl again myself! Samuel! You behave yourself now! We have to set a good example for this child!"

"Fiddle. She's a well-grown young lady herself! It certainly won't hurt her to see old married folks like us having a little fun!"

It happened it was Catherine who struck the final note of the play. Watching sparkly-eyed for a moment or two she saw an opening and neatly poured a glass of cold water down Samuel's back, leading all three of them to shriek with laughter. Sarah laughed so hard that she sat suddenly on a chair, gasping for air.

"My! I haven't had that much fun since I was a girl in my father's house!"

"And I suspect your father was as much a rascal as any of you children," Samuel offered.

"Oh, definitely! We had a wonderful childhood. My mother was quieter, but she was really as mischievous as Papa. We had wonderful games in the evenings. And on Sunday afternoons."

"On Sunday? Wasn't that sinful?" Samuel smirked.

"My, no! Papa used to give thanks for our fun. He always said God wanted us to enjoy our journeys through life as much as possible. He said perhaps the fun we had and gave our gratitude for, helped someone else out who had a life without any fun. Do you think that might be true, Samuel?"

"I don't know, love. I only know I give thanks every day for you, my Sarah." Sarah had risen as they talked and he drew her into a close embrace, where they lingered long moments. Then Samuel reached out an arm and drew Catherine into the family hug, planting a gentle kiss on her forehead.

"All right," Sarah finally remarked. "We still have some work to do here," and they reluctantly broke contact and sat again on their chairs around the white-scoured pinewood table.

"All right," she said. "I think we have a good idea here. We can teach languages and math and geography and I know it little bit about science. I don't know how important that would be to young ladies. What do you think, Samuel?"

"I think the idea has a good chance of working. Miss Emily would be the head of the school, because she's a lady herself. It would be her estate and her name that would make it all possible. I think the parents would be more interested in seeing their girls properly trained as young ladies than having them learn academic subjects."

"Then we're agreed. Catherine, you will propose this to Miss Emily at lunch tomorrow. All right?"

"Yes, ma'am. I'm a little nervous about it, though. May I practice telling you so I'll be a little more comfortable with it tomorrow?"

"Of course. Excellent idea." And so she rehearsed and rehearsed again until she was content that she could present the idea competently and professionally to Miss Emily. All slept peacefully in the cottage that night.

~ ~ ~

"And now, my daughter, you are a bride of Christ. Wear the veil humbly," Mother Clare spoke gently.

"Yes, Mother. I know I'm not worthy. I don't think I could *not* be humble..."

"I think you're confused about the meaning of humility, Sister Mary Joseph. Being humble simply means seeing ourselves as we are, not as we wish we might be. To be humble we must see our strengths as well as our weaknesses."

The young nun looked at the prioress in confusion. "But I was always told that I should be humble, that I was like the dirt under our feet or the garbage we discarded."

"Oh, no, child. Humility isn't like that at all. Many people think so, but see it this way: we are so important to God that he sent his only Son to die for us. And God has chosen you to be a bride of that Son. Think for a moment. What do you do especially well?"

Sister Mary Joseph looked about the office where they sat, and remained silent.

"You won't find any questions or answers in the room," Mother Clare said gently. "All of the significant questions and all of your answers are within you. As God himself dwells in you."

The young sister in the white veil looked away from Mary Clare. "I don't know, Mother. I don't understand what you're saying." Her eyes were moist and bright. "I don't do anything well, it seems."

"You have a wonderful voice in the choir," the elder woman remarked. "What else do you do well?"

"I sing?" the young nun reflected. "That's not something important. That's just something that I enjoy doing..."

"Make a joyful noise unto the Lord," Clare nudged gently. "God gave you a wonderful voice so you could praise him. It's an important piece of our spiritual journey to praise God. The more we can see of God the more we learn about our true selves. God is a part of us, you know. We are a part of God."

"Oh, no, Mother." The tears now came in earnest and rolled unchecked down her cheeks. "God couldn't be a part of someone like me. And I'm certainly not anything like God."

"That's your spiritual task for the present, my dear. As much as you are able, reflect on the Silence within you. It may be easier for you to do that in the chapel, where the Lord is present in the consecrated hosts resting in the tabernacle. Or you may meditate in the peace of your own cell if that better suits you. As you gradually learn to become more silent within yourself, you will realize the presence of God within you. And your dwelling within God."

"But, Mother!" She spoke in anguish. "You don't understand. You don't understand what I've done. I'm not worthy to be here. But I have no other place to go," she said, almost inaudibly.

Mother Clare hesitated and listened within her own being. No, the young woman needs to listen first within herself. She motioned gently toward the door. "This will get you started with your task. Understand that this is a lifetime task. You will not learn everything quickly. No," she mused, "you will not learn *everything* in this lifetime, likely. But your journey is well begun. Peace, Sister. Come back in a few days and visit with me again."

Mother Clare meditated for some time after the departure of the young nun. Yes, she thought. I was right. This is one I needed to provide spiritual direction for myself. It is well that we are here, she and I.

~ ~ ~

Will held his breath. James presented the draft on the Water Street Bank for the full price of the boat. The beautiful steamboat that was to become his. He saw her in his mind's eye as she would soon be refitted. The *Genevieve*. Spotless white and trimmed in red. Genevieve was already talking about taking a trip on her.

"Where shall we live, Genevieve? Here? Or in St. Louis? I might get to see you more often in St. Louis, but we wouldn't have family there..."

"I'd rather stay here, Will. I want my maman nearby. You'll be gone a lot, I know. And your mother and brothers are here. And Jubilee. I've asked her to be my maid of honor, you know. She's nearly as excited as I am."

"She's a great friend to have. I'm glad you like each other so well. Maybe it won't be so lonely for you when I'm gone. So. When is the great day to be and where are we to live then? Have you talked with the Father about posting the bans?"

"The bans will be published beginning with the last Sunday of next month, April. You said you'd likely be back here in the middle of May, so that will be well timed. Father Andre understands that your schedule isn't firm, especially since you'll be operating your own boat. Your own steamboat! What a wonderful opportunity!"

"Yes. James has been more than a brother to me. I'm still gasping a little at his generosity. I never expected..."

"You earned this," Genevieve interrupted. "You've worked hard and honestly for James for years. He's a good man and generous, but you earned this."

"I have always done as well for him as I could. That's the way Momma raised me. Raised me by hand to always work my best," he chuckled.

"Your mother is wonderful. I'm so lucky to be getting her along with you. She's already teaching me how to cook the things you like, and she insists that we share her summer house. She's sure it's big enough for everyone. And she's been going with me some days to look for a house for us here. We found one yesterday that I'd like you to look at.

"It's got four bedrooms and a wonderful kitchen. It's yellow stucco and it has a balcony on the front, like I've always wanted. A wrought iron railed balcony. We can sit out there in the evenings and watch people go by. It's only about a mile from your mother's house and just a little bit further to my family's house. It's on a levee, so it won't flood. And the price is right, a little less than you said we could spend."

"If you like it that's the one we likely should buy. It will be your house, after all. A woman should have a house to belong in. You'll spend months on end there without me. Are you sure we need a house that large to begin with?"

"Ah, yes! We both want children. We need room for the children. The beautiful little brown-skinned children that you and I will make together..."

The kiss interrupted her declaration. Long and tender, it began to build into passion. He loosed his hold around her and stepped back. "We can wait. We *must* wait. Both your mother and mine would be so disappointed if we did not. You are a treasure that I want to unwrap...but not just yet. Everything should be right..."

"Everything will be right," she murmured. "With you it will be right."

## Chapter Ten

Samuel silently forked hay from the loft to the mangers of the stalls below. One of the horses whinnied its appreciation. I need to take these horses out and work them more, he mused. I guess I should just turn them out, but if I do that, I'd need to take them to the far meadow because there's not enough grass left in the meadow nigh. And sure as I do that Miss Emily will need to go somewhere and it will take too long to fetch them in. Thank goodness, we don't have milk cows anymore. I just wouldn't be able to keep them milked properly.

Milk was delivered every morning just about dawn, since the Durrant estate had sold off its cows. In tin buckets, the man from the dairy farm down the road entered the kitchen door and set the milk on the countertop in the pantry just beyond the kitchen. After Angel had skimmed a day's supply of cream off the milk, it was lowered into the cistern just off the kitchen door in the summer, or set into a low cupboard on the north outside wall of the pantry in the winter. If the cupboard door was kept closed to the heat of the kitchen, the milk would stay chilled and sweet all day. On occasion, if the day was especially cold, as it sometimes got this far north, milk left in the bucket would be rimmed with ice.

What will Miss Emily think of Catherine's idea? Samuel pondered. I am so afraid of being split up. I guess Momma's stories about my first papa being sold South made a real impression on me. It certainly did on her. Eleven days of hiding and nights of running, just to make sure I'd be free and nobody could sell us and split us up. And now this fear in my heart... I'm not sure I could live without Sarah. I'm pretty sure I wouldn't want to.

Samuel took an occasional turn at meeting runaways who still came through the tunnel that led to the church basement and knew well their terror and exhaustion. Often they hadn't eaten for days and had no belongings more than the ragged clothes on their backs. Samuel was especially touched by the young women who fled in order to make a chance for their babies, born or unborn. The journey to freedom was harder for the women and more terrifying if they had children.

And Catherine. My goodness. Whatever will she do if she's taken away from us? She's an able young woman, but we're the only real family she's ever had. I can't imagine what it would be like for her if we can't stay together. All those terrible years alone in the attic and then being lent to us. I'm not sure I could bear it if she should be torn away. She's the daughter of my heart, and she'll always be so, no matter where she herself is.

Nearly noon, he mused. Mayhap it won't be long before we find out what Miss Emily thinks of the notion. Dear God in Heaven, he thought. Do whatever you like with me, but protect Sarah and Catherine. Women are so fragile when they're alone. Especially black women or orphaned white girls.

The luncheon was proceeding smoothly. Miss Emily continued to be impressed with Catherine's ease in handling complex table settings and her poise in sitting with a woman who had done so much to harm her since her birth. Catherine had assumed the baking chores for the house and now presented her grandmother with fresh bread each week.

"Catherine, you really shouldn't be doing Angel's work," Emily had protested. "That's a job for a servant, not a ..." Her voice fell off and her eyes looked bleak. "What I mean is..."

"Miss Emily, please don't mind if I do things around the house. I do enjoy it, and we all have to work together so we can stay together, don't we? Angel has extra chores now and so does Sarah. I enjoy doing the baking and I've been doing some of the ironing for Sarah. I feel good about learning things like that. It gives me... I'm not sure. I think maybe it gives me a feeling of being competent. Of being somewhat in control, perhaps."

The girl's hands reached out as she spoke, carefully pouring fresh tea from the pot for her companion. "Please allow me to continue to work at these things I enjoy. They give me a feeling of belonging here. I really need to belong somewhere. Is it all right if I continue with such chores?"

"Yes, child. Do as you like if you truly enjoy it. Heaven knows I've taken enough away from you. I don't want to add to my debt!"

"Miss Emily, please don't be concerned for my sake. Yes, it was a difficult time but I'm stronger for it, and better fit to live a useful life.

"Miss Emily, may I tell you about an idea I have? I'm sure no one meant to meddle or nose about in your business, but it's common knowledge that there were some investment problems and there is not the money to continue to live as we have been." She hesitated, but Miss Emily did not respond, so she continued.

"I've asked about with folk who go down to town and find there is no school for young ladies here. There are enough people here to make a real town, now, and there are a lot more across the river in Louisville. It seems to me that we could offer a real service to those families with young ladies to be trained. The girls from here could come to a day school and if families from other cities are interested those girls could stay in the empty rooms on the second and third floors."

Catherine continued to relate the details she and Sarah and Samuel had discussed. Miss Emily sat silent and unmoving. Finally, she said, "Catherine. It's dear of you to think of this, but I don't see how we could actually do this. I have no notion at all of how to run a school and I certainly can't teach anything."

"But that's the core of the idea, Miss Emily. You know how to raise young ladies. You can teach young ladies to *be* young ladies. You have all the knowledge anyone could want of manners and social graces and such that a young lady needs to know. Miss Sarah will help me learn to teach and I can teach languages. I don't mean to boast, but I am very good at languages. If it might be allowed, Sarah can teach languages herself, and she can teach mathematics. Samuel can build anything we might need. Will you consider it, Miss Emily?"

"Child. What an ambitious scheme! My, my. I'll need a little time to think about this. Do you really think it has a chance of working? Have you discussed this with Sarah and Samuel?"

"Yes, ma'am. That's where the details of the idea came from. We all discussed it together. They think it would work."

"It's extra work for them..."

"But none of us minds work, Miss Emily. We like doing things that we do well."

"What do you think would need to be changed here for this to work?"

"You would have to decide which rooms could be used for the girls, and who would stay in that area at night to supervise the girls. We can clean the rooms you choose and get them ready to use.

"We'll need to get more help. Maybe we could get some of the same people back who have gone to other jobs, but I rather doubt that they would be available. In any case someone would have to interview and choose help. You're the only one who's done that before.

"We'll need someone to help with the stable work, too, so the carriage or wagon would be ready whenever it might be needed. For the day school girls, their parents might send a carriage for them or perhaps we might do that. I expect you and the parents would work that out when the parents come to get their girls enrolled in the school. I expect you would need to decide which girls are appropriate to enroll and how much to charge them. I'm sure there will be other things, but those are the things we've thought of so far."

"I believe I need to talk to the banker about this. He's been planning on selling off the house and land and putting the proceeds into an annuity for me." Emily was silent for several seconds. "Do you really think this might work? Truly?"

"Yes, ma'am. We've talked it over for three days now and each day it seems to be a better idea than it seemed the day before."

"Very well. I shall send Samuel to carry a message to the banker. We can talk to him together here, so he can see the house again. I believe it really is appropriate for a school for young ladies and he can see that too. I'll want you and Samuel and Sarah to sit with us and help plan, so we're held down by common sense, not flying away on some cloud of wishful thinking. And so that he can see that we have the resources we'll need. I hope he isn't too prejudiced against colored to listen to them... I know *I* used to be," she added wryly.

"Miss Emily," Catherine said hesitantly, "do you think I might ride with Samuel when he goes to town? I don't believe I've ever been off this place except to walk to church. If you don't mind, I'd like to see what a town looks like up close, instead of 'way up here on the bluff."

Emily sat silent for several moments. *Momma, may I go to Memphis with Papa? Please, Momma. I've never been any place but here. I'd like to see how other people live. Please, Momma.*

*Good heavens, girl. Young ladies ride in carriages. They don't ride on riverboats. And they don't go traipsing off to wherever. Young ladies stay at home and learn how to be young ladies.*

"Ma'am? Have I said something I shouldn't have? Please forgive me if I've upset you. I didn't mean to..."

"No, Catherine. I was just woolgathering. Yes, by all means, you may go with Samuel. Yes, you may go with him anytime he is willing to take you. He's always shown himself to be of excellent judgment. Yes, go and enjoy yourself."

"Thank you, Miss Emily. Thank you very much." The younger woman was hard put to conceal her eagerness.

"Catherine, do you think you might..." Her voice fell off into silence.

"Ma'am? What would you like me to do? I'm sure I'll be glad to do whatever it is..."

"Nothing important, Catherine. Perhaps another time."

~ ~ ~

The May sunlight was bright and hot in New Orleans. Genevieve woke at daybreak and rose from her bed, too excited to be her usual languorous morning self. The day! At last, after all the planning and endless waiting and anticipation. She gently tugged her dress from the clothespress, admiring the ivory satin with eyes and hands, pulling a fold of it up to brush lightly against her cheek.

"Genevieve! Time to be up you sleepabed!"

"Maman! I am up before you this morning! I couldn't sleep anymore," she added as she ran lightly down the staircase and found her mother in the kitchen. "It's glorious weather, is it not? What a wonderful day!"

Her mother smiled indulgently. It was Genevieve's day.

The morning was the longest of her life. Her hair, dressed in rag curlers the night before, was released and lovingly brushed into soft curls by her mother. "Your hair will look fine if it's just brushed out without curls tomorrow. I don't expect you'll want to bed tonight with rags in your hair."

Genevieve giggled in response. She and Maman had talked into the night the evening of her engagement. "Be sure you see to your own pleasure," Maman had said. "He will be engrossed with his own and may not consider yours," adding in detail the mechanisms with which the young woman could find pleasure and the means of pleasuring her husband.

Maman helped her choose her garments for the wedding night, and the two women together removed from the cypress wood chest the linens put aside for Genevieve's use in her own home. Beautifully embroidered, some by Genevieve and some by Maman, there were ample items for the first years of her marriage. Together with Will's mother, they had looked at houses, and with Will's blessing, had purchased one with funds advanced by James. Together they had shopped for dishes and silver and myriad other items needed to run a house comfortably.

"I wish I could have given you a sister for company," Maman remarked on the morning of the day.

"I have a sister, Maman. You have been as much sister to me as mother, for you have always listened and guided, but have never judged. I have never missed a sister but I would be bereft without you."

"Know that our relationship will change now, with your marriage. Your husband will be first now in your heart and considerations, as I know I have often been until now. You must take care that after you have seen to your own needs, you next consider his needs and wishes in all matters. You should not yield to him blindly when you disagree with him..."

"I could never disagree with him, Maman," Genevieve interrupted, dreamily.

That elicited a giggle from her mother. "I assure you, beloved daughter, there will be disagreements. He is a *man* you are marrying, not a god. You must have disagreements from time to time or you do no honor to him or to yourself. You must stand firm when your belief about a matter is different from his, but you must listen and respect his views.

"If you make a real marriage, sometimes things will be done his way, sometimes yours, and sometimes you will compromise and neither of you will truly get your own way. But by these disagreements and decisions and compromises, you will build a true marriage. The secret is to always talk about differences and always honor and..." she paused, smiling, "...to remember that on occasion you might not *like* him or what he does, but always *love* him."

"Was it so with you and my father?" Genevieve quizzed.

"Ah! Yes, it was so. Your father was such a wonderful rascal and we loved each other so well. But there were times... I threw an egg at him one day, I was so angry with him."

"Maman! You didn't!"

"Oh, yes. We truly loved and we were at times truly in despair at the beliefs or opinions of the other. Our disagreements occasionally amused the neighbors. I remember one time..." Her voice trailed off. "Look at the time! We must hurry now!"

"Maman! Don't leave me in suspense! What happened that time?"

"Oh, child! Another time! There truly is no time today. When is Jubilee coming?"

"She will be here any moment."

"Let's get your dress and petticoats out. She can help dress you when she comes. Everything is ready for your journey?"

"Oui, Maman. I am *so* excited about everything! My marriage, our journey together...my new relationship with you, Maman. It is no longer as if I am child and you are mother. It is more as if we are two women together. Is it not strange?"

"Oh no, cherie. Not at all is it strange. I remember when I was a young married woman and my mother and I were as close as two good friends. I've been waiting for the relationship with you to mature. I've been anticipating the joy of knowing you as another woman rather than as the child whom I must guide and guard. I am so pleased with you and so happy that you are marrying a good man."

Jubilee's voice broke into the conversation and attention shifted to dressing Genevieve in her ivory satin.

"I do," Will asserted. He turned and bent, kissing the bride gently. "My wife."

The festivities continued into the night, with both bride and groom in demand as dance and conversation partners.

Will suddenly became aware that Genevieve was missing from the gala throng still gathered in the hall beside the church. Peering about he realized that Jubilee and Genevieve's mother were also gone. Before an anticipation could fully bloom there were excited murmurs from the side of the hall nearest the door.

Genevieve entered, flanked by her mother and her best friend. Radiant in a gown of warm rosy silk, she embraced and summoned Will with her glance in his direction.

Walking gracefully toward him, they joined in a final public embrace and turned to leave.

Genevieve had retained the mass of flowers she'd carried during the ceremony, symbolic of her joy in this venture, and now tossed it toward the onlookers, not even trying to conceal her determination that Jubilee should catch it as indeed, she did.

A number of the merrymakers scrambled into carriages and followed them to the docks. Genevieve held her breath when she saw the boat. No longer the dingy drab she had been when Will and James bought her – and as Genevieve had seen her – she sparkled in the lights of the torches carried by friends. Glistening white, her paddlewheel and trim were a bold, clear red, and the red was yet more decorated with gilt shadows and highlights. Her name blazoned across her sides was no longer the *Wildwood*, as it had been when they bought it, but now proudly proclaimed itself the *Genevieve*.

"She's been completely overhauled and refitted. I think you'll like our cabin... Are you sure you want to do this? A riverboat isn't a place for a lady..."

"Yes! This is exactly what I want. You live on the river, Will. I'm your wife. I want to share your life and your home, at least this once." She shrieked suddenly as Will grabbed her and lifted her easily, carrying her up the stage onto the boiler deck.

"There, wife. You are on board your new home, for however long you choose to stay." He clasped her hand and led her to their cabin. "Your mother helped me fix this up for you," he said. "I think you'll like it." He lit one of the gimbaled lamps mounted on the bulkhead and she drew in her breath in surprise and appreciation.

The quilt on the double bunk was a double wedding ring design – chosen, of course, for its symbolism – tough enough to survive life on a boat but colorful enough to be pleasing to the occupants of the cabin. "Ah, Maman knows I love bright colors!" she exclaimed. A chest of drawers on the starboard side was secured to the deck; a rail around the top of the chest ensured that articles set there would not easily slide off as the boat moved. A clothespress occupied the corner starboard and aft. Genevieve brushed the bold red curtain of the press aside and saw her clothes that she had chosen to bring on the boat.

Windows on the port side were curtained with copies of the quilt. Will picked up the bottom of a curtain and showed her that it was actually a small quilt, with batting and a backing. "This might help a bit when it's really hot and the sun is in the windows, but mostly they're to help keep the cold out in the winter. The river can be bitterly cold in January."

Genevieve and Will exchanged last hugs and handshakes with their well-wishers and Will gave the order to cast off when the stage had been hoisted back onto the forward boiler deck. The crew, who had been standing by for the midnight departure, had taken the boat out earlier for a shakedown run a couple of days upriver and back. Both the crew and the boat performed well, and Will was confident they could manage safely without his immediate supervision for the balance of the night.

~ ~ ~

The Westmont Finishing School for Young Ladies was a reality. Sixteen girls comprised the first class. Two were from nearby in Indiana and were brought and returned home by carriage each day. The others were clustered, two in each room, on the second floor of the great house. Miss Emily occupied the seventh room on that level, ensuring that the girls would be properly supervised at all times. Other inquiries had been received and it was likely that the school would grow.

Miss Emily had the advantage over other schools the parents might have chosen. She herself directed the "finishing" of the young ladies, but additionally the students had their choice of four languages they might acquire, practical mathematics, geography and a bit of history, and literature. The academic work was not deep, but it ensured that the young ladies could converse intelligently in any cultured setting and the foundations laid for theater and opera, when such might be available.

As the students became comfortable in their new environment each took a turn, week by week, supervising the household staff so they could learn that important task. The work was assumed gradually, so that during her first week the assigned student did little but shadow the housekeeper, learning the roles of the various staff members and discovering the look, feel and taste of excellence.

In successive weeks the students gradually assumed more responsibility for the tasks of the household until they were comfortable leading the staff. Miss Emily assured the girls that they needed to excel at this task, as there would be no one but them to guide their own homes once they married. Since the housekeeper, Mrs. Engle, and Miss Emily determined together the marks each girl would receive, the young ladies learned to be courteous without being familiar to the hired help. Most of them were rather timid about the task when they started, but they were patiently taught and learned to enjoy doing such work well.

A request for riding for the students resulted in permission being sought and given by the girls' parents. Sidesaddles were obtained, and Samuel and his young assistant taught them a confident seat. The girls had been riding on this cold November afternoon and came rosy-cheeked to the kitchen afterward, seeking hot chocolate. Angel accommodated them cheerfully and they gathered around the kitchen table, babbling eagerly.

As her teaching duties allowed, Catherine had occasionally continued her work as bread-baker for the household. She was absorbed today in punching and kneading before covering the dough ball with a floured towel to rise. She looked fondly at the girls. All were working to learn at least one language other than English; one bold girl worked on two.

"Miss Catherine," Ellen said, "why are you baking bread?" Although she would have been unable to recognize the task before her stints of household supervision she now knew, and could not understand Catherine's work. "You're a teacher, Miss Catherine. Why do you do the cook's job?"

"Do you have something that you do well and really enjoy doing?" Catherine responded.

The girls talked among themselves for a moment and then they all responded affirmatively. "Is this thing that you like to do a task appropriate for a girl?" queried Catherine. Most again replied in the affirmative.

"What is it about that task that you really like?" she continued.

"I like cutting and arranging flowers for the house," replied Estella. "I am good at the arranging because I seem to have a good sense of balance for different flowers and colors. I feel good when I've made the house cheerful with flowers, and I feel good because I've done something I do well."

The other girls related favorite occupations ranging from writing nice letters to an elderly family member to helping care for younger siblings during childhood illnesses. All agreed they experienced pleasure in doing something well.

"That's how I feel when I bake bread. Angel was willing to teach me and I have a nice feeling of accomplishment when I butter the loaves after they come out of the pans. I might have done one or some of the things you young ladies have related, but I happen to love fresh bread and Angel didn't mind. I don't think any task is beneath us. I think we have a need to do something that we take pride in. My thing is bread."

"Yum! Very good bread," added Gloria, whose plump waist testified to an appreciation of good bread. The other girls nodded in accord.

"Might I be allowed to bake bread?" asked Joann.

"You must discuss that with Miss Emily. If she gives permission you must ask Angel if she has the time and energy to teach you."

"Or you might teach us..." suggested another student.

"First Miss Emily. No speculation or planning without her consent," Catherine directed to a chorus of 'yes, ma'am' from the girls.

~ ~ ~

The *Genevieve* was wonderful. Genevieve, the woman, quickly habituated to the thwack-thwack-thwack of the paddlewheel and the smells of steam and the river. They left New Orleans in early summer and boated northward back into spring. It had been a cold and wet winter and spring dallied above Memphis.

Genevieve lounged comfortably on the bow of the boat as it entered the Ohio. "This is so exciting, Will," she remarked as he took a chair beside her. "I understand now why you love the river so. I believe I'm in love with it also." She took immense pride in the *Genevieve* and in her role as wife of Will.

She spread their bed up early each morning and neatened their cabin, refusing to allow any crew member to assist, despite Will's attempt to treat her as a fine lady on her honeymoon whom others should care for.

Genevieve had cautiously approached the galley, understanding that the cook might not appreciate the intrusion of an outsider. She had a gift for recognizing inner strengths and pride and when she had the cook "wrapped around her little finger," as her mother would have said, he welcomed her incursions. She was soon the biscuit-maker for the boat, and by the time they reached Louisville, she was regularly sharing the galley with the cook and contributing Creole specialties to season the plain, good fare.

Other crew members were treated with equal respect and soon discarded any reservations they might have had about having a woman on board, or for that matter, shipping under a black captain. None had so worked before, but Will was quietly authoritative and appreciated their work when it was good. When it was less than good, he simply looked at the careless crew member with a raised eyebrow, as if to say "Hey! You know you're better than that!" and soon the crew was functioning as a well-trained unit. The *Genevieve* was a happy boat on which to serve.

# Chapter 11

Emily padded softly up the stair to the third floor. More girls were expected next month and she thought to assess the rooms under the eaves for their livability. Carrying her keys and tablet, she entered first the dormer room on the south. A comfortable, well-aired expanse, it would comfortably house two girls. The furnishings would be adequate with the addition of another chest of drawers and a table with chairs for the girls' study efforts.

Word had quickly spread among the well-off families in the area that Mrs. Emily Durrant operated the best finishing school available for their daughters. Students coming home for the winter holiday were observed to be poised and confident. They interacted well with servants in their respective homes, leading to a comfortable ease in which the servants knew well that they were expected to do their finest work but equally, they were respected for their humanity and their service.

When appropriate moments arose, the students also demonstrated academic gains, but it was important to their families – to their mothers in particular – that they reserve any intellectual prowess for moments in which it was fitting. Joann, for example, had carefully acknowledged the introduction to the guest in her home, Francois Monpere, in well chosen and nicely accented school girl French, bringing her father to even stronger appreciation for the daughter who already held the most of his heart.

Emily smiled as she reflected on the greetings she had received from some of the families of the students. The school indeed filled a need in the region. Most families were reluctant to send their girls far off to school no matter how large the reputation of such a school might be. She remembered considering Stevens Finishing School for Marian. Clearly the best available, but so far away! She would have been able to come home only for the summer, and a servant would have had to go to accompany her home. She would...

*Momma! I'll be alone all that time! May I not even come home for Christmas?*

*No. The trip back home will take two or three weeks. Your vacation would be ended before you even got home. There will be other girls there over the holidays also. Yes, you will have friends there. And staff to care for your needs.*

*Mother...*

Emily jerked her thoughts back to the task at hand. Had she any memories not loaded with anguish? School would resume on Monday, and she must have rooms ready for five more girls. How fortunate that Catherine had conceived this notion of a girls' school. How fortunate... Emily's thoughts trailed off as she passed the door of the slitted room.

My god. Great god in heaven, how could I have done such a thing? How...

Pausing, she unlocked the door. A few dust mites skittered along the floor as the door swung open. Strange, there had been no noticeable dust when Cathe... Breaking the thought off sharply Emily crossed to the slit of a window. Such a small world. Silent even now, with the door to the hall open.

With a great groan, Emily sank to her knees in front of the window, shaken by sobs wrenched from her innermost being. Bracing her hands on the bottom of the window, she dropped her head to her hands and sobbed until there were no more tears.

Spent, she yet lingered in the room as twilight fell, dozing lightly with her body leaned against the wall under the window.

Lamplight fell softly into the room, lighting Miss Emily's figure where she sprawled, exhausted from the tears held back for so many years. She stirred, consciousness aroused somewhat by the light, and turned toward the doorway.

"Miss Emily! Are you all right? No one knew where you were. We were worried when we couldn't find you. Are you all right?"

"Catherine. You are so like your mother. She was gentle and loving too. She was my heart... Can you ever forgive me?"

"Miss Emily. Your tears and mine have washed this room and our spirits clean. Yes. All is forgiven. Nothing is left to cause pain."

"Catherine. Do you know that this place – this house, land, everything – is as much yours as mine? Your grandfather left it to your mother and uncle and me, equally. Your uncle is gone and dead. Your mother may be also; no one knows where your grandfather took her. You have a right to your mother's share."

"Miss Emily. Come downstairs and get a warm cup of tea. We can talk then if you like. I would like it very much if you could tell me about my mother. Would you do that? I remember her a little bit from when I was very small. She was so warm and loving. I adored her..."

"Yes, Catherine. I will tell you about your mother. She was warm and loving and such a wonderful daughter, and then we sent her away..."

~ ~ ~

James lingered at the landing. His men loaded the wood and the owner of the landing was not present today, leaving James to his own devices. His attention was drawn, as it always was, to the walled monastery up the hill from the river. It owned an aura of peace, as if an actual presence emanated from within it. Glancing at the men engaged in their loading task he saw that he was not needed and walked off, wandering toward the monastery. At closer range, the pull of that presence was even stronger.

He gazed for long moments from a hundred yards away, then reluctantly changed direction and moved back down hill, toward the farmhouse above the landing. The farm wife had been watching and met him by the kitchen door.

"Wood's the same price as usual?" he inquired.

"Yes. The husband's gone to town today. I saw your men loading. He told me I never had to worry about the *Marian Dee* if you came by for wood while he was gone. He left the double-barreled shotgun for one or two others though. Not everybody wants to pay for what they get!

"That there's an interesting place, isn't it? Hard to imagine a lot of women living alone like that. They've got a mule and work the fields nigh. The husband hauls stuff to market for them. He uses some of their land on shares, too, and pays them their share after he sells it. Guess that's what they live on. Don't know, but reckon I wouldn't want to be living without no man to take care of me, myself. Seems like it would be right scary sometimes. Don't you think?"

"I don't know what to think about something like that. But there is a feeling about the place. I don't know as anyone there would need to be afraid of anything," James replied pensively. "It just seems so peaceful, like there's a power around it, protecting it."

"Yeah, well, I've noticed sometimes that it seems like that, now as you mention it. The husband says to keep away though. He doesn't want me to get any notion of leaving him to go live with a bunch of women," she giggled.

James returned her good humor with a broad smile of his own. "We've loaded all of your wood, ma'am. I calculate about seventy cords. Does that tally with your figures?"

"Yes, the husband said there was seventy there. He's got more seasoned wood coming in a couple of days. He sends a couple of men out to bring in the deadwood from the knobs about here. So there should be more waiting for you, when you come back down. The husband always appreciates you coming by, you know."

"Yes, ma'am," counting out the price of the wood into her upturned palm. "I thank you for your wood and your hospitality. I'm sure we'll see you on the trip back down. Your husband is our most reliable supplier of good wood. Have a good day, ma'am."

~ ~ ~

Louise's eyes twinkled. "What are you afraid of? Let's go!"

"Miss Emily said we're never to go out at night," Delia remonstrated. "We'll get in trouble."

"Fiddle. No one will see us. That's the advantage of going in the dark. Come on!"

Carefully listening at every junction of hallway and stair, the girls slipped out silently. Sandy, waiting patiently at the kitchen door, saw himself as protector of the students as well as of Catherine, and followed them silently, alert for any possible peril.

Creeping through the shadows, the girls gained the small apple orchard without incident. Finding apples mostly by touch, they each chose a few and filled their pockets.

Going back as they had come they were nearly to the house when a man's silhouette suddenly stepped from the shadows behind the great red oak in the kitchen yard and loomed above them.

Delia gasped and the girls faltered. Joann, feeling some responsibility for the safety of the others as she had readily supported Louise in her proposal, stepped between the group and the interloper. "Who are you and what do you want?" she demanded. "You should know that our excursions are carefully supervised by Samuel, the head groom. You don't want to irritate him, I assure you!" Joann was puzzled momentarily when Sandy walked ahead, sniffed the intruder, and wagged his tail.

At just that moment a deep contralto voice behind them queried, "And why do you think Samuel would protect you when you're out for mischief? Hmm? Whose idea was this excursion anyway?"

Recognizing the voice of Sarah, Louise spoke up immediately. "It was my idea, Miss Sarah. We came out to get some fresh apples."

"There's a big bowl of apples in the kitchen, girls. You knew about that. You didn't come out here for apples, that's certain."

"No ma'am. I also urged the others to rebellion," Joann stated firmly. "We just wanted a change of scene, I guess. Sometimes a little flavor of danger makes life more interesting. At least I know I was a little bit bored with everything so predictable and I was ready for some change. I'm as responsible for the rule infraction as Louise is."

"I'm glad to see you stand up for your own actions. That's an important part of character for everyone to learn. You'll have to tell Miss Emily, you know. It is she who made the rule about going out in the night."

"Yes, ma'am. We'll go now and tell her." They trooped in through the kitchen door, walking around Samuel, who was struggling to control a grin threatening to take over his face.

"Samuel, you are a rascal! You enjoyed this as much as the girls did, didn't you?"

"Yes, I did. But I do have a concern about their safety if they go out alone at night."

"A group like that should be quite safe. No one intrudes up here from town. None of the neighbors ever come here except Svenson when he brings the milk in the mornings."

"Yes. And he was mightily pleased when this became a school and we suddenly needed a lot more milk. Yes, I think this is a safe place for the girls, but they must not take that for granted. If they learn to be loose with their behavior here, they might be overconfident of safety in some other place where they could be in real danger."

"Well, I hope Miss Emily doesn't hold them to much punishment. I was obviously ready for a little change myself."

~ ~ ~

Catherine wiped the snow off her log and seated herself, gazing toward the breathtaking beauty of the ravine below. The tree trunks and branches stood out starkly against the snowy backdrop. Her mind slowed and her attention shifted to inner thoughts. Sandy, fur thick against the winter cold, flopped down beside her.

The trees lose their leaves in winter so we can see their limbs uplifted in praise, don't they? And the little cedars remind us that life goes on, no matter what the appearances may be...

As she sat in motionless meditation, a movement brushed across her consciousness and her eyes refocused on her immediate environment. The doe flicked her eyes nervously at the young woman, but she continued to paw for browse when Catherine did not move. A sudden shift in the light breeze brought the human and dog scents to the deer, however, and she spun about, crashing into the underbrush. Catherine followed her progress by ear as the doe broke dry sticks on the ground in her flight. Sandy roused at the deer's movement but sat motionless at a quiet command from Catherine.

Yes, she thought. I need to leave also. It must be nearly dinnertime and they will worry if I'm not there. She had formed the habit of walking back through the knobs, as the hills there were called, long before, at times when the company of others pressed on her after her years of solitude.

This particular place always soothed jangled nerves and lifted her perspective. Of late, she had come daily, as the weather permitted. She enjoyed the schoolgirls with their quick minds and quiet mischief, but she found that her daily quiet kept her centered and in balance for whatever might occur.

Catherine had learned that she loved to teach. Her years of enforced silence made language priceless to her and a suggestion of that regard was communicated to her students, enhancing their attention and appreciation for the words with which they built their lives. Several of the girls already could carry on simple conversations in French or Spanish and one was struggling with German.

She found the girls now clustered in the drawing room with Miss Emily. "It's nearly Christmas time, young ladies. Some of you will be going home and several will spend their holiday here, since you live too far away to go home. How can we make Christmas something joyful, for both groups? What suggestions do you have? Will you please share your ideas with the group? Perhaps your families have some wonderful customs that will help enrich the season. Yes, Louise?"

Louise spoke up confidently. "We go from our church each year and sing carols for our neighbors. Everyone enjoys it. Some of the families invite us in for hot chocolate, and we have a bit of time afterward to visit with each other before we go home to our own families."

"Excellent. Is that something in which you students might be interested? We could plan an expedition for a few evenings before the town students leave for the holiday so everyone could enjoy it."

"We could put up a Christmas tree after the caroling. We can make wreaths if you'll allow us to cut some evergreens. Perhaps the people going home could make wreaths to take with them, or we might put them on the doors to our rooms."

Joann spoke up. "I think we should do something for the Christ child, a birthday gift."

"How could we do something like that?" Delia queried. "He's not real... You can't give something to someone who only exists in a story..."

"But I think he's real," Joann replied earnestly. "What if we give something to someone who won't have any Christmas otherwise? Wouldn't that be like giving a gift to the baby Jesus? Didn't the Father say that if we do something for someone in need it's the same as doing it for God?"

The girls murmured among themselves, moving toward the dining room as the dinner bell rang. The topic continued around the dining tables. Each girl in turn was hostess for a table, polishing a skill that would be vital for them after their schooling was ended. Delia presided hesitantly at the third table. It was her first turn at the chore and her attention shifted back and forth, as she tried to please everyone. Joann was at her table this week and had been privately reminded twice already by Miss Emily that she was only a guest at this table and must allow Delia to find her own style and confidence.

"Do you really think we might do something for someone as a gift for the baby Jesus?" Delia asked. She was among the group of Protestant girls who were escorted by Samuel to the Presbyterian church in town each Sunday morning. Others were taken to the small Catholic church, which Miss Emily now also attended, and the pastor of the Baptist church sent a trusted driver each week for two other girls.

Miss Emily offered the religious options to the parents when the girls were registered. She believed that her students were to become leaders in their social groups and it would be to their advantage to have some training in religious matters as well as acquiring a firm grasp on table manners. Each girl who had a church then was taken to it weekly and those without specific beliefs might visit their friends' churches as their parents permitted, but except for three girls exempted by their parents, each attended somewhere. It would widen their experience and perhaps give them an added touch of self-confidence or even a bit of selflessness that Miss Emily had come to believe was the best foundation for her students.

"I do agree with Joann," Miss Emily was saying at Estella's table, where she was this week in a guest role. "I believe Christmas will be more meaningful if we share it with others. What do you think?" she asked Gloria, seated at her right.

"I'm not sure," the girl replied. "We've really never done anything for Christmas in our family except put up a tree and exchange gifts. It does sound like a good idea, though," she mused. "Do you know someone in need for whom we might prepare a gift?"

"Perhaps our local girls might know of someone," Miss Emily replied. "I haven't lived down in the town for many years, and I'm afraid I'm no longer well acquainted there. Do you know of anyone?" she asked Madelein.

"Perhaps," the young woman said thoughtfully. "I'll ask my mother this weekend when I go home. She's always lived here and knows a lot of people. The other girls who live here could check also."

The girls left for an evening walk in the orchard and fields behind the house, taking advantage of the last vestiges of evening light. Catherine joined Miss Emily at a western window, appreciating the colorful sunset spread before them. "We certainly have students to be proud of," Catherine remarked.

"Yes," Miss Emily murmured. "It will be good to see the house decorated for Christmas again," she continued. "I guess..." Her voice trailed off as her eyes lost their focus. "I guess it will be good..." she tried again. "It was always wonderful..." Her voice caught and Catherine, glancing at the older woman, saw two tears roll down her cheeks.

"You decorated the house for your son and daughter," Catherine offered quietly.

"Yes. It's been so long. I couldn't bear to do it again after they were gone. It was never important to Mr. Durrant. Turning her head sharply she said, "No. It was never important to your grandfather, Catherine. And you were shut away... I've cheated you for all of your life, child. How can I ever make it up to you?"

"There's nothing with which to concern yourself, Miss Emily," Catherine responded quietly. "What's gone is gone. We can't remake yesterday nor borrow any tomorrows. And right now, everything is all right. It truly is," she finished, gently touching Miss Emily's hand.

Miss Emily reached out and grasped Catherine's hand. She opened her mouth but no sound came out. "I, I..." She dropped her head and the tears came more quickly.

Catherine leaned forward and softly kissed Miss Emily's cheek, then turned soundlessly and slipped away, leaving her grandmother in the growing dusk.

~ ~ ~

Genevieve nestled warmly under Will's arm, smiling in pleasure as the students from Westmont caroled them, tied up on the Indiana side of the Ohio. Some of the boat crew joined in and declared "Oh come, all ye faithful" with the girls. After they closed with the exhortation to "Go tell it on the mountain," Will invited them on board for hot chocolate.

The girls stood about in groups under the watchful eyes of Sarah and Samuel, visiting with crewmen. Catherine looked about the spotless deck as if studying something she'd need to remember later.

"Good evening, miss," Will greeted her. "Thank you for sharing your music with us."

"Of course," Catherine replied. "The pleasure is ours, I assure you."

"Is this the first time you've been on a boat?" Will queried.

"Yes, it is. But..." her voice trailed away.

"Thank you for the music," Genevieve said, joining Will.

"My wife, Genevieve Isaacs," Will offered.

"I'm glad to meet you," Catherine replied. "I'm Catherine Durrant, a teacher at Westmont. It was the girls' idea to go caroling, and when they saw you tied up, I think they sensed some adventure. I saw your wife and thought it must be safe for the girls to come. We'll need to be away soon; we were on our way home when we stopped here."

"This will be my last trip for a while," Genevieve offered. "As you may have noticed, we're expecting our first little one soon, and I'll be too busy for a while to come up the river."

"My–"

Catherine was cut short as Samuel announced "We must go, young ladies. All back to the carriages, please."

"Good night..." rang out from several voices. "...and Merry Christmas!"

They clambered aboard the carriages and "Oh come, all ye faithful..." rang through the streets again as the horses trotted off toward the westward bluffs.

~ ~ ~

*Adeste fideles,*
*Laetum triumphante,*
*Venite, Venite,*
*In Bethlehem...*
Sister Mary Joseph's lovely voice led the procession toward the altar. As

the others of the community filed in behind her the song swelled and rang in the small chapel. The newest postulant carried the Baby Jesus and laid him tenderly in the manger prepared for his coming, with Mary and Joseph in adoring attendance at the crèche.

~ ~ ~

The music wafted faintly to the farmer's wife, standing outside the kitchen door, huddled in her shawl. Returning from the outhouse, the music had caught her attention and she stood, quiet within, listening. The door opened behind her and her husband joined her, slipping his arm around her shoulders.

"Did you hear the music, Robert? They were singing Christmas carols. I wonder what all they do up there," she murmured. "I guess I didn't expect them to celebrate Christmas. I guess I don't know anything about what Papists do..."

"Come inside, Martha. I have a message from them to you..."

"You *what?*"

"Come." Walking through the kitchen the farmer seated her on the front room sofa, saying, "Close your eyes now."

Martha obediently closed her eyes but opened them immediately when he laid a small bundle of cloth in her hands.

"What is this? Oh!" as she unfurled the folded piece, "this is beautiful! Where did you get it?"

"Mother Clare sent it for you for Christmas. She's the head nun up there; sometimes I talk to one of the other nuns, but usually I talk to the mother nun when I sell their produce for them, or pay their share for their land that I work. She said she'd like to send a token of their appreciation to you. One of the nuns sewed it especially for you."

The cloth was embroidered with a brilliant peacock, tail spread, each tiny stitch precisely sewn. The edges were neatly hemstitched.

"She said it can be made into a pillow or hung on the wall, whatever you'd like to do with it."

"Oh, my! It's so beautiful. This took months for someone to sew! I think I'll hang it on the wall here" – gesturing at a space unadorned on the wall – "where we can see it all the time. Please thank her for it when you go up there the next time – Robert, do you think I might go with you the next time you go there? I'd like to thank her in person."

"I don't see why not. You're my business partner as well as my wife. You take care of everything when I'm not here and you take care of all the paperwork for everything. I'm sure Mother Clare would be glad to have you visit."

~ ~ ~

James stood quietly in the wheelhouse. Another Christmas come and gone. There had been generous bonuses for each crew member, but no other suggestion of Christmas aboard the *Marian Dee*. Most of the men had no family but each other; only two had taken leave to share the holiday with family.

It had been a good year, especially with the rivers still open and high enough to navigate. The ice was beginning to form at the edges, though. This would likely be the last trip up the Missouri this year. Even if the rivers didn't freeze over entirely, when shore ice formed up firmly, blocks of it could break off and damage the boat's hull.

One more year laid by, he thought. I miss having Will to talk to. No one else ever seemed to be enough like me to really talk to. So Will and Genevieve are about to become parents, he mused, thinking of the letter left at St. Louis for him. I don't regret much about my life, but I do wish I'd had children. It seems a shame when I look in the mirror and see gray hair that there's no one to carry on the Mason family after me.

I just never found anyone who suited me after Marian died. Of course, being on board the boat all the time didn't help, since I never met young women. I wonder if any women I might have liked saw the name Marian Dee, and thought there was no point in looking around for the captain. Oh well. I was never really interested in finding anyone after her, anyway.

The silence of the river and of the boat, largely sleeping in this watch, settled comfortably around James. I have a lot to be grateful for. A lot. I earn my living and more on the rivers I've always loved. I had Marian for only a short time, but I had her.

We truly shared our souls. I miss Anson; he was a good friend. I hear they moved his body last year back to Indiana. I'll miss visiting his grave as I did in New Orleans. Wonder where he's been laid now...

"Evening, Captain. I'm your relief. Good night, isn't it?"

"Yes, it is. A good night for accounting our lives and being grateful. And good night to you," he said with a grin. "I'm just on one of my reminiscing kicks tonight. See you in the morning." And he was gone below with a wave.

# Chapter 12

Spring came softly that year. The fields and roads were muddy and the branches bare, but the buds crept out overnight, it seemed, and then the leaves and blossoms were everywhere.

Catherine stood near Samuel and Sarah's cabin talking with Samuel. She'd moved into the big house a year gone, partly to give privacy to her foster parents, and partly to help supervise the students, but primarily to reduce the risk of the nightriders coming to Samuel and Sarah. Miss Emily had requested the move; she recognized the danger as Catherine could not, and as Sarah and Samuel seemed unwilling to do. It did make her feel easier also to have the once-thrown-away young woman living in her rightful place as heir to the family.

"I feel like just walking down the road and walking on forever. Isn't that strange? This place is home, the only home I've ever had..."

"Part of it is probably just because it's spring," Samuel rejoined. "Part of it might be the wishing to know your parents."

"I think that's right. Do you think either of them might still be alive?" she queried. "Do you think I'll ever find either of them?"

"I think there's a good chance that one or both of them are alive. I don't know about the finding them. I'm going to town this afternoon. If you don't have any classes, would you like to ride with me?"

"Oh, yes. Maybe that will help my feeling that I'm wandering around lost." It was on the ride back home that Catherine saw the *Marian Dee,* steaming away down river. "Samuel! Do you see that boat?"

"Which boat? That one with the blue trim?"

"Yes. Look at its name! It's called the *Marian Dee!* That was my mother's name, wasn't it?"

"Yes. Yes it was. Marian Durrant. I guess that could be shortened to Marian Dee."

"Do you think it has anything to do with my mother? It said Port of New Orleans," she continued in a smaller voice. "I guess maybe it's just a coincidence."

"Likely."

"But my father was a boatman, wasn't he?" she mused.

"Yes. He was a pilot or something that sounded like a responsible position on a boat. Sarah says that's where you get your strawberry blonde hair. He was a redhead."

"You saw him?"

"Yes, once I saw him."

"When? How did that happen?"

"Your uncle sent a note to your mother when they were going upstream, the second year after he left. Said they'd stop coming back down, 'cause they'd likely have to wait for the locks. Your grandparents were still angry with their son, so Mr. Durrant left in a hurry for Chicago and your grandmomma said she had a sick headache and went to her room for a couple of days.

"I brought your momma down when the boat came back. I left the buggy with Mr. Anson, but James brought her back home. He said Anson had gone with a friend whom he met downtown, and asked him to bring Miss Marian home. Everything seemed to be in order when they came. He said he'd sooner walk back down, so I put the horse up. We didn't know until a couple of months later that you were on the way."

"My father's name was 'James'? What was his family name?"

"I don't know, child. I've tried to remember, but I'm not sure they even told me his last name. I just don't know it."

Catherine sat silently on her log above the ravine westward from the great house. My father, she mused. James. James who? I wonder if Miss Emily knew he was red-haired. I heard her say once that there are no redheads in the Durrant family. I wonder if that might have contributed to her revulsion – Catherine paused.

She was not quite able to voice, even in her mind, such feelings as might have led to her long imprisonment. Even now, a few years after her freedom had been granted, she had successfully worked through the flashes of hot, defensive anger, but she still could not rationally work out the maze of feelings that her grandmother must have experienced. She had forgiven her grandmother. Perhaps understanding would come later.

Catherine rose from the log and strolled in the general direction of the house, unable to keep her body at rest while her mind was not. She could not stop thinking about her parents, to wonder about the unknown father who had called her forth from her mother. Nor was she able to think about her parents without having a bit of the old anger revisit her.

Though she could not forbid such thoughts, she did find, with a bit of practice, that she could replace them with other thoughts. Here and there, violets and wild anemones peeped from beneath the early spring green of the land. She found that concentrating on the flowers, concentrating on finding the flowers, eased her mind away from its discomfort.

~ ~ ~

James huddled in the evening chill on the stern of the Texas deck, watching the shadowed Indiana shoreline. Marian. Despite his longing for her presence, he pondered how his life had been richened by her, no matter how briefly he had known her. Now and then other women had attempted to attract his attention, but there had not been enough room in his heart to consider another. Abruptly cut off though it had been, he and Marian had been truly well mated. He grieved that she had not worn his name before her life was cut short.

Though James was not a churchly man, he had lived too long on the rivers to believe he was alone in his life. The life of the river itself had wakened him to a great, warm silence within himself. He smiled at the thought of a rough, unschooled man such as himself talking to angels, but over the years, he had come to enjoy at times quiet conversations – sometimes with words, sometimes without – with those whom he could identify in no other way. Tonight, as he retired to his cabin for the night, he breathed again a "thank-you" to those angels and to the Silence, for the gift of Marian. He was a rich man.

~ ~ ~

Martha glanced up through the growing dusk toward the monastery, noticing one of the nuns seated on the white oak bench on the near side of the enclosure. Robert had taken real pleasure in crafting that bench, fitting each piece precisely and pegging the pieces together with hickory, spending hours with a carefully held blade, smoothing it. He'd worked oil into the wood to protect it from the weather, and painstakingly rubbed it down with rags so the oil would not stain the clothes of a person seated on the bench. The work had occupied many cold evenings, and was finally finished, ready to deliver.

"Let me help you carry it up, will you?" Martha queried. "I'd like to meet these ladies. Do you think they might like some fresh bread?"

"Likely they will," he responded. "Of course you'll come with me; this is too awkward for me to carry alone," smilingly said. He knew how she'd hoped to meet the nuns since they'd sent the peacock for her at Christmas time. He'd seen her often pause and settle into a peaceful mien, looking up toward the monastery. He'd been aware for a long time of the aura of peace emanating from that place, though he would have described it in much more informal terms. At bottom, although he'd been uneasy at first about "Papists" moving into the area he now simply recognized that the nuns were very desirable neighbors. He had anticipated being able to present Martha to their acquaintance.

~ ~ ~

Mother Clare sat quietly on the sturdy wooden bench that the farmer, Mr. Stevens, had given the nuns. He had noticed that one or another nun was often outside the enclosure, reading or gazing off at the river. Although they sometimes seated themselves on an old log there, the log was cracked and full of bugs and dirt. He thought to give them a place of clean comfort for their meditations.

Mother Clare's attention was caught by a riverboat descending, by the clearing near the farm below. I wonder what life on a riverboat might be like, she mused. Surely it would be a privilege to live in proximity to the river. I do love the river, she thought. Always changing, always the same... She rose and pulled the shawl closer about her shoulders and returned to the cloister for the evening Vigil. She had a very good life.

~ ~ ~

"I wish you could see the continent before you settle down," Miss Emily remarked. "I'd planned to take your mother with us when we went...but, ah, circumstances had changed then..." she broke off, realizing that such a dream was only that. While the school paid their living expenses and kept the property intact and well-maintained, there was no excess with which someone might travel. "I'm sorry," she faltered. "I really would like to be able to give such a trip to you, but of course we can't."

"That's no problem, Miss Em–Grandmother," Catherine said. "I'm perfectly content here." Miss Emily had asked her to call her grandmother, but Catherine's long habit of watchful caution had not yet been fully retrained in the presence of the older woman. Leaving Miss Emily, Catherine left the house for a brief walk before lunch.

"Hello! I don't remember seeing you before," the young man with touseled, curly brown hair exclaimed. "Are you one of the teachers here?"

"I am. I teach languages."

"And what might your name be, beautiful young woman who teaches languages in Westmont School for Young Ladies?"

"I beg your pardon. I don't believe we're acquainted, Mr...."

"Elliot. Wilbert Alfred Elliot the Third. But my friends call me Bert. I'll wager that Bert would sound especially nice coming from such a glorious young lady as you..." His face suddenly changed from a broad, mischievous smile to sober alertness, left eyebrow raised.

Catherine felt, rather than heard, the presence behind her. She was aware, at the same time, that her dog, Sandy, had stationed himself beside her, eyeing the stranger watchfully.

"Well, Mr. Wilbert Alfred Elliot the Third. I expect you have some sort of business here today?" Sam's deep voice was gentle but both Catherine and the youth heard the restrained power poised to lash out at such an intruder.

"I've come to bring Miss Louise Harvey home to visit with her uncle and aunt, who've just arrived from Baltimore. Oh, yes. And her cousin, Wilbert Alfred Elliot the Third, son of Alfred and Jessamine Elliot, Miss Harvey's aunt and uncle."

"And there's a reason why you've come, a total stranger, to pick up Miss Louise, instead of sending their coachman for her as usual."

"Well, I've never seen a girls' school before – I thought it might be interesting."

"Indeed. Interest yourself in the road back down to town. We don't allow strangers to pick up our students."

"Excuse me, but aren't you getting a bit above yourself here? I don't take orders from – servants. I give them. Fetch Miss Louise at once."

"Sorry. Our young ladies don't accept rides from strangers..."

"I don't accept conversations with inferiors. Get my cousin immediately."

"How dare you!" interjected Catherine. Sandy, hovering protectively beside her, tensed and growled as the young man's voice became demanding.

"The young gentleman is just leaving, aren't you?" Miss Emily's voice had the effect of a whip singing through the air. "Get off of our property now." Her voice was quiet but level and impelling.

"I beg your pardon, ma'am. I meant no harm. I've just come to fetch my cousin, Louise Harvey."

"You'll 'fetch' no one, young man. Leave immediately."

Red-faced, the youth muttered, "Yes, ma'am" under his breath and turned away.

Getting back into the carriage, he slapped the reins across the horses' backs and drove back down the lane toward the town road.

"Why, Miss Sarah, did he call me beautiful and smile so?" Catherine quizzed her mentor, who also had heard the tense quality of the voices of Samuel and the young man, and had come in response. They walked together to Samuel and Sarah's cottage.

"Ah. That's called 'flirting'. It's done when a young man wants to get the attention of a young lady and impress her. Or sometimes, it's a young lady who flirts with a young man. For the same reason."

"Did Samuel flirt with you before you were married?"

Sarah giggled. "Samuel spent a great deal of effort looking sober and stable before we were married. He was trying to impress my father."

"Did it work? It must have worked; you got married."

"Yes, my father was favorably impressed with him. Meanwhile, *I* was flirting with Samuel, to keep him interested in trying to impress my father."

"But she was very subtle about her flirting," Samuel remarked. "She just did innocent-seeming things like falling down, where I'd catch her..."

"Go on with you!" Sarah exclaimed. "Where did you ever get such a notion?"

"You told me, my rascal wife. Remember?"

"Oh my. And you believed that?"

"I think it's time for me to be getting back to the big house now," Catherine offered with a smile. "I seem to be an extra person here right now..." Laughing, she slipped out of the cottage, leaving her foster parents exchanging teasing insults with each other. How lucky they are, she thought. I wonder if I'll ever find anyone like Samuel to marry me.

Louise had been picked up by her father to spend time with her visiting relatives. Bert had accompanied him and apologized to Miss Emily for his rude behavior. Louise's father, meanwhile, thanked her for protecting his daughter. "I wasn't at home when this scamp left to come up here or I would never have permitted it. I certainly don't want Louise ever to accept a ride with a stranger. The last time she saw Bert they were both just babies. Thank you again, Mrs. Durrant."

~ ~ ~

"Isn't he simply elegant, cheri? Look at his long, graceful fingers, and the way his hair curls so. He has your nose."

"And your crinkled-corner eyes," Will added with a smile.

"Maman says that my eyes – and his, of course – are from her grandmother, who was Caddo Indian."

"Caddo – I never heard of Caddo Indians. Were they from here? What were they like?"

"They were from north of here a ways, Maman said. She said they lived in grass houses."

"Grass? How can you make a house out of grass?"

"Maman said they built a framework for a round house with tree branches. Then they wove bundles of long grasses into the framework to make the walls and the roof. The roof was just the top part of the wall, bent in toward the middle so it all came together at the top. The grass was put in going up and down, starting at the bottom of the walls, and then putting the bottom of the next row on top of the first one, like shingles, so it shed rain. Inside they built a little floor up high in the house so they had a loft for storage. Or someone could sleep up there if they needed more room. Maman said sometimes the children would sleep up in the loft."

"I guess it sounds bigger than I imagined at first."

"Maman said they were maybe twelve or fifteen feet across, at the bottom, and about the same height, so there was a lot of room overhead."

"I'd think the wind would blow it to pieces in the next little storm, not to mention a hurricane."

"I guess a hurricane would probably tear it apart, but they lived too far inland to get more than a little wind and a lot of rain from a hurricane. Little storms, like thunderstorms, didn't usually damage them. Maman said her mother told her that the wind went around the houses because they were round. There were no corners to catch the wind as there are on our houses. Of course, the grass bundles were tied tightly, and if a few bundles of grass blew off they'd just replace them after the storm."

"Life is a lot more complicated now, isn't it? If a storm blew our house apart, look at everything we'd lose."

"Yes, but do we really need all of these things? They make life easier or more pleasant, certainly, but we could survive without them."

"You're right, Genevieve. We don't need all these extras. I need you. And I guess now I need young Lawrence William here. As long as we have each other and food to eat and a place to live in, we have everything we need."

"Yes. I am so pleased that you agreed to name the baby for yourself and my father. My mother grieved so when he died; she's so pleased to have his name go on."

"Sweetheart, I'm so delighted with this son that you could have named him Jehosophat for all I cared. Just so you're safe and happy."

"I'm very happy, Will. Very happy indeed."

Genevieve's ten-day rest after Lawrence's birth passed quickly. Will had planned his boat schedule to be in New Orleans at about the time the baby was due, but they'd had no guarantee, of course. Will thought it amazing great luck that he'd been at home for the actual birth.

He gave most of the crew two weeks off, leaving a skeleton crew on board to protect the boat, strip and repaint as needed, and supervise loading goods to ship back north. The crew thought it amazing good luck to be paid for their time off, or for the on-board crew, to be paid extra wages for that period. Will had heard of other boats that skimped on the treatment of their crews, but he remembered well being a boy growing up as a crew member on the *Marian Dee*.

Will had always been treated respectfully, even though he was just a youth at first, and he'd been well-paid since James' first salary advance to keep Will's mother and siblings on his first trip north with the boat. In return, Will had worked as hard as he could, even as a scrawny fifteen-year-old, as had most of the rest of the crew. Those who did not join their loyalties to the boat made a trip or two with them, and then were gone.

Will was very proud of his boat. Earned by his own work with James' sponsorship, named for his wife, the *Genevieve* was always spotless and orderly, from the immaculate galley to the least coil of line on the decks. His men took pride in themselves and their work. As had James, Will sometimes hired someone whom his instincts said was worth a trial, even though they presented themselves in a dirty or rude condition. Those who stayed on quickly came to conform to the standards of the boat. If they were not interested in keeping themselves up or taking pride in their work, they were soon cut loose to seek a boat more suitable to their slovenly habits.

Genevieve snuggled tiny Lawrence into the crook of her arm. "Aren't we lucky to have such a family as this," she murmured to Will. Both her mother and Will's were seated with them in after-dinner comfort on the long balcony that fronted their home. Lawrence moved his head from side to side and then, finding a nipple, settled down to nurse. Marc d'Vonne, Will's youngest brother, was home from school, working to put away some of the money he would need for his last year in college.

"So, Daniel. You're a doctor now. I'm very proud of you! You worked hard to accomplish that. I'm proud that you're helping the younger ones now too."

"You worked hard, Will, so I could go to school. It's my turn to help the others. You've got your own son to support now."

"I had all the breaks I needed to accomplish what I wanted to do. I just wanted to pass the opportunity on to you that I'd had myself."

"You made your breaks, son. I've never seen anyone work harder than you have, from the time when you were still just a little boy."

Will shifted uncomfortably at such praise from his mother. "Nothing more than any man would have done, given the chance. Do you think it might rain this evening? It's so humid we almost need umbrellas now," turning the focus away from himself.

~ ~ ~

"Miss Catherine," the Reverend Abram had said, signaling with a touch on her arm to wait while the last stragglers passed by, leaving church. "It's time for you to go to your own church now," he said when they were alone. "You know we'll always care about you, but you can't be a grownup young lady and go to the black people's church. Some of the white folks here already upset about that."

"But I don't have any place to go," the girl protested. "I don't know anybody who goes to the white churches. I don't belong at any of the white churches."

"Did you know anyone at our church when you started coming here?"

"Of course I did. I knew Sarah and Samuel."

"But you were just a child then. You're grown now. It's time for you to take on grownup ways. It's time for you to begin to make your way among your own people..."

Catherine looked into his eyes then, and saw the fear behind his kindness. "They'll hurt you if I stay here, won't they?"

The Reverend hesitated, but then nodded his head. "Yes. They will hurt us."

"Thank you for all of your kindnesses, Reverend. Please thank the others for me." Turning, she was several steps away before the tears flooded her eyes.

Father O'Malley had thus come into her life again. Miss Emily observed her lingering about the house or slipping off alone at church times. Unsure of the reason for the young woman's change of habit, and not a party to the decision to change, after a few weeks she decided some tactful intervention might be of value. Having thus decided, she sent a message to Father O'Malley, requesting his presence at the going-away luncheon for the students. All but Anna, recently matriculated after the death of her parents, would be going home for the summer.

The good father, of course, questioned such a dramatic change in Miss Emily. Never warmly welcome before the death of Mr. Durrant and unwelcome entirely since that occasion, he wondered about the motivation behind this invitation. Ah, well, he breathed inwardly, I wouldn't be invited without a purpose. I'll just have to wait and see.

Miss Emily appeared proud and pleased with her students. "The language award for this year has been earned by Delia, our fluent French student. Please congratulate her." Delia looked shocked, but prodded by the girls beside her, rose and approached the dais temporarily erected near the fireplace in the large drawing room. Delia bowed her head slightly, allowing Miss Emily to slip the medal over her head.

Holding it in her open hand she looked at it, at Miss Emily, and finally at her schoolmates. "I'm very surprised at this... I had no idea..." The clapping of the others rescued her from a further need for words. Still holding the medal in her hand and with a bemused smile on her face, she resumed her seat.

"Our mathematics award goes to Louise. She has made additional studies into algebra and geometry after mastering the required work in household accounting. Perhaps this suggests," to Louise face-to-face, quietly, "that you will need to be observant throughout your life to find activities to busy your mind. I've noted that you already have a penchant for mischief, the work of an idle mind."

Louise giggled a "Yes, ma'am," in response and bowed her head so the medal could be draped around her neck. Dropping a graceful curtsy – as a young girl might – she smiled affectionately at Miss Emily and returned to her seat.

"The 'Most Gracious Hostess' award goes to Gloria." As the young woman walked toward the front of the room Miss Emily continued, "Gloria has a gift for drawing others out of themselves. She observes their strengths and complements them, while overlooking weaknesses. Her guests and friends will be blessed, indeed."

"I'm pleased to announce that Miss Louise and Miss Joann have completed the course of study here. I believe that Miss Louise has an additional announcement for you. Louise?"

"Yes, Miss Emily," Louise said as she stood and addressed the group. "I'm delighted to announce my coming marriage to Thomas Black of Baltimore. He's a solicitor with the firm of Johnson and Albatrony. We're to be married on August 17th in the Fifth Presbyterian Church in Wilkes-Barre and honeymoon in France. We'd be delighted if any of you might be able to attend the wedding. You'll receive proper invitations, of course. Mustn't let Miss Emily down so quickly on something so basic!"

The other young women laughed softly. The ceremony quickly concluded, the girls scattered into twos and threes around the room, moving momentarily into the dining room and finding their place cards as lunch was announced. Catherine, hostessing one of the tables, found Father O'Malley on her right.

"I'm glad to see you again, Father. I'm so grateful for your assistance when I needed it. How thoughtful of Miss Emily to invite you since today is in a sense a recognition of a new beginning for me also, in completing my first year of teaching."

Father O'Malley smiled warmly and remarked to the other young ladies at table, "Miss Catherine is an excellent role model for any young woman. She has great courage and resilience. You are fortunate to have her as a teacher."

"Courage is sometimes hard to hold onto," remarked Anna. "Living can truly be discouraging at times."

"I see that your introduction to the events of life that can be difficult has begun early," Father O'Malley remarked. "If at any time you'd like to talk about anything I'd be happy to be a listener for you. You need only mention it to Miss Catherine or Miss Emily and they will see that an accommodation is made for a visit with you."

"Thank you – Father." The title appeared to be difficult for her to speak.

"That would be helpful, I'm sure, but I'm not Catholic."

"That's not important, child. What's important is to be yourself, and sometimes it is easier to define oneself with a listener. Religion tends to be something we inherit from our families. I suppose most often our inheritance fits us, since we tend to turn out very much like our parents. Religion is just a form, child. What's real is our relationship with ourselves and with God. I'm glad to be available for anyone who needs to talk."

"Thank you – Father. Perhaps some time that might be helpful."

Catherine also resolved to be easily available to Anna. I know what it's like to lose one's parents, she thought. I wonder if it's easier or harder to have them for fifteen years or so, as Anna did, or to never know one parent and to lose the other when still not much more than a baby – of course, I had Sarah and Samuel...

The festive luncheon soon finished, attention was claimed by the ring of silver on crystal, as a toast was proposed. The happy group, after several such, scattered into small factions about the second and third floors, completing packing and waiting eagerly to leave for summer at home. Long before the sun dipped behind the western knobs, the house was extraordinarily quiet.

## Chapter 13

Miss Emily stood forlornly, supported by Catherine's hand on her arm, gazing at the subsiding mound of clay-colored earth before them. "He was such a wonderful person," she remarked to the younger woman. "He was always pleasant to everyone around him, and always well-mannered. I always put him to bed myself when he was little. Then when he got too old for that he would come to me in the evenings when he was ready to go up to bed and hug me and say 'Momma, you're the best mother in the world...'" A silent spasm passed through her.

Catherine said nothing, but only moved slightly toward her, understanding that the woman needed to come to terms with her grief and guilt herself.

"I'll never forgive myself for not going to meet him that last time. He sent word that they would be back in a couple of days and I didn't go to him. I was angry with him for causing an upset in the family because his father was so angry with him. Edward left town as soon as he got the message, and I went to my room and said I was ill. He never came back! He was my own son. My only son. And I refused to see him. God will never forgive me for that!"

"Are you sure it's God who's not forgiving? Or is it you who's not forgiving yourself?" Catherine moved then, putting her arms around the woman in a comforting embrace. At length Emily turned and they walked back to the carriage. Neither of them noticed the solitary figure walking toward the cemetery as their carriage left, driven by Samuel.

~ ~ ~

"How do you do," Charles said. "It's a distinct pleasure to meet you, Miss Catherine. I understand you are an instructor in the Westmont School for Young Ladies."

"And a pleasure to meet you, Mr. Balsom. How nice that you could be here for the ball."

"And that said, may I have this dance?" They slipped smoothly into the rhythm of the music. "What is it that you teach?" he queried.

"I teach languages," she responded. "French, Spanish and German."

"Goodness!" He held her away from him for a moment. "I'm afraid I'm out of my league here! I sometimes find it a challenge to speak English!"

"Oh, it's not anything remarkable," she responded. "My – the woman who mothered me learned those languages from her father, who was European. So I learned them as naturally as I learned English."

"You make it sound too simple," he asserted. "It can't be that easy."

"Truly, it is easy. Did you find it difficult to learn to talk when you were a small child?"

"Of course not. I suppose I learned like any child does."

"Exactly. I learned that way also. I just happened to learn four languages as naturally as a child learns instead of one."

The dance ended but Charles kept a hand on her elbow. "Would you like some refreshments?" he asked. "I must admit I didn't have time for a proper dinner and I'm famished."

"I'm not hungry but I could use something cool to drink."

The large drawing room had been converted into a ballroom for the evening. While the ball was part of the training of the students, Miss Emily had been careful also to invite young men to whom Catherine might be attracted. She smiled in satisfaction as Charles and Catherine selected refreshments and wandered out into the garden, lantern-lit for the occasion. Young men from the Dahl Academy mixed with the Westmont girls and quiet laughter could be heard around the room above the sound of the music.

"What sort of work do you do, Mr. Balsom?" she inquired. "I've not seen you before. Are you new in this area?"

"I've just completed my schooling at Harvard," he replied. "And no, I am not new to this area. I was born and raised here; I've just been away for some time at school. I'm now a very junior partner in the Scribner Furniture Works here. I don't really know anything about wood or building furniture, but I am good at managing money and books and I'm quite good at managing people. I think I can be an asset to the company. It seems that the expertise they already have is in the making of high-quality product. They seem to have difficulty with some management areas and in marketing."

"How interesting! I'm sure you will do well."

"Are you from around here?"

"Yes, this is my home; I grew up here. Miss Emily is my grandmother."

"Oh! I didn't realize I was in the nest of this lovely bird," he smiled at her.

"Mr. Balsom, I believe you are flirting!"

"I believe that also, and I'd like to provide some competition," a deep male voice asserted from behind Charles. "Would you be good enough to provide an introduction sir?"

Amid laughter, the group of young people swirled in graceful dance patterns under the watchful eye of Miss Emily and her minions. Promptly at midnight, Miss Emily began working her way through the guests. "Thank you so much for coming this evening," she murmured to this one and that. Recognizing the polite dismissal, guests in twos and threes voiced their appreciation for the occasion and left for their homes or dormitories.

"What a pleasant evening," Catherine remarked, helping clear up the evidence of the dance. "I didn't realize dancing could be so pleasurable. I guess I thought it was just an exercise set to music..."

"A pleasant partner can make nearly any experience pleasant," Miss Emily rejoined with a smile. "Leave the rest for morning, everyone," she counseled. "It will be easier when we're refreshed."

*"How are you finding business going here, Mr. Durrant?" she asked.*

*"Business here is very good, everything my father could have wanted for me when he arranged my position in the firm. My best business at the present, however, is making life a pleasure for you," he responded archly. Although his words were bold, his embrace in the waltz was light and respectful as they whirled about the floor, weaving in and out of other couples. "I'm delighted to have the privilege of escorting you this evening, Miss Emily."*

*"It is marvelous, isn't it, Edward?" So engrossed in the pleasurable moment was she that she failed to notice the intimate address, although he did. "It seems that winter is flying away, isn't it?*

*"The warmth of good company always sends the seasons spinning."*

Yes. Good company. I wish you hadn't gone, Edward. I wish with all my heart you could still be here. You would be so proud of our little girl, Edward. Yes. I believe even you would have to be proud.

~ ~ ~

Anna had spent the summer quietly, sometimes seeming more like family than student. Her manners were gracious as a matter of childhood training. Her mind, as she began to recover from the anguish of her parents' deaths, was open and alert, quick to absorb whatever was presented to her. She'd taken a particular liking to Sarah, whose motherly warmth sheltered the bereaved child through the worst of the storms of her loss. She also displayed an aptitude for mathematics, often spending afternoons in the cool shade of the orchard with paper and a book, solving equations or speculating about such things as infinity. Her father had been a lover of mathematics and had noticed her affinity for the subject well before her sixth birthday, as she brought to him such questions as "If I take 6 away from 3 [her amazing mind having mastered such basics as addition and subtraction early and effortlessly] how many would I have?" Or, on another day, "What is the highest number, Father?"

The notion of negative numbers she assimilated without difficulty. Infinity, however, she failed to grasp. Lacking any possibility of a concrete answer, her father finally asked, "Can you understand the Master of the Universe?"

"No, Papa. No one really can, can they?"

"No, daughter. Even those who spend their lives in study cannot understand the incomprehensible. Infinity is like that also. Perhaps it is the same... No one can know."

"Oh," the child had responded. "Oh."

The start of the school year was difficult in some ways for Anna. She'd come to know comfort in the company of Emily, Catherine, Sarah and others of the staff. Now defining a social niche in the camaraderie of other girls was far more challenging. She'd always been quiet and something of a recluse, and – an only child who was tutored at home by her father or other adults – her early life had not included other children.

Her preference to find a secluded nook and people it with her books had been less noticeable at home. Here, where the girls busied themselves with each other, with dreams of romances and notions about dresses, with the myriad secrets girls share with other girls, she was uncomfortable.

"Anna, come with us to the orchard," Mary called. "We're going to pick the last of the apples."

"Thanks, but I'd like to finish my book," was her ready response.

Catherine had taken note of the difficulty but didn't want to intervene directly because she wanted the girl to learn to associate comfortably with her peers. At length, she approached Gloria early one evening, as the group was scattered about the grounds, enjoying the artistic bounty of autumn.

"Have you noticed that Anna is finding it difficult to get acquainted and make friends?" she asked. "You know she lost both her parents just several months ago. Do you think you might enjoy spending a little time with her each day? I think it would be easier for her to get acquainted with one person at a time instead of the whole group. Do you think you might be able help her feel more comfortable? Maybe it would help you think about other things than food," she teased gently. Plump Gloria tried so hard to divert herself but still ended up thinking most of the time about food and her love for it.

Gloria flashed a quick smile in response. "Of course, Miss Catherine. I'll give it a try. And you're right; it can't hurt me to think about something besides food!"

~ ~ ~

Charles and Joel climbed into the wagon, pleased to be free for the day. "Do you think there'll be many girls there?" Joel quizzed.

"I don't know, but we can hope, can't we?" Charles laughed back at him. "It's a perfect day for a picnic. Not too hot or too cold."

"How far is it? Have you been there before?"

"No, but I've got the directions here," gesturing toward a folded square of paper. "Let's pick up Amanda first. Then we need to pick up Catherine at the girls' school."

"Do they let girls just go out on dates like this?" Joel asked, astonished.

"Oh no. Catherine isn't a student. She's one of the teachers there."

"Oh. Sounds old. Is she?"

"Ha! As if I'd tell you. Get your own dates, Joel Archibald!"

Still laughing, the young men rode up into the knobs behind the patient mare.

Hours later, the sunburned quartet clambered back into the wagon, this time dropping Amanda, who'd complained frequently throughout the afternoon about the heat the bugs the food and the company, at her home first. "Would you like to sit back here in the straw with me?" Joel asked as they drove away from Amanda's house.

"Thanks, but I came with Charles. I'll ride up here with him," she answered, shaking her finger playfully at Joel. "Do you two spend a lot of time together?" she queried.

"Yeah, we do seem to bump into each other a lot," Charles replied. "I guess that's pretty easy, since we work at the same place and live almost next door to each other. We started school together and seem to have just stuck to each other since then."

"Where did you grow up, Catherine? Did you go to school here?"

"I grew up in my grandmother's house, Miss Emily Durrant." She hesitated briefly and continued "I was tutored at home. I never went out to school."

"I guess that's why we haven't met before, then," Joel remarked. "I would like to meet with you again, if that's agreeable to you," he dared, glancing as he so said toward Charles.

"You rotter!" Charles said. "Trying to steal my date!" Handing the reins to Catherine, he hopped over the low seat back, picked up a handful of the sweet oat straw with which they'd lined the wagon, and stuffed it down Joel's shirt.

Catherine giggled as the mock battle continued, the horse content to find its own way back toward home. By the time they reached the Durrant lane, both young men were leaking straw out of most of the openings in their clothes and there were even bits caught in Catherine's hair where straw had lodged when it was tossed. Espying Samuel, paused by the stable to wait for the wagon to come down the lane, Charles scrambled back over the seat back and tried to look dignified as the wagon stopped in front of Samuel.

"I trust you've had a pleasant afternoon," Samuel said dryly, holding his hands up to help Catherine dismount from the wagon. "I thought another girl was going with you."

"We had a glorious time," Catherine replied. "We did have Amanda Farris with us, but she was not having a good time, so we took her home first." Feeling audacious, she turned to the young men and asked, "When are we going out again?"

"Inside with you, young lady," came Sarah's voice from behind her. Catherine heard the smile in her voice, however, and remained beside the wagon. "Sarah and Samuel, may I present Mr. Charles Balsom and Mr. Joel Benson. Sarah and Samuel were my foster parents," she explained to the young men.

Seeing the shock on their faces, Catherine thought, Yes, if you're going to think me strange or less than you for being raised by black parents, now's the time to find out. Both men found their voices rather quickly, though Charles' eyes were still wide and evasive.

"Ma'am, sir," Joel spoke, touching the brim of the hat he'd replaced on his head after the straw scuffle with Charles. "We've really been careful of her this afternoon, really we have. We were just letting off some steam with each other on the way back." He carefully neglected to tell Samuel the trigger for the straw-shoving match.

Charles, meantime, just nodded his head, barely, and said, "We'd best be getting back. My father may need the horse this evening." So saying, he slapped the reins across the horse's back and drove away down the long drive that circled the big house. Samuel looked after them thoughtfully but said nothing.

~ ~ ~

Catherine saw just a flicker of motion past the head of the staircase to the third floor. No one should be up here, she mused. I believe all of the girls are outside. She hesitated at the closed door by which she'd seen the motion. It was the room with the slit window; she still had trouble being unafraid near it.

Pausing with her hand on the doorknob, she gathered up her courage and quietly opened the door. Shocked into silence, she stared at Miss Emily, rigidly upright on a prie-dieu, a rosary clasped in her hands.

"You are intruding on my private prayer," Miss Emily finally said, breaking the silence.

"Miss Emily! Please don't do this! This isn't necessary! Please come back downstairs..."

"You are intruding. Please leave."

Although her words were harsh, her voice trembled. Catherine entered and stood in from of Miss Emily, her hands on the older woman's hands. "Please don't do this, Miss Emily. Please..."

"Leave me," the woman ordered. "Leave. Now." Her eyes squinted tight but moisture escaped them despite her best efforts. She sagged, resting her head on the upright of the prayer bench. "You only make it more difficult. Please leave."

The movement of the woman had freed her hands from Catherine's. Seeing the determination of her grandmother, Catherine reluctantly turned and left, closing the door behind her with a quiet click.

When she checked the room again the following day – verifying first that Miss Emily was busy with a lesson for the girls – the door was locked, as it was again several days later when she again tried it.

~ ~ ~

Father O'Malley roused from the doze he fallen into after dinner. With the washing up done, the housekeeper had gone and the house was quiet. Tamping his meerschaum, he walked to the front porch, overlooking the now still street, and sat on the old rocker there, striking a match against his thumbnail and lighting his pipe. He sprawled his legs out comfortably and relaxed. After his pipe, he'd go next door to the church and say his office directly to the Lord. An amazing privilege.

Matthew Robert O'Malley was born seventh (and thankfully, last) in the family of Sean and Bertha O'Malley, late of Derry and Essen. Sean was a hard worker, but the hard work – at a furnace of the great steel mill – broke him and killed him while young Matthew was but a small boy. He'd scrambled for odd jobs to help keep his mother while she was taking in laundry to provide for him and his siblings. There'd been a large fuss over his going to school. "I can't go, Mum," he'd piped in his treble voice. "I'm a man. I have to work and take care of you."

"You're a small boy, no man, and you will go to school. The Fathers won't charge for you; you can do chores and errands for them to pay your tuition. Your father was very clear, that his sons are to finish school and not be melted at a steel mill as he was. You'll be off in the morning to St. Patrick's and you'll pay particular attention to the teaching of the Fathers. Perhaps you'll be my priest, laddie," adopting the affectionate address of the boy's father toward him.

His parents had openly hoped for one of their sons to become a priest. Ronald, the eldest son, had crossed words with their father and left home at fifteen, not to be heard from again. Matthew had heard his mother's grief one night when she thought she and Sean alone. Perhaps if he worked hard enough he could make up for Ronald.

It developed in the next few years that Matthew was the only hope for the family dream of a priest of its own, if Matthew should show a bent toward it. Shamus and Ian had proved no aptitude for the books and now – with families of their own – toiled in the mill as had their father. Shamus with his three sons and his wife poked out to there with the next one; Ian with a daughter and hopes for sons from his young wife. The girls were soon married and gone, busy with their own mates and little ones.

Perhaps Matthew was shaped by those early hopes of his mother. In any case, he did have a real aptitude for learning and showed no urgent need to socialize with the neighborhood girls. Father Arthur had enrolled the boy in the minor seminary at the age of 12, and 10 long years later, Bertha knelt gratefully at the communion rail to receive the first blessing of the new priest, and then knelt again to receive the sacred Host from the consecrated hands of her own son.

It was a blessing beyond hope. In the quiet aftermath of that first Mass Bertha relaxed at last her grim grasp on this life, and peacefully slipped away to rejoin Sean. It was Matthew's first funeral Mass. It made the leaving easy when he was sent to work the mission in Indiana; for with his mother gone and siblings scattered, and little but haphazard acquaintance with his other kin, wherever he was sent would be home.

~ ~ ~

"What are you going to do if she says 'no', Joel?" Charles asked. "Aren't you kind of jumping the gun on this? I'm not sure you have any good sense at all, wanting to marry someone with a background like than, but this is really ridiculous!"

"Look at the pantry area," Joel said. "The big cupboard has a tin-lined floor bin and a sifter built into it. I should think it would be quite convenient to cook in this kitchen," he continued, gesturing at the large, well-polished range. "It's got a good cistern right back here," pointing out the kitchen door. "It's deep enough to stay cool, and the pitcher pump pumps it right up into the kitchen. There's enough roof area to keep the cistern filled.

"Look here," he moved to the next room. "Wouldn't a nice oak dining table look good here? And an oak stand with a big Boston fern on it right there," pointing to the front parlor, just past the double French doors from the cozy sitting room. "See the pocket doors here? They don't take up any room at all, but the room can be closed off..."

"Joel!" Charles insisted. "Do you really know what you're doing? Buying a house is a major investment. How can you be sure that she'll like it? Actually, how can you be sure she'll even want to marry you? Maybe being raised like that she'd rather have..."

"Oh, Charles! Don't even say that! She has to marry me – don't you think? I don't think she's going out seriously with anyone else..."

"But have you even hinted that you want her to marry you?"

"No. No, I guess I haven't. I guess I've been afraid she might say no... But I've already bought the house. I guess all I can do know is hope?"

"Man, you'd better hope!"

Chapter 14

Sister Mary Joseph smiled at the couple standing before her. "It's my task today to respond to anyone who rings the gate bell. I'm glad to see you again. Has everything been well with you?"

"We have been well, Sister, and fortunate," Martha replied. "It's been a very good year."

"Yes, Sister," Robert continued, "we've brought you your share from our crop on your land."

"Will you have a seat here and be comfortable for a moment, please? I'll get Mother Clare for you. I'm afraid I don't know anything about the share-cropping."

Martha unconsciously opened herself to the ambient peace, sitting with legs uncrossed and arms at her sides, allowing the utter silence to quiet her being. Robert also was affected, but somewhat less comfortable than his wife in this place of only women. He remarked, only half-teasing, "Don't get too comfortable here! I can't have you running away to live with anyone else, even just a houseful of women!"

Mother Clare entered the room as he spoke. Her quiet laugh joined that of Martha. "We'll try not to lure her away, Mr. Stevens. The sisters are at dinner now; this is a recreation period for us, when everyone may speak freely. Would you like to see around the cloister? I believe the sisters might appreciate seeing the friends who help make our lives here possible."

Martha nodded eagerly; she'd not been able to imagine how such women would live or what they might do all day. Robert slipped his arm around his wife's shoulders and assented also. They followed quietly through the hall to the chapel, where the Silence was sentient. Both were aware of the Presence there, though without words to express their perceptions.

"Each sister spends two hours daily at individual prayer and an hour in spiritual reading," Mother Clare informed them. "Some like to spend their prayer time here, while others prefer the quiet of their cells, or outside. I personally enjoy sitting on the bench you made for us, Mr. Stevens."

"How could anyone pray for two hours?" asked Martha, amazed.

"We have the Liturgy of the Hours that we pray together," Mother Clare explained. "That's mostly readings from the Psalms or other books in the Bible. Then we try to just be silent for a part or all of the time we spend alone in prayer. We need to learn to be quiet so we can hear what God says to us, yes?"

Martha listened thoughtfully, left eyebrow raised. She'd never thought of prayer as a two-way communication. In her experience and religious training praying was just talking to God, and she'd never had much to say.

"Our work is a part of our prayer, also, of course, although we don't count that time in our two hours. Each sister works for five hours each day."

"I don't understand..."

"You wash dishes and mend clothes and do all of the other things you do as a part of your love for your husband. As he plows and cuts wood and all of the other things he does for love of you. Yes?"

"Yes," both agreed, "but..." Martha hesitated.

"We work for love of each other, also. If I sweep the hallway it makes it more pleasant for the other sisters to walk in it. When Sister Ruth or Sister Mary Joseph or whoever cooks a meal it is a celebration of our love together. Do you see?"

"Yes, but I still don't understand how love of another person can be prayer," Martha rejoined.

"God lives in each of us. He lives in everything and everybody, but when we are loving to those around us it's a part of our loving God. Just another way of expressing our prayer. Do you remember that St. Paul says in the Bible to 'Pray without ceasing...?' Our work then, our eating, our sleeping, our enjoyment of each other's company must be a part of our prayer because we can't live without those things."

"I think I understand," Martha murmured, shifting a bit closer to Robert. Mother Clare smiled and opened the nearest door in the hallway where the sisters' cells were. The Stevens glanced at the austere interior and Martha remarked "This seems so bare. Are all the sleeping rooms like this?"

Mother Clare nodded. "We try to have few distractions. It makes it easier, perhaps, to become aware of God in our lives."

"But I expected that the sister who made the beautiful tapestry for me would live in a, a ,a – more artistic place, maybe? How could someone who lives like this make something like that?"

"Sister Magdellen has an artistic gift, Mrs. Stevens. It was she who drew the peacock. She and Sister Mary Martha did the stitchery on it."

"Sister Martha! That's my name also."

"I didn't know that. I knew you only as Mr. Steven's wife. Perhaps we have more in common that we realize," she smiled. "I'm glad you liked the gift. Please come this way," she continued. "This is our kitchen," motioning toward an open doorway, "and here is our refectory. Sisters," she announced, "please greet Mr. and Mrs. Stevens, our benefactors who help crop our land and sell our crops for us."

There was a quiet murmur in the room as the company of nuns, surprised at the unexpected guests, rose to greet the couple. "Sister Mary Martha, Mrs. Stevens, who is also Martha, would like to meet you and Sister Magdelen..."

"I'm glad to meet you – this is so unexpected," Martha Stevens said. "I want to thank you for the beautiful peacock. It's brightening up our living room, where I see it every time I walk into the room. Robert made a frame for it for me."

"We took real pleasure in sewing it for you, Mrs. Stevens. You do so much for us here."

"I'm afraid that's Robert's doing. I don't really have anything to do with the farming itself, or the banking."

"Ah, but you take care of all the bookwork for the farm, my dear," Robert asserted. "And you do the cooking and cleaning and wash and mend my clothes – and provide me with the company of my favorite woman... But we're just ordinary farmers, Sister, doing what we do. It's no bother to sell your produce for you and there's no more work on your land than on ours. You do us a large favor by making it possible to farm more land than we could buy."

"Sister Ruth, Sister Naomi..." One by one Mother Clare presented the nuns to the visitors. "And Sister Esther," she finished, indicating a tiny, bent wisp of a woman. Sister Esther turned her head sideways and up, her smile almost lost in the maze of wrinkles on her face. "Sister Esther was our abbess until a few years ago, when she asked to be relieved. She continues to be a blessing for us."

"It's an honor to meet you, Sister," Robert said gently, taking the withered old hand in both of his hands. "You remind me of my mother. She was a wonderful old woman. I suspect you are too."

The giggle was unexpected, as was the warmth of the handclasp she returned with her bony old hand. "I try to be a blessing," she chuckled, "or at least to stay out of trouble!" Robert's mouth opened in amazement, and Sister Esther reached her other hand to Martha. The old nun took the younger woman's hand and held her gaze with her smiling but penetrating eyes. "Oh yes," she remarked to Martha without explanation. "And you, my son." Still smiling, she released their hands, grasped her cane, and shuffled away, bent almost double by the collapse of her vertebrae as she had outlived her supply of bone-making minerals.

Martha and Robert looked quizzically after her, and then at Mother Clare, who merely smiled and said, "Shall we go to the office?" The business transacted then, the two walked back down to their riverside home, hand-in-hand, wordlessly.

~ ~ ~

James walked pensively, head down, never noticing the carriage driven by the black man leaving the cemetery as he approached. Entering and finding the plot without difficulty, he sat quietly on the grass near the foot of Anson's grave. "I still miss you, my friend," he remarked. "Will helped fill your place for me for a while but he's gone and busy with his own family now. Did you know that they have a little girl now too? Antoinette.

"She's going to be a beauty like her mother. Genevieve and little Lawrence went with Will on his last trip to St. Louis. The boy acted as if he'd been born on a boat, Will said. Coiled up lines as neat as you could ask for and even watched forward and pointed out riffles and sandbars. Handsome little fellow, and a mind that will be hard for his parents to keep up with.

"Kind of leaves us out, doesn't it, with no one to follow behind us and carry on our families? Well, have to leave, friend. I guess I don't need to wish you well..."

~ ~ ~

Anna had spoken with Father O'Malley numerous times on the visits he increasingly paid to Westmont. His graceful silences and kind words allowed her to voice her feelings and to begin, finally, to truly heal.

The good Father had tried during each visit to be available also to Miss Emily and Catherine. The younger woman had finally confessed that she'd been unchurched because of the color of her skin. "Perhaps you might like to visit us of a Sunday," he'd remarked casually. "You'd find us very different from what you're accustomed to in a church, of course, but many find it fits their needs. You're certainly welcome if you'd like to visit from time to time."

Miss Emily was a deeper challenge. Father O'Malley suspected that she was mired in her own guilt, but months – and a number of visits – passed with none but casual, social remarks from her. The occasion of Anson's reburial in the family plot might have been a likely opportunity, had she allowed herself to grieve openly then, but she held herself rigidly in check, going through the motions of the burial with little sign of her inner turmoil.

The Father had come upon her trimming the rose bush next to the front door one morning, with slow tears running down her cheeks. She'd simply swept them aside and invited him to seek out Anna or Catherine. She'd turned away and attended the bush again. He touched her arm briefly in leaving, unknowing that the gentle touch had opened the silent fountain of tears again.

~ ~ ~

"'Toinette! You little rascal!" Genevieve's voice rang through the dining room as the child, just turned three, raced away, skirts flying. "Lawrence! Don't even think of rescuing her!"

"But Maman," the boy started.

"Not a word, young man, not a word!"

Genevieve would have been hard put to consider what her life might have been without the children. Lawrence, a proud schoolboy who delighted in reading to his mother or little sister, and Antoinette, who seemed to have bundled all the mischief that might have been latent within the family into her small body. Antoinette, who kept them on the run all day, every day, flying from one piece of impishness to the next.

"Right here, young lady," Genevieve asserted, just as the front door opened and Will entered. "Will!" Genevieve cried. "I didn't expect you until next week! I'm so glad you're home early – " Her words were cut off in Will's warm embrace.

"Aha, wife. I caught you unaware. Chasing after that scamp of a daughter again, eh?"

"What else?" she laughed back at him.

Antoinette had stopped her headlong flight and hovered in the doorway to the dining room. As she determined that her parents were too busy to fuss with her, she raced into the room and grabbed Will's leg. "Papa! Papa! Lift me! Lift me now!"

"Ah. Her imperious highness, Antoinette," Will said, lifting the small girl and tossing her upward as she shrieked with delight. Seeing Lawrence, he plunked the girl down with a loud, smacking kiss, and held his hand out to his son, drawing him into a warm embrace.

"Papa! What did you bring us?" 'Toinette demanded.

"Hugs and kisses!" Will declared.

"I want mine!" the girl shrieked, as Will swooped down and picked her up again.

"I met James in St. Louis, going up as I was coming down. He was talking of maybe settling down somewhere. I think he's lonely."

"Perhaps he could live close to us," Genevieve offered. "No, I guess when I think about it that wouldn't be much company for him, since you're gone more than you're here. It's too bad he never found a wife." Genevieve knew the story of Marian but thought James might have recovered from that loss somehow and settled on another woman to wife. "He's not thinking of selling his boat, is he?"

"I don't think he's thinking of it seriously," Will replied. "I don't think he *could* sell it as long as it wears that name. And thinking of boats and their names, I happen to have with me the last of the money to pay on our boat. As of this payment, she will be utterly, entirely ours. As the house already is, of course."

"I'm so proud, Will. I'd like to go on a trip with you again. What do you think? Could we tie Antoinette to the railing or something to keep her from jumping overboard?"

"Do you think your mother might enjoy her company for a bit? I'd like to have you with me but I would really be concerned with her safety on the boat."

"I'll ask her this evening. She's coming to dinner. Should we take Lawrence with us if Maman will keep Antoinette?"

"I'd like to. He acts as if he was born to the river and the boat. Do you think Antoinette would be jealous if he goes and she doesn't?"

"Fiddle dee! If she's a scamp here, she'd be more so on board. We'll just explain to her that Lawrence has earned the trip because he is well behaved so we don't have to worry about him falling overboard. That might help tame her a bit for Maman..."

"I doubt that. I doubt if anything will ever tame that child."

~ ~ ~

"Please come to church with us for Easter, Anna," Gloria said. She was unprepared for Anna's reaction. As if terrified the other girl backed away, holding her hands in front of her as if to ward off a blow. "I'm sorry, Anna! I didn't mean to frighten you – what is it?"

"No. No thank you." Her voice was higher pitched than normal. "I, I've got some school work I need to do."

"You? You always have everything finished early."

Unseen, Father O'Malley had happened upon this conversation. "May I borrow Anna for a bit?" he asked Gloria.

"Of course, Father O'Malley," Gloria responded.

"Shall we walk in the orchard?" the priest invited Anna.

"All right," she answered, still tense and afraid, but willing herself away from the girl who had become her friend, but who had now come to represent a terrible threat to her.

"You seemed frightened by the idea of going to church," the priest said gently when they were ensconced on a wide bench under the apple trees. "Is there something I might help with?"

Anna had gathered up herself into a tight bundle, pulled away from the Father as far as possible without falling off the end of the bench. "Thank you, Father, but I'm fine."

"You know, Anna, I have a friend you might enjoy visiting with sometime. His name is Ezra Goldsmith. Rabbi Ezra Goldsmith." He let the statement hang in the air. The girl's eyes widened but she made no response.

"Perhaps the Master of the Universe would like for you to visit with the rabbi. What do you think?"

Anna began to sob.

"Gently, girl. It's been a long time," the priest said softly.

At length the sobbing slowed to an occasional hiccough and sob. "Please...please, you will help me?" she asked.

"Yes. I will help you and so will my friend the rabbi. You don't need to hide here. You're perfectly safe. No one will harm you."

"But the Christians killed my grandfather. He didn't do anything, they just killed him. My father hid with my grandmother or they would have killed them too."

"Where did they live then?" the Father asked.

"They were in Poland. They were Polish, and the Christians just killed them because it was Easter." Her voice began to rise again and her hand, raised to brush her hair back, trembled.

"Let me find Miss Emily and get permission to take a little trip to town with you, child. Are you all right if I leave you for a bit?

"Y,Yes, yes I guess so..."

"No one will hurt you here, Anna. You are safe here."

He returned shortly, bearing Miss Emily's permission and with Catherine in tow. "I thought you'd be more comfortable with another woman riding with us," he said kindly. Miss Catherine knows where we're going, as does Miss Emily. They both approve."

The carriage returned a few hours later, bringing Anna, now relaxed and peaceful. Anna and Catherine climbed out of the conveyance near the side door of the house. "May the Master of the Universe bless you, child," Father O'Malley said gently to Anna, "and you also, Catherine, for your understanding and care." Dusk was falling as the carriage drove back westward out of the drive.

~ ~ ~

While other young men also took advantage of any excuse to visit at Westmont, Joel had become a regular visitor. He escorted Catherine to St. Patrick's now on Sunday mornings – Father O'Malley having given the young man to understand that *he* also was a protector of the young woman – and to various social activities. While Catherine had dated others, she preferred the company of Joel.

"I need to talk with Samuel for a minute, Catherine. Will you excuse me?"

Catherine thought nothing of the request, for Samuel and Joel had been comfortable with each other from the first meeting. She wandered away and relaxed on a bench under the arbor, gazing pensively at the wisteria splurging its lavender over the arbor and around the stable, thirty feet behind the arbor. How marvelous, she thought. Three days – or some years, a few more days – of glory every year and then the blooms drop off and it masquerades as just another vine for the rest of the year.

Her appreciation of the flowers was interrupted by the return of Joel. "Did you find Samuel?" she queried.

"Yes. Yes, I found him and yes, I got his approval."

"His approval? For what?"

"Catherine. Will you marry me? I got this for you, hoping that your answer would be yes," opening a small box and revealing a lovely ring.

"Mercy! I used to wonder if I'd ever find a mate whom I could honor as I honor Samuel..."

Taking her hesitation as a possible refusal, he spoke "You don't have to decide right now, if you need time to think about it. I can wait for your answer... Please, will you consider it?"

"I don't think I need to consider that," she replied archly.

"But Catherine..."

"Joel! Yes. Yes, I will marry you. Yes, I'd be honored to be your wife."

"Catherine! You've made me the happiest man on earth!"

"Remember that feeling when we have our first fuss," she chuckled. "Oh yes. I think I've been waiting for you since I was a little girl." She looked admiringly at the ring he slipped onto her finger and leaned forward (for he had, indeed, knelt before her to ask the question), giving him a gentle kiss, their first. Both then rose, and joined in an embrace that fulfilled their early dreams and held a promise of more dreams later.

Silently, each rapt in the presence of the other, they strolled hand-in-hand through the orchard and stopped, gazing out at the fields and hills. Then their lips met again, and they returned to the house in order to share their newfound joy with Sarah and Miss Emily.

# Chapter 15

James paused, hands still on the wheel but mind suddenly jerked back many miles away. I didn't see it! Why didn't I think of it? he scolded himself. It was there, it had to have been there...it must have been there. Where was it? I would have seen it? Maybe it's somewhere else, some other city, some – no, they brought Anson's body home to the family plot. They couldn't have been much angrier with anyone than they were with him. Even if she died somewhere else, they would have brought her body home. I didn't see it, I didn't search for it, I should have searched, I would have seen it. Where is she?? They said she was dead. The maid or whoever that was. She said she was dead and I just believed her. I didn't talk to anyone else. I was too shocked and hurting too much to think; I'd so looked forward to going and claiming her for my wife...if she was buried there I'd have noticed, wouldn't I? Surely, I'd have noticed...I didn't search...it's as if I forgot her...

No, I didn't forget her; I just knew from the caretaker in New Orleans that Anson's body had been moved, finally. That's all I was thinking about. I should have searched. I should have gone back and asked for her again. I have to go back. How could I have not thought to look...?

He disposed of his load with as much dispatch as possible and turned the *Marian Dee* back upstream in record time. The paddlewheels thumped a quicker rhythm than on previous runs; the crew looked askance at each other, but no one had the intimacy of relationship that might allow a question to be put to James. So they kept their own counsel and were still more careful than usual that everything on the boat be spotless and entirely in order.

The *Marian Dee* tied up to the Stevens' pier twelve scant days out of New Orleans. Robert and James chatted while the wood was being loaded. James glanced up toward the monastery, seeing a brown-clad figure seated on the bench near the cloister wall. "Hm," James mused. "I've never seen anyone around there before. I didn't know they came outside of the wall."

"Yeah, that's Mother Clare," Robert responded. She likes to sit on that bench and say her prayers under the trees and near the river."

"Oh! I didn't know you knew any of them."

"We met them a couple of years ago. I've been sharecropping most of their land, so I was up there a couple of times a year, usually, but they sent a gift down for my wife, so the next time I went up she went with me and Mother Clare introduced us all around. We were up again last fall. Old Sister Esther died and Mother Clare sent word for us to come for her funeral if we'd like."

"Do you mean one of the nuns comes down or something?"

"No, the priest who comes there every day and says Mass for them came down and told us. We do have an emergency signal; if they need something immediately they will hang a sheet out over the wall there. We worked that out with Mother Clare one time, but they've never used it."

"Are they really sisters? Is that Mother Clare really their mother?"

"No, we were kind of confused about that at first too, because we're not Catholic either. Mother Clare says we're all brothers and sisters; they're just a little bit more formal about it there. And she isn't really a mother. She's just the head nun. Old Sister Esther used to be the Mother there, but when she got real old and doubled up, she asked them to choose someone else.

"Sister Esther was a prize! She was so old she was all doubled over – I'm sure that had to hurt – but she still giggled and teased like a schoolgirl. The time we met her she said she tried to be a blessing to everyone but if she failed in that, she hoped at least to stay out of trouble!" Robert laughed quietly at the reminiscence.

Something about the figure caught James' eye as the nun up by the monastery rose and walked around the wall. He stared for a moment, then shook his head.

"What's that?" Robert queried.

"Oh, nothing. I thought she looked familiar, but of course, I was mistaken. I've never known any nuns. I've never been able to understand it. It has always seemed like something up there at that place was pulling me up, every time I've been here."

"It's a rare place," Robert replied. "I think I know what you mean. I always get a real peaceful feeling, a kind of a pull toward there too. I noticed it in the chapel especially when Mother Clare showed us around.

"Well, I see the men are finished loading. We'll be on our way," James said, counting out the money to pay for the wood into Robert's hand. "Hope the rest of your week goes well, Mr. Stevens," he said as he walked back toward the boat, nodding politely at Martha, who came out of the kitchen door and waved as he passed.

The stage was pulled as soon as James boarded, the crew working smartly to make time as they had since New Orleans, to accommodate James' hurry to get upstream. James stood at the port railing on the boiler deck as they pulled out, gazing at the bench beside the monastery wall. The bench was now empty.

~ ~ ~

Father O'Malley looked surprised as he opened the front door of the rectory to see Catherine and Joel waiting there together. "Come in, come in," he boomed heartily, suspecting their mission by their presence together.

Father O'Malley brought freshly squeezed lemonade, kept chilled in the cistern outside the kitchen door, and they sat briefly chatting. Joel assured the Father that his business prospects were strong. He agreed that the weather this week had been ideal for the season. He paused shyly, looking lost, after each response to Father O'Malley's conversational offerings. At last, the Father simply let the silence hang among them, so Joel finally glanced at Catherine and plunged into the topic at hand.

"Catherine has agreed to marry me," he announced. "Samuel and Sarah and Miss Emily have given their blessings. We'd like yours also. And we'd like you to marry us."

"Ah. I suspected it might be some such thing to bring you here together. I'm very pleased to add my blessing for you. I'd been hoping for a while that this might come to pass. I think you're both of excellent character and ready to form a family of your own. I do congratulate you."

"Have you talked about such things as having children and managing money? Or where you will live?"

Joel blushed but Catherine grasped his hand and lent her support to him. "We definitely want children, Father," she responded. "We haven't talked much about money."

"It's important to talk about things that will be important to your family, and money is certainly one of those things. For instance, who will decide where you live?"

"Ah, Father, there's a little complication about that," Joel said tentatively. "I guess I haven't told Catherine yet; I've been so busy being so happy that she agreed to marry me..."

"What's this? What have you not told me?" Catherine queried curiously. "I hope you're not planning to move to Timbuktu or someplace," she added. "It would be very hard for me to leave my family..."

"Ah, Catherine – ah, would you like to take a little ride with me? Father, if you aren't busy would you like to come also? Please," he added in a small voice.

"Joel, my son, I hope you aren't proposing a pattern here, of seeking support for your positions before you reveal them to your wife," Father O'Malley said only half-jokingly.

"Um, I guess I don't have anything to offer about that, except that we came here first because we wanted to share our excitement with you. Would you like to come with us to share something I have to show Catherine?"

"All right, you've gotten my curiosity aroused. Shall we go now?"

Driving down Main Street they chatted, excitement suppressed, about various goings-on around town. Joel turned down, then, to Dewey Street and stopped the carriage in front of a modestly neat house, two stories of brick with glistening white trim and a front porch, with a generous balcony on the second story, a door from it leading into the house.

Joel hopped out of the carriage, barely concealing his anxious excitement. Reaching up, he handed Catherine down from the carriage and pulled a key out of his vest pocket, which he gave her. "The key to your house," he said, a firmness suddenly in his voice. "I hope you like it. I guess if you don't we can sell this one and get another..."

Catherine's mouth dropped open. "Our house? You bought this house for us?"

"For you, yes," he replied quietly. "But if you don't like it, we can get another. Or we can live here until we save enough to build whatever you'd like. I guess I should have asked you first, but I hadn't even asked you to marry me. It certainly isn't what you're used to – will you come and look inside?"

"Oh. I love this," she said, glancing around the sitting room. "And here! Look at this wonderful stove! I can bake a lot of bread in this oven. And a pantry..."

"Come up here," Joel urged, leading her up a broad stair and through a large bedroom to the balcony. I've heard you mention a lot of times that you enjoy watching the river. You can see the river from here and this house should be high enough away from the river to be safe from floods. Or at least from most floods."

"I do love to watch the river. I've never understood why, but it has always seemed that a part of me belongs to the river. Joel, I'm so delighted with the house! I'm so delighted that we're going to marry and that we're going to live here. You know, I've waited a long time to consider marriage until I was sure I knew myself, and the man I was to marry. I believe this is the time and you are the man and I'm so happy about that."

Assured of her consent to marriage and her affinity for the house, Joel finally looked again at Father O'Malley. "Will you marry us?"

"There are some formalities to take care of, but yes, I'd like to do that. Shall we go back to the rectory and discuss it?"

Catherine held Joel's hand all the way back.

~ ~ ~

"Joel! Have you heard the rumors about war?" Charles asked.

"I've heard a bit," Joel said cautiously. "What are you hearing?"

"A river man said yesterday that the Southern states are calling themselves the Confederacy. He said they fired on Fort Sumter last month."

"Yeah, I heard about the same thing. They want to be their own country, separate from us. What do you think? Do you think there will really be a war?"

"I don't know. I suppose we'd be officers if there is a war."

"But that would be terrible. Who could go around the country killing people?"

"Well, in a war you don't just kill 'people', you kill enemy soldiers."

"Well, why are they 'enemy'? Just because they're different from us? Because they believe differently from us? Aren't soldiers people too?"

"You're just shying away from the notion of war because you and Catherine are being married soon. Goodness sake, Joel. Would you not fight to protect your own home and family?"

"Of course I would. But my home and family are *here*. I don't see anyone threatening us."

"Well, no, no one is threatening here, but other peoples' homes may be threatened. "Oh well. I guess we'll just have to wait and see what happens."

~ ~ ~

"Do you have a moment, Father? Miss Emily asked from the shelter of the arbor, seeing the priest leave his carriage near the stable."

"Of course, Miss Emily. What can I do for you today?" he asked with a smile.

"I think – I, I think I would like to make my confession, Father."

"Of course. Would you like to come in to the church to do that, or is there a place here where you'd feel comfortable?"

"I, I – you may not approve, but yes, there is a place here. Will you come with me before I lose my courage?"

"You're a very brave person, Miss Emily. You have started anew and made amends such as few people would have been able to do. Please lead the way."

The Father hesitated at the doorway of the room; Miss Emily produced a key and opened the lock. He carried, as she had directed, a chair from an empty room here on the third floor. Glimpsing the window as she moved into the room he involuntarily caught his breath. The slit in the stone wall was so small. Barely six inches wide and about three feet in height, it was a tiny opening on a circumscribed world. "Bless me Father, for I have sinned," she intoned.

When at last she felt emptied, she raised her eyes toward him, seated on the chair in front of her prie-dieu, her hands still rigidly clasped atop the kneeler. "Can God ever forgive such things?" she asked, almost reduced to a whisper.

"My dear Miss Emily," Father O'Malley responded. "God forgave you long ago. I think you have not been able to forgive yourself. Is that true?"

"No. Oh no. I can never really forgive such behavior." She repulsed the notion.

"Only a truly evil person could do such things. I've tried, Father. I've tried so hard. And I've tried to do penance for Edward. I've been so frightened for him. I loved him, I truly did, and if he's condemned to hell for what we did, I don't want to go to eternity without him. I've tried, Father," she broke into sobs.

Father O'Malley reached out and covered her hands with his. "Cry it out, my dear Miss Emily, cry it all out."

When at last the wrenching cries subsided, he continued, "Miss Emily. God has forgiven you, long since. As God's priest, I formally forgive you. Your penance is twofold: you are not to come here again. You may keep the prie-dieu if you wish, although you may find other places and postures as effective for prayer as on your knees. If you choose to use the prie-dieu it is to be moved to your room or another appropriate location. You have used this room to punish yourself most cruelly for a long period of time. You must not do it again.

"The second part of your penance is that each day, for the rest of your life, you are to do some thing for your own pleasure. It need not be anything lavish. It can be as simple as enjoying a sunrise or sunset, or admiring a perfect apple, or talking with someone you love or enjoy. It may be singing a song, or listening to someone else sing. It may be taking time to appreciate some special thing in one of your students..."

"Father! That's so selfish! That's how I got into this predicament, being selfish."

"No, Miss Emily, you weren't so much selfish as you were concerned about appearances. It might reflect poorly on the family if your son did common labor, even though he was doing what he loved. It might have looked bad if your Marian had given birth and the community found out about it. Others might have judged her poorly, or judged you and her father.

"Unfortunately, you judged yourself far more harshly than others would have. You've worn a hair shirt, as it were, for these many years. You must learn to come closer to God by accepting his loving forgiveness. It will not be easy. You've gotten into a very deep rut here. Will you accept the challenge to begin to extract yourself?"

"Yes, Father," she replied in a very subdued tone. "I will try, if you are sure this is what I must do."

"What does your heart tell you, Miss Emily? You are the mediator of your own spiritual journey. I can only know generalities. God wishes to communicate with you directly about the details."

"Father! Is that not heresy?"

"Fiddle dee, Miss Emily. You don't really believe God expects us to be puppets, do you? If you believe I know what's best for you, then you would have to allow that only my bishop knows what's best for me, and the cardinal for the bishop, and the pope for him... Do you see, my dear? It would be a dreadful chore to have to know all things for all people."

There was a lightness in Emily's step as they left the attic. The prie-dieu was left in the hall to be moved later. The room itself was locked. It was not to be reopened in Emily's lifetime.

Chapter 16

James hesitated at the gateway to the cemetery. Almost 1400 miles, running the paddlewheel ragged – literally, a board broken by a floating tree trunk just past Memphis was only now being repaired – to look for a tombstone. Walking cautiously, as if he expected to be challenged at any moment, he moved toward the Durrant grave plot.

When he didn't find it immediately, he looked again and then widened his search. Surely, it was here... It is here, it is here, it is – not – here.

James stopped at the livery on his way back past town and rented a horse and buggy. Turning the tired old nag's head out into the street, he put the late morning sun behind him and began easing the horse up into the river bluffs above the town. When he reached the Durrant lane, he paused. To hope, to fear – finally he turned down the lane, where he encountered Sarah walking from their cottage to the big house.

"Excuse me," he said. "Can you tell me where I might find Mrs. Durrant? I understand that Mr. Durrant has passed away— "

"Yes. Mr. Durrant died a dozen years ago," Sarah responded. "If you'll come with me I'll locate Mrs. Durrant for you." Leading him to the drawing room, she left and returned shortly with Miss Emily.

"Mrs. Durrant," he said. "My name is James Mason. I've come to beg information from you."

"Indeed, Mr. Mason," glancing at his workaday clothes and boots but seeing also his square shoulders and a habitually confident posture. "How is it that I can assist you?"

"In 1833 I met a young woman named Marian Durrant..."

With a start Emily realized that she was looking at the man's hair, somewhat dulled by age but still unmistakably red. She gasped and clutched at her throat. Both had been standing, but James quickly leaned forward to support her. "Please, ma'am, let me help you." She offered no resistance and he led her to a chair and helped her sit, pulling another chair near and maintaining a protective grasp of her hands.

Sarah passed by the doorway and he summoned her with a gesture. "Please bring some tea to refresh Mrs. Durrant. I believe this is a difficult moment for her." Sarah returned almost immediately. "The tea will be here directly. Angel is bringing it. Is there something I can do?"

"I think not," he replied. "I need to speak with Mrs. Durrant about some family things— "

"Let her stay. If you are who I think you are, she's as much involved as I am. Pray continue, Mr. Mason."

"As you wish. Anson Durrant came to work on the riverboat the *Daisy Lee*, where I was employed at that time. He and I worked together for two years and became close friends. He wrote his sister, Marian, frequently. I met Marian at the same time I met Anson, and she agreed to exchange letters with me. My letters were enclosed with Anson's, and she sent letters to me in her letters to him.

"In 1835 the *Daisy Lee* returned here. Anson had left word on the way up to Cincinnati that we would stop on the way back. A black man named Samuel brought Marian to the riverfront. He said that neither Mr. Durrant nor you, Mrs. Durrant, were able to meet us. He left Marian in Anson's care and we walked about a bit.

"Anson met a young woman friend of his and left Marian in my care to return her here in the evening. I'm afraid we were young and irresponsible – but I did return her home about 9 o'clock that evening, as Anson told me you would expect her. The *Daisy Lee* was able to get through the locks in the middle of the night, headed back down to New Orleans.

"We received no more letters. Anson blamed himself, saying he had forsaken his father's dreams for him. We assumed that Mr. Durrant was destroying our letters to Marian and forbidding her to write to Anson. Or me, of course, although we believed he had no knowledge of her doing that.

"We came back through here after Anson's death. I'd received no acknowledgement of my letter telling Mr. Durrant of the accident, so I came up to speak to him in person. A servant met me at the door and said he was not in and Marian had died, and I was not welcome here. I was so shocked – I'd planned to ask Mr. Durrant's permission to marry Marian that day also.

"I used to stop at Lafayette in New Orleans when we had a layover there, and sit by Captain Marat's family vault and kind of visit with Anson. The last time I went there the caretaker told me he'd helped remove the bag, um, he told me that Anson's body had been moved to your family plot here. I stopped to visit with him the next time I could when we were going through here, but I was clear to New Orleans before I realized I hadn't seen Marian's tombstone.

"Mrs. Durrant, is Marian really dead? If she's married someone else, I'll leave and cause no trouble, but please, just put my mind at ease. Where is she?"

It was well that this visit had been prefaced by Emily's confession and reconciliation. Without the belief in God's forgiveness imparted by Father O'Malley, she would have been ill prepared to hear this request. She had gained a bit of spiritual peace since that event, however, and she straightened her spine and spoke directly to James.

"I'm sorry, Mr. Mason. It breaks my heart, but I don't know where she is. I don't know if she's dead or alive," she continued, explaining Edward's action and her failure to take any action to protect Anson or Marian.

She then added, "I have a question for you, Mr. Mason. You said that you and Marian were young and irresponsible. Is it possible that she might have gotten with child while she was with you?"

James blushed, nearly matching the color of his face to that of his hair. He dropped his head, but then – modeling from Emily's courageous behavior – he straightened in his chair and said, "Yes. Yes, ma'am. That's the only time in my life that that might have happened, but yes, it did." Realizing then the meaning suggested by that interchange, his eyes widened. "Is there a child? Please, if there is a child, please tell me."

"Yes, Mr. Mason. There is a child. Sarah, will you please bring her? And perhaps Samuel should share in this conversation also."

Sarah rose quickly, as Angel came in with a tea tray, complete with biscuits and oatmeal cookies. "Please try the cookies, Mr. Mason. We'll have a bit of lunch soon, but I believe the person who baked the oatmeal cookies is your daughter."

When Catherine appeared in the doorway, James' eyes misted with tears and he sat rooted to his chair. Sarah gently brought Catherine forward. "Mr. Mason, this is your daughter, Catherine. Catherine, your father, James Mason."

James rose to meet her and stood, still speechless, with her hands in his. It seemed that neither could get their fill of looking at the other. Finally, Catherine spoke. "I've dreamed so long about meeting my parents. I have some rather vague memories of my mother, from when I was a small child, but the only thing I knew about my father was that his name was James and it was likely that he had red hair."

"You look so like your mother, Catherine. Only your hair is different. Your hair is like mine, only softer." Only then did he realize, "Your name is Catherine. Do you happen to know how that name was chosen?"

Sarah answered that question. "I can tell you that. I was present when Catherine was born. As soon as she knew the baby was a girl, her mother said she was to be called Catherine because your mother," gesturing at James, "was named Catherine. Marian wanted to acknowledge your father, and join you to him, um, spiritually, even though she didn't know where your father was physically, except on a riverboat."

"You are then," James calculated quickly, "twenty-five, no, twenty-four years old. You would have born late in the year; it was early spring when your mother and I were together. I've missed so much of your life! I'm so sorry I wasn't here for your childhood."

"Sarah and Samuel were here to love and guide me. May I present my foster parents, Sarah and Samuel Freeman," motioning to the couple.

James offered his hand to Samuel. "I believe I met you before, didn't I? On the day Marian and I were together. You brought her down to the river in the buggy and then left the buggy for us to use."

"Yes. That was me." Samuel at first hesitated to take the other man's hand, but realized both that there was much of the story he wasn't privy to, and that Catherine needed a father who was respected. He then met James' hand with a firm clasp.

"And Mrs. Freeman. Thank you so much for caring for her."

"We were the fortunate in the situation. We wanted children but could not have them. Catherine filled a great gap in our lives with abundant joy and love. She will always live in our hearts."

"Perhaps you'd like to show Mr. Mason around a bit, Catherine, while lunch is being readied." Miss Emily recognized a need for the two to spend some time getting acquainted. James' bearing and words led her to believe the girl would be safe with him, but if they were just walking about there would be many eyes to verify her safety, as the students were wandering about, also waiting for lunch. It never hurt to have a backup plan for a young woman's safety.

"Is this a school or something?" James queried as they met a second small group of girls.

"Yes. This is Westmont School for Young Ladies. There were some financial difficulties after my grandfather's death. We opened the school to serve girls whose families wanted them trained appropriately while being sheltered from untoward influences."

"And do you have a role in this enterprise?"

"Yes. I teach languages."

"Languages! What languages do you teach?"

"French, German, and Spanish."

"Where in the world did you go to school yourself to learn so many languages?" James exclaimed.

"I was tutored here," Catherine replied. "Sarah's father was European. He knew those languages and taught them to his children. Sarah then taught me. It was very simple, actually, since I was learning to talk – in English, of course – at the same time." She didn't know Miss Emily had revealed her imprisonment or not, but she was not going to offer the information needlessly.

"How many students do you have here?"

"This term there are seventeen. Three of those will graduate in May. Nearly all of the students go home for the summer. I suppose Anna will be here again this year; her parents were killed in an accident about a year ago and she's been here since. Sometimes she seems more like family than like a student. She's very bright, though, and applies herself to anything we can give her academically. She already knew Polish, Russian, and Yiddish when she came here, so she mastered German in a flash, so to speak. She's competent now in Spanish and beginning to work on French. You'll meet her – and the other students – at lunch."

As she spoke, the bell was rung for lunch, and they walked back toward the house.

"I don't want to impose. I'll go back down to the river and make some arrangements for my boat and then come back later this afternoon."

"Please. It wouldn't be an imposition. Angel already cooks for so many, there's always an abundance of food. Please stay and have lunch with us."

"If you're certain," he responded, after a brief hesitation. He tucked her hand under his arm and accompanied her to the dining room, where an extra place had been laid at Catherine's table.

Catherine kept to her feet while the students were being seated, and then brought James' hand forward clasped in hers. "May I present my father, Mr. James Mason," she announced to the girls. The students dutifully bobbed their heads in acknowledgement of the introduction and Catherine and James seated themselves as the staff began serving lunch. Catherine noticed that Angel, who did not help serve, came to the dining room doorway and looked long and carefully at James. At length she turned her attention to Catherine and nodded her head, smiling.

Seats at Catherine's table had been rotated, putting her at the head of the table for this occasion, with James seated at her right. Catherine then set about putting him at ease. "On my left here is Isabel, who has a gift for Spanish. Beside her is Sonja, an excellent French student. She's also our resident romantic," she added with a smile. "Anna is our mathematician. And Mary Annette is our resident rascal. She's also quite good in mathematics, but I believe her primary role here is that of rascal. Mary Annette pointed a finger at herself and said "Me??" The girls laughed and James relaxed a bit.

"Would you share a bit of yourself for the girls?" Catherine requested.

James looked at her with a gentle smile, saying, "Of course. Although this," gesturing at the group around the table, "is a bit more than I expected.

"I am a riverboat pilot on three rivers, the Ohio, the Missouri, and the Mississippi. I've worked the rivers since I was thirteen. I am captain and owner of the steamer the *Marian Dee*, named for Catherine's mother."

Catherine had not known, and her eyes glistened with moisture.

"Where are you going with the boat now, Captain Mason?" Isabel asked.

"I'll look around here for a load for St. Louis or New Orleans. If I don't find anything here I'll go on up to Cincinnati. There's always freight there waiting to be shipped downstream. I came up with a light load this time, because I was in a hurry to get here."

"I think it would be exciting to work on the river," Sonja offered.

"I believe I see how you came to be labeled a 'romantic,'" James remarked with a broad smile. "Riding up or down a river can be romantic. For that matter, sitting beside the river and watching it flow past is romantic for some.

"Working the river is sometimes pleasant. It is often too hot or too cold, though, and loading and unloading are hard, heavy work. Piloting a boat is much easier physically than being a deckhand, but the pilot has to keep his attention on the river every moment, or the boat might run aground on a sandbar or be damaged by hitting a snag in the water."

"What is a snag, Mr. Mason?" asked Anna.

"A snag is anything floating on the river, or worse, just under the surface of the water, where it's harder to see, that might damage the boat. Trees often get uprooted in high water and float downstream. If the tree 'snags' on anything it may be there for months, until a boat comes along and gets caught on it.

"We broke a board in the paddle wheel on the trip up this time. An old dead tree was caught against a bank that jutted out into the river. I suppose if I'd been more careful I might have seen and avoided it, but being to the side like that there weren't many clues that it was there. The crew is replacing that board now, while we're made fast here."

Lunch past, Catherine and James resumed their stroll about the grounds. "You've not married," James remarked.

"No, I realize that most young women already have families by my age, but I wanted to get acquainted with myself first, I guess," Catherine rejoined. "I am engaged to be married to a man named Joel Benson. He's a manager at the Allison Furniture Works. I expect he and you might have a number of things to visit about."

"I'm sure he's a fine young man if you've chosen him," James said. Shaking his head, he muttered, "I just can't believe how lucky I am."

"What do you mean," quizzed Catherine.

"Honey, I've lived so long alone and have believed for so long that I would always be alone and now to find that I'm related to a treasure like you. It's just so amazing." In the flush of mutual admiration, neither noticed the endearment.

"You never married? There was never anyone after my mother?"

"No. I guess there were several good women who would have been available if I had been, but I just couldn't face up to anyone else. Your mother and I wrote each other for two years before we met again in person. And got you started," he added with a self-conscious chuckle.

"I wish I could have known my mother that well. I was only three when – when they took her away. I've never known where they took her nor if she might be alive or dead."

"Would you like to read your mother's letters?" James offered. "No one but me has ever read them, of course, but I kept every one of them."

Tears shone in Catherine's eyes. "Oh, please. Please let me read about my mother."

"Do you have anything scheduled right now?"

"No, the term is essentially over. The girls will have a few informal sessions with me before they leave, but graduation is next Sunday afternoon. We can take the day today; no one will mind."

"Let's check in with Mrs. Durrant then. If she doesn't mind we can go to the boat now and get them."

"Everyone calls her 'Miss Emily.' I used to call her that too," Catherine added without thinking. "I don't think she'll mind if you call her Miss Emily. What should I call you?" she asked suddenly.

"What do you think you might be comfortable with? My name is James; you may use that if you like. Or 'Father', or..."

"Perhaps I need to reflect on it a bit, to give time for some relationship to develop. Likely when I've known you for a while something will come naturally."

"All right. In the meantime you may use 'James' if you're comfortable with that."

"I think not. Perhaps 'Father' for now – it would seem very rude to use your given name. And much too cold to call you 'Mr. Mason.'"

"As you wish."

"Father. Father. Fa – I think I never believed there would be a father in my life. I'm grateful that we found each other."

"And I you. By the way, you make very good oatmeal cookies."

Catherine laughed in appreciation, and arm-in-arm they walked back to the house.

"Have you heard talk of war, sir?" asked Joel.

"Yes, I'm afraid I've heard more than just talk. There's actual shooting, some places, I've heard, and I met three or four riverboats coming down from Cincinnati that have been armor clad to fight in the war. Whatever happens, the river will be vital. It's the only way to move a lot of goods quickly."

"Do you mean the Ohio?"

"The whole central drainage system for the middle of the continent. The Ohio to the east, which will likely be more important than the Missouri, to the west, since there's less population along the Missouri and by and large they're much less involved in politics than those closer to Washington D.C.

"The Mississippi, of course, picks up the Ohio at the corner of Kentucky and Missouri and Tennessee, and the Missouri joins it at St. Louis. Then it goes through the whole Southern heartland of the country. Culture there is more easy going in some ways, maybe somewhat more communal, and there's a sort of laissez faire belief system among the big plantations there."

"I'm not sure what you mean by that," Joel said, thoughtfully.

"It's sort of like 'This is our way, we've always done it this way, we're always going to do it this way, and we won't tolerate anyone interfering.'"

"Specifically what sort of thing are they defending?"

"The main thing is that there seems to be a serious problem with tariffs. The North controls the tariffs on imports by its influence in congress. They set high tariffs on manufactured goods, because if those can be imported cheaply it interferes with the Northern manufacturers selling their products

160

in the South. Europe has too much competition for the Northern manufacturers to make as much profit exporting there.

"The federal government then uses the money they get from tariffs collected on Southern ports to do things like subsidize fishermen in New England and Northern shipping interests, which in effect have a monopoly on the use of Southern ports. The *London Times* last November said the war is really for 'empire' on the side of the North and for independence on the part of the South. Of course, I'm not sure how unbiased their assessment is.

"Here and there a few people are saying that slavery is at the bottom of the problem, but I think that's incidental and not the real cause. The South is agricultural and their agriculture – indeed, their economy in general – requires that slavery be continued.

"So even though I don't think there's any direct link between slavery and the war, I do think there's an indirect link, since the Southern economy in its present form couldn't survive if they should loose their slaves.

"From some of the plantation owners I've known, I think maybe they believe they're supposed to live in big houses while slaves do the work. Sort of a divinely established system. But especially when I hear about the tariff problems, I can see the Southern point in saying that the federal government is trying to interfere with the way they live their lives and conduct their business."

"Do you think then that money is behind this war?"

"Well, I'm certainly not a statesman nor the best informed person in the country, but I do see a lot of different places and hear different people, and I get newspapers when I can at my stops along the river, and at the bottom line, I suspect that in any war if we follow the money we might have the real cause."

"Are there others with money at stake in the war, sir? Other than the plantation owners and the Northern manufacturers?

"I'm hearing of armaments being sold here from European countries, and of course if the cotton which usually goes to mills in New England goes instead to England or another country that country is getting it cheaper, while the shippers may actually be getting a better price, since the Northern markets seemed to be keeping the prices depressed. And if they ship back finished products such as cloth into what has become essentially free ports, that's a saving for the South and more profit for the Europeans.

"I think a lot of people on both sides will die for their beliefs about the war, but I misdoubt the accuracy of their beliefs."

"You say the rivers are essential to the war; will you become involved, with your riverboat?"

"I don't know. If I did, I truly don't know which side I would serve. I just find it hard to believe that killing people is a solution to a problem."

"Samuel was born slave. His mother brought him here to freedom when he was just a baby. He says his mother told him his real father was sold South because their master was angry about a horse that died. Samuel says he saw his mother's back one time, and it was crisscrossed with deep scars, where she'd been whipped when she tried to keep his father from being taken away. They don't know which state they came from; his mother had never been off the place where she was born before. She walked all night every night for a long time before she finally got here."

"His mother was a very brave person. I've heard such stories before and I always question if I'd have the courage to do such a thing. Just follow the North Star and not know where the journey will end, or how.

"I don't think there's any way I could support a system that believes it can enslave other human beings. I just couldn't do it. Perhaps we'll be lucky and the conflict will end before we should have to make such a choice," Joel remarked.

"I hope so, but I misdoubt it. I'm afraid there will be many dead and few families on either side not scarred by the agony of war. God protect us all."

Chapter 17

It was decided then, that Anna should accompany her. Miss Emily claimed to be too old for such gallivanting, although she'd told of begging to go with her father to Memphis when she was a young woman, and no one would consider risking Samuel or Sarah on such a journey. Having another young woman with her would serve propriety as well as give Catherine company, and both would be enriched by the experience of such a trek. A local attorney had been named Anna's guardian subsequent to the death of her parents, and he readily acceded to Miss Emily's request for permission.

"Please stay safe while I'm gone," she said to Joel. "I hate to leave you for so long, but I've waited a lifetime to get acquainted with my father. And once I'm married and start a family there won't be any opportunities for such travel. Or if we wait now, the war may catch up to the rivers so it wouldn't be safe for us to go."

"You have Will Isaacs' address so you can send mail that Catherine will get when we get to New Orleans," James reminded him, "and Catherine can send mail back by northbound boats along the way."

All of the students had had the adventure of a day trip on the *Marian Dee*. They had trekked down to the waterfront to admire the boat and the desire had been born in several of the students, unusual as it might be for a young lady to voyage aboard a boat. Miss Emily had given permission for the excursion, thumping upstream toward Cincinnati and floating back downstream.

Catherine, standing in the pilothouse now with James, remarked "We were on a riverboat before, when we were out Christmas caroling. We saw a woman on a boat queued up waiting for the lock so we thought it would be safe for us to stop and carol them. Of course there were a dozen and a half of us, so that in itself was quite safe, and Samuel and Sarah were both with us. It was as neat and spotless as this boat, and the owner and his wife very pleasant."

"Do you remember the name of the boat by any chance?"

"Um," Catherine paused, "I think it was the *Genevieve*. Do you know of such a boat?"

"Yes," James smiled. "I certainly do. I guess since your Uncle Anson's death, the owner of the *Genevieve* is my best friend. He's the Will Isaacs whose address we left for Joel to send you letters."

"That's amazing!"

"The river can be a pretty small community, although there are probably a few thousand riverboats working now. The woman you met on that boat was Will's wife Genevieve, for whom the boat is named. I predict that you'll like her when you get to meet her."

"Have you known them long?"

"Actually, I've known Will since he was fifteen years old. He worked as a deckhand on this boat and I trained him then as a pilot. He bought the *Genevieve* when he got married. I've known Genevieve – the woman Genevieve – since then. They have a couple of children now. You'll meet his son Lawrence when we get there. He's about five or six. And I expect Antoinette will intercept and meet you before anyone has a chance to introduce her. I think she's three now, and she was born a rascal. Genevieve still makes trips occasionally with Will, but they leave 'Toinette with Genevieve's mother; they're afraid she'll fall overboard if they take her on the boat. Lawrence, on the other hand, acts like he was born to be a boatman."

"I look forward to meeting them again." There was a long, peaceful pause in the conversation before Catherine spoke again. "Where will we stop next?" she queried.

"We'll stop at the Stevens' landing and load wood. Perhaps you can meet Martha Stevens. I believe you'll enjoy her. There's also something unusual in that area that I'm curious to see if you'll notice."

"What is it?"

"If I tell you it will spoil the experiment!" he laughed. "Of course you'd notice something you were told to watch for." Her teasing bore no fruit; she would have to wait until they got there and then perhaps she would notice whatever it might be. He did agree to solve the mystery for her if she did not discover it herself.

Anna had shown an immediate love for the river, but her deep curiosity about everything was now being satisfied by the engineer. "If you'll notice this, you'll see that both sides of the piston provide power. This part here is called a 'D' valve. It controls the steam going into the cylinders. And the long rod there moves the paddlewheel. That engine over there is the same as this one. It supplies power to the portside paddlewheel."

Anna had to learn about steam pressure and expansion along with the mechanical parts that changed the steam into power to move the boat. She almost asked more than the engineer knew, as his knowledge was practical while some of her questions involved the physics of the machinery and the water vapor, but a friendship was quickly formed between the two agile minds who both loved to understand how things worked.

~ ~ ~

*It's so quiet*, Emily thought. The last of the girls gone this morning, and Miss Alison and Miss Agnes gone with them. When I was alone before Catherine, I didn't know what I was missing. Now I know. Oh my! I do know. And when she comes back she'll only be here for a moment – and then gone to wed Joel and living in town. Of course, perhaps there will be children then. And she insists she'll teach next term. What a marvelous gift for language she has. I guess, in a perverse way, I contributed to her hunger for language. Yes, certainly perverse!

*Momma, what did that man say?*

*Hush, Emily. Not everyone has the privilege of being born to speak a civilized language. When they wander into our country like this, they show their ignorance by speaking gibberish.*

*But what did he say, momma?*

*Emily! Come away and don't gawk like some lower-class person. It's better to just ignore such people, then perhaps they'll go back where they belong.*

"Miss Emily. Would you like to come to lunch now? It's laid in the dining room."

"Oh, yes. Thank you Sarah." Emily began to walk toward the dining room. "Sarah," she said tentatively. "Would you do me the favor of lunching with me?"

"Ma'am?" Sarah said, in shock at the notion.

"Miss Emily? Young Joel is here to see you." It was perhaps ten o'clock the following morning when she was summoned.

"Whatever? I hope nothing is wrong – why would he come to see me?" she mused, anxiously, as she walked to the drawing room where the young man had been shown.

"Miss Emily, I apologize for not giving you more warning, but my mother is expecting you for lunch today. Actually, I thought that giving you more warning would give you time to realize why you can't come, so I waited until the last moment on purpose." His air of innocence while so speaking was so complete as to be obvious in his mischief. "Do you need a few minutes to freshen up? I did allow a little extra time for that, knowing a bit about how ladies are about such things.

"Why, Mr. Benson. What a rascal you are! If you're so well versed, you must know that luncheon dates are always made at least a day or so in advance. It would be rude to just barge in on your mother; I can't be a party to that."

"Well, Miss Emily, the date was made last week. I just neglected to tell you about it until today. And I'm almost your grandson-in-law. You really must call me Joel, ma'am. My mother is eagerly looking to make your acquaintance, since we're all to be family soon. I believe you'll enjoy her company. She's a lot like you, gracious without seeming to work at being so. And she's delighted that you're coming to visit her."

"Joel. All right, Joel. It's well that the students have conditioned me to the ways of young people. How audacious of you to make such a date between your mother and myself! However, you've succeeded in raising some anticipation in me also. If you'll wait here I'll 'freshen up', as you put it, and I'll be down directly."

Mrs. Eleanor Benson was indeed as gracious as Miss Emily. The impromptu luncheon – impromptu on the part of Miss Emily, that is – was a comfortable occasion and the women began to lunch and visit back and forth, providing Miss Emily with her first real friend, other than Sarah, on whom she'd come to rely for a bit of companionship, since her marriage to Mr. Durrant.

~ ~ ~

Catherine and Anna ate in the crew mess – with extra flourishes added by the young cook, who was smitten with Anna's beauty – and shared the captain's stateroom, while James moved into the extra stateroom usually saved for passengers. They reached Stevens' landing late in the afternoon.

Catherine was walking toward the stage, just dropped, when she suddenly stopped, not as if she had reached a destination or had been paused from without, but rather as if she had been stilled into inner silence. James, walking to meet her, smiled to himself and thought, yes, she senses it too.

"What is it?" she breathed, as James came abreast of her. "Is there really something here? What is it? Where does it come from?"

Martha Stevens, seeing that it was the *Marian Dee,* and with two women on board, had walked down to the landing. At James' nod, she came aboard as Catherine was gazing up the hill.

"What is that up there?" she asked. "Where the stone wall is?"

"That's a monastery, a place where women live together so they can work and pray together," Martha offered. "They're Catholic nuns," she added.

"Miz Stevens, please meet my daughter, Catherine, and her friend, Anna Goldsmith."

Bemused, Catherine reluctantly turned toward the other woman. "I'm very pleased to meet you," she said softly. "So you know about that place up there."

"Yes. We sharecrop some of their land and sell their produce for them. I went up with my husband once when he was settling accounts with them. It was their supper time, when they talk and visit with each other, and Mother Clare, the nun in charge, showed us around a bit and introduced us to everyone there."

"What do you mean when you say at suppertime they talk?" Anna quizzed. "Do you mean at other times they don't talk?"

"No, they don't, except during dinner and supper. They have some gestures they make with their hands so they can communicate if they need to, but Mother Clare said they don't talk the rest of the time because the silence makes it easier for them to pray. Actually, she said 'to communicate with God.' She said the Bible says we should pray all the time. She says the important part of prayer is being still so they can hear what God says to them."

"There are a few nuns in town now, who teach children, but I didn't know there were groups of nuns like this. I should think it would be difficult to live without men to work to earn a living for them," Catherine mused.

"I think maybe I understand a bit," offered Anna. "My religion is mostly just for men, because women are considered too busy with home and family to have time to be religious. I can see where they'd be free to pray if there are no men around for them to have to take care of. In one way that might make more work, but in another way it would be a lot less work, because men are always wanting women to do things for them."

"Hey! Careful there, Cherub!" James cautioned with a grin. "You women are outnumbered here, you know!"

Anna, who'd acquired the nickname 'Cherub' from James when he perceived that she went to some lengths to bring him small comforts, flashed a smile back at him. "Mildred, please bring my slippers for me," she mocked, leaning back slightly and posing one foot in the air as if to have a shoe removed and a slipper added. "Oh, yes, and Mildred, while you're going to get my slippers, would you bring me that book that's lying on my desk please? By the by, is dinner nearly ready, Mildred? Oh, Mildred, did you buy new *shabbot* candles? How about a kiss for your tired husband, Mildred?"

James and Mrs. Stevens were laughing together at Anna's superb imitations. Mr. Stevens was somewhat less amused, asking himself if perhaps Anna's parody fit him, also, and Catherine realized that this was the first time Anna had been able to speak of her parents without weeping. She stood close to the girl, giving support by her presence, but also smiled at the mischief being spoken. Anna's eyes did tear up, but she did not cry.

Mrs. Stevens recognized that something was being withheld. "Is Mildred your mother?" she asked.

"Yes, ma'am. She and my father were killed in an accident about a year ago. But that's what it sounded like nearly every day when my father got home. My mother was very much still in love with him, so sometimes she'd mock the things he said until we were all laughing together. I guess that's where I learned to do it."

"They sound like wonderful people," Martha Stevens offered. "I'm sorry you lost them."

"Yes, it still hurts a bit sometimes. But I've learned from getting acquainted with other girls my age that I had a lot more love in the years with my parents than some get in a lifetime. So I'm very grateful that they had me."

Seeing a figure walk outside the monastery walls and sit on the bench, Martha waved to her, getting a friendly wave in return. "That's Mother Clare," she remarked. "She's a lovely person."

Catherine lifted her arms as if to reach toward the figure, but realized where she was in a moment and dropped her arms. James reached out with a strong arm and clasped her about the shoulder. "I think I understand how you feel," he told her. "I always feel drawn to that place too."

"I'm not sure what I feel," Catherine responded. "Except in some strange way I feel like I might belong there or something."

"Yes. I have that sort of feeling also, and it's obvious that I don't belong in an institution full of women," he said.

When they had visited with the Stevens a bit more and the wood was all loaded they raised the stage and reversed the engines, pulling away from the shore. Catherine stood aft, cooled by a mist from the starboard paddlewheel, gazing toward the dusk growing in the clearing around the monastery. As she watched, the nun there rose and looked toward the river, then turned and went back around the wall out of sight. Catherine, alone at the rail, breathed in the silence.

~ ~ ~

Mother Clare's attention was drawn to the boat below, at the Stevens' landing. She's seen it there often, a blue-trimmed sidewheeler, but this time there were women on board. *Passengers?* she mused. As she watched, Mrs. Stevens came out of their house and boarded the boat, talking evidently with the women on board. Clare's attention was drawn then to her meditation.

When she returned to the moment, the boat was slipping away from the landing. One of the women on board was at the aft rail, seeming to gaze upward. Mother Clare paused for a moment in rising, watching the figure now dwindling in the dusky distance, and then walked back There remained something in her heart strangely unsettled, but having learned concentration and meditation over years, she brought her errant mind back to the task at hand, and entered the silence of the chapel. It was time to raise voices in praise at evening Vespers.

# Chapter 18

The trip up the Missouri was peaceful. The Mississippi churned with war news and work, but above St. Louis, the war was only a distant murmur. There was bustle around Omaha, but more that of an ordinary city than of a war zone. Sioux City, the head of the navigable river, was a quiet town, gathering in the grains and livestock from the surrounding bluffs and fields, processing them, and selling and shipping the products away by boat, by barge, by freight wagon.

"Look!" said Anna, resisting the urge to point. "An Indian! It is an Indian, isn't it?" she asked, looking at James.

"Yes, he is Indian. There are two tribes pretty close here: the Sioux are right around this area and north and west of here. I think they used to live east of here, around Minnesota, but they got pushed out as white people settled and took the land. Then I've heard that the government just made a treaty with the Omaha Indians, making a few thousand acres a reservation for them. We came past that a few hours ago, in the bluffs on the Nebraska side of the river."

"Are we really in Nebraska? I never imagined I'd see a place so far west," Anna murmured. "And think how far this is from my parents' first home, in Poland."

"I imagine that is far away," James assented. "Over there," gesturing to the left, "is Nebraska. Over here," gesturing to the right, "is Iowa. Just a few miles up river it is South Dakota."

"Mercy! Can we go on up to South Dakota? We've come so far it seems a shame not to see it too," Catherine said.

"I don't want to take the *Marian Dee* any further upstream; the stream bed is pretty unreliable and most of it is too shallow to be safe. If you like, we can hire a hack and drive on up to South Dakota. Shall we do that?"

"Please," Anna replied. "I guess maybe I should have been born gypsy. Once I've begun to travel I don't seem able to be content with what I've already seen."

"Her father knew gypsies in Europe, Sarah said. Do they have them in Poland also?"

170

"I think so; at least my parents talked about them sometimes. I know that some of the Spanish or French words I've learned are about the same as the Polish or Russian. Papa said that was because the gypsies traded in languages as well as pots and pans and other things for sale."

"They did what?" Catherine asked with a puzzled look. "How can one trade in languages?"

"I think he meant that the gypsies moved among various countries to trade. When they didn't know a language, or didn't know it well, they sometimes used words from the languages of western European countries, and gradually some words got sort of blended in where they hadn't been to start with. For example, the word for 'bean' is almost the same in Spanish, French and Russian. A lot of other words are similar, or are the same except with a different accent. Anyway, I suppose if I really were a gypsy, I'd get tired of traveling eventually. When I had a home I enjoyed living in it."

"You have a home now at Westmont. I know Miss Emily will welcome you for as long as you'd like to stay there. Perhaps you might think of doing some teaching – after I have children, I don't expect I'll be wanting to gallivant clear across town to teach, or at least not every day. You're nearly as proficient in Spanish and German as I am, and your French is improving all the time. And you know a great deal about mathematics and I know only the simplest arithmetic."

"My father loved the study of mathematics."

"Yes. It shows. He also loved to teach the mathematics he loved to the daughter he loved!" Catherine remarked with a warm smile.

The jaunt to South Dakota was the pleasant work of an afternoon. Leaving Joe, the first mate, in charge of supervising the loading of the materials James had agreed to take for shippers, he took up the reins instead. They found the long hill down Military Road to Riverside Boulevard a challenge to the brakes of the hired rig.

"I doubt if it will be easier to drive back up hill," James laughed, watching the buggies and wagons lumber up the hill on the opposite side of the road. "But once we get to the bottom of the hill it's all easy going. The Missouri wanders off west and then runs up north inside of South Dakota. There's another river between Iowa and South Dakota, called the Big Sioux. It's a small stream though, and I believe there's a bridge across at the end of Riverside so we can drive across."

There was indeed a bridge, small but sturdy, and the trio ate their picnic

171

lunch in South Dakota and then ambled back to Iowa and toward the waterfront. The horse proved able to lug the carriage up the long hill toward downtown Sioux City and they arrived at the *Marian Dee* as the day began to darken. James took the hired rig on another block to the livery stable and returned on foot.

"Back to the Missouri," he said, walking up the stage. "As they say here, it's too thick to drink but too thin to plow. Fortunately for us, it supports steamer traffic!"

The young women smiled dutifully at his joke, then continued their conversation, which was of a more philosophical bent. "Just think, Anna. We're only half-way across the country from east to west and about in the middle from north to south. Isn't it amazing how big this country is?" Catherine, ever aware of communication subtleties, had noted the flat tones of the Midwestern accent, different from the drawls of southern Indiana and Kentucky, and from the crisp accents of visiting Easterners. "There's always something new to learn, isn't there?" she remarked.

"Yes, it seems so. Perhaps it's as Papa said about infinity, that no one can know it. I think likely no one can ever know all the knowledge that's available on the earth."

"I think that's a good comparison," Catherine responded. "I'm sure no one can ever know it all."

~ ~ ~

"Woman, leave off! The house looked wonderful before you started meddling with it. It looks wonderful now, and you're still not satisfied. Come here," he said, patting the seat beside him.

"No," she replied. "There's too much to do before they get here. And it's becoming so hard to buy the things we need. Almost everything is going for the war."

"Speaking of getting things," Will remarked, "bring your handsome husband a nice cup of chicory coffee, please?" He ended on a rising inflection, trying to tempt her to ease up rather than to make another task for her busy hands. "And while you're fixing the coffee, fix a cup for yourself too, will you please? And one for your mother."

"Maman isn't here," Genevieve said. "She hasn't been here all day."

"Ah. You're wrong about that," Will said gleefully. "She is indeed here, and I'm sure would appreciate a nice cup of your wonderful chicory coffee, wouldn't you, Momma Two?"

The appellation "Momma Two" had come from Will's affectionate regard for her. He had fallen in love with his mother-in-law, who was always available for companionship or if help was needed, but melted away immediately if a tiff arose between husband and wife. She told them frankly that she loved them both, but they were no longer children, so she had no responsibility to negotiate their fusses.

And as if on cue, as Will spoke, the front door opened and a melodic voice said, "Cherie! Mon cheris! Are you at home? Oui, of course I would like a cup of your wonderful chicory coffee!"

"Of course we are here, Momma Two. We're always at home for you," Will welcomed her. "And I believe your daughter is about to make that wonderful coffee..." He ducked as Genevieve, relaxing into a mischievous grin, threw a small pillow at him.

"Oh! Genevieve! You must have worked all night and all day. The house looks so lovely!"

"Oh, Maman. Do you really think so? It seems like there's so much more that I should do," she rejoined.

"Oh no, Cherie. If you do more, it will begin to look artificial and unwelcoming.

It will be very good to receive James' daughter, won't it? I'm so pleased that he found her at last."

Joel had sent a letter to the Isaacs with the first letter to be saved for Catherine's arrival. He introduced himself briefly, but spent the bulk of the letter on the news of James finding Catherine. He told them James said they would probably go up the Missouri before coming to New Orleans, so Catherine and her young woman companion could spend more time with James and see more of the country.

Will was on the river when the letter, addressed to Mr. and Mrs. Will Isaacs, arrived. He came home two weeks later and calculated the probable time of arrival of James and the women. "That's if the war doesn't hold them up," he qualified. "There's quite a lot of war traffic on the river now. It still seems safe, except for those who are armoring their boats to fight, or maybe the boats commandeered as troop ships.

"A lot of the steamers now are ferrying supplies, but that really can't be easily identified. A load of cotton bales would identify a boat as Southern, but most of the growers are trying to get their cotton to the coast, to ship to England now."

"I hope this conflict will be brief," Genevieve said. "It's a terrible thing to kill people you don't agree with."

"Well, I'm staying clear of it for the present," Will remarked. "I'm not sure, if I had to choose sides, which side I would pick. I guess I'm Southern born, but my spirit might be more Yankee. At least the Yankees don't think they own people."

"I hope you always stay clear of it, Will! What would happen to the children and to me if you should be killed in the war?"

"Actually, you'd be cared for at least in part," he responded. "You remember I told you I'd started a small fund with the Merchants' Bank? There is enough there now to keep you and the children for a few years, if you're careful. And it's in your name, so you'd have no problem accessing it."

"Oh no, Will. I'm very grateful for your care for us, but I don't want to talk about you dying right now. We have guests coming and I could use a bit of your help in preparing for them." And so the dragging out and rug beating and sweeping and scrubbing and airing and changing had begun and had gone on and on...

"Enough, child. Stop now and don't work any more. You do no honor to guests if you are too exhausted to enjoy them."

"Yes, Maman." After a brief reflection, "Thank you, Maman." And so the yellow stucco house with the black cast iron railed balcony awaited the coming of Catherine, child of the friend and benefactor. As James had predicted, both Catherine and Anna immediately loved Genevieve, with her quick movements and flashing smiles. And they loved Lawrence when he was presented to them, and Antoinette, who flew into an acquaintance with Catherine's lap before the lap was formed by sitting in Genevieve's house, and before the child could be presented.

~ ~ ~

They had lingered, hungry for time to know each other, to make up for the years lost. The comfortable leisure of Will and Genevieve's home gave them time and the warmth of their friendship was a catalyst to the process. Finally, the war talk became too close to ignore longer.

Will broached the subject first. "I think you and the children should go with me this trip, to stay out the war in a safer city. There's talk now of attempts to take New Orleans. It's the richest city in the South, so I suppose it's inevitable. With its international port, Louisiana had hoped to remain neutral, but that hope is long gone now. Now the hope is just to keep the Yankees out."

"Several of the men we know have joined the Native Guards, to defend New Orleans."

"Yes. I'd heard that too. It's part of what makes me think you and the children will be safer on the river with me. I think the city is vulnerable because it is both a river port and a seaport. That gives two easy ways to get into the city, and the North has plenty of boats and ships. And armies to follow behind and make life precarious for the citizens.

"Your mother must go with us also, if she will. With my mother staying at the summerhouse in the country, I'll feel much easier with all of you with me. Daniel's the only one of the children in the city, and since he's a doctor I think they'll tend to leave him pretty much alone, don't you think?"

"Yes, I wouldn't think they'd trifle with someone they might need."

"And it's always the women and children who suffer in an enemy occupation," Will added. "I simply can't risk leaving you here."

"Please come and visit with us, Genevieve," Catherine interjected. "It's summer, so the great house is nearly empty. Grandmother will be delighted to have guests. And should the war keep you from home more than a few months, Joel has bought a spacious house for us, where you'll be equally welcome. Please come. I'd love to have you and the children and I would fret about your safety if you stayed here."

In the end, Genevieve acquiesced but her mother chose to join Will's mother. They had shared the summer home – away from the hurricanes and yellow fever and malaria of the sweltering city – for a few years and were affectionate friends. The *Genevieve* and the *Marian Dee* began the beat upriver in tandem, staying close each to support the other through the now unknown conditions of the wartime rivers.

There was some difficulty in slipping back upstream past Vicksburg. Armies of various Northern states had gathered there, besieging the town, and cannon fire could be heard miles downstream. James kept some distance below the town, with Will in the *Genevieve* astern, just out of the wake of the *Marian Dee*, until the dark before dawn.

They then ran all ahead slow, engines *whoof, whoof, whoofing* almost silently, paddlewheels turning so slowly there was almost no splash. They ran dark, without lanterns or markers, but with a man on the bow of each boat, in dark clothing to be visible to the eyes of the pilot against the scrubbed white oak deck, to look to their path ahead, so they might pass the siege without becoming targets themselves.

The night was clear but moonless, and they'd hung, dark, under the shadows of the trees that lined the riverbank, to avoid detection, but more importantly, to allow eyes to adjust to the darkness so the spotters and pilots could steer in relative safety. Steam pressure had been built to the boilers' capacities, to avoid the glow of an open firebox and to avoid the smoke that would boil out of the stacks, should a firebox smother a bit under a fresh load of fuel.

A lookout at the east end of the ditch being dug to try and straighten the oxbow in the river so they might pass out of range of the cannons on shore, saw the boats pass, silent shadows, but believed them to be their own boats coming upstream to reinforce the attack, and failed to raise an alarm.

A sentry in what was to become the final resting place for hundreds of men, both Union and Confederate, near the shore, assessed the silently moving silhouettes as unknown and therefore possible threats, but by the time the alarm had been passed up the hills to the cannons, both the *Marian Dee* and the *Genevieve* were safely out of reach of the artillery.

Anna slipped onto the boiler deck and kept to the starboard rail during that passage, her sensitive spirit attuned to the agony and terror that crept about or tunneled under the land. She was silent throughout the following day, replying in monosyllables to questions or remarks, refusing food. Both Catherine and James had had enough experience in pain to give her time and space to come to terms with her feelings, and she spent the day and evening sitting near the stern, gazing back toward the battlefield passed.

Finally, she murmured to Catherine, as she sat down near her, "Why do they kill each other? Is the earth too small for all? It is not that one faction is all evil and the other all good, although perhaps they sometimes think so. How is it that one person – or one government – arrives at a belief that he or she or they have a right to determine the fate of other human beings? The life and death of other human beings?"

Catherine merely took and held her hand, knowing the questions were ageless and unanswerable. At last, the young women rose and moved softly into the silence of their stateroom. Anna's sleep that night, when finally she slept, was deep and dreamless.

~ ~ ~

*16 December 1834*
*My dear James,*
*We trimmed the great tree in the hall today. Samuel, the young groom, took two boys with him and went out and tramped around yesterday until they found this magnificent fir. They brought it in on the sledge and set it up for us this afternoon. We had a glorious party, trimming and singing carols and drinking hot chocolate.*

*Mother is almost as girlish as I, when we decorate for Christmas. She put a bright scarlet ribbon in her hair and directed the placement of each ornament just so, so the tree was balanced and symmetrical and utterly wonderful when it was finished.*

*The only thing lacking for my happiness is the lovely bright scarlet of your hair--I wish that you could have been among the friends at the party. I would love to be able to spend time with you, to share the many things we enjoy, but I am resigned for the moment to sharing my friendship on pieces of paper. You are often in my thoughts.*
*Warm regards,*
*Marian*

*****

*27 July 1835*
*My dear James,*
*The summer heat presses on us day after day. There has been no rain and the flowers droop despite the yard boys carrying buckets of water from the cistern. They've been bringing our drinking water from one of the springs recently: the cistern has gone stale in the drought.*

*The cool of the river would be lovely right now. Of course, the company of the river man would be better still! I am eager for your coming, that we may speak unslowed by the handicap of quill and ink.*
*Fondly,*
*Marian*

*****

*4 January 1836*
*Dearest James,*
*Christmas is past, the tree and wreaths removed, with all the brightness of the season. The house seems so ordinary after such a splash of color and excitement. I was delighted to get your missive, with the warm greetings from you and Anson.*

*Yes, I do believe we are well matched, and I would like to spend a great deal of time with you. I look forward to the moment when I can again see that wonderful crown of yours instead of just remembering it.*

*Give Anson my love also –*
*Affectionately,*
*Marian*

\*\*\*\*\*

*9 February 1836*
*Dearest James,*
*I am so glad that you are at last coming back up river. It has been so long since we've been together – it's hard to believe that we had such a brief encounter when you were last here. I feel I've known you all my life. Our beliefs and hopes and dreams fit together so well. I await eagerly your coming.*

*Your dear companion,*
*Marian*

\*\*\*\*\*

*24 March 1836*
*Dearest Heart,*
*I will treasure always the moments we had last week. I regret that Father was not here so we might ask his consent for me to become your bride. I suppose it may take some 'suasion to bring him around to the notion, but I know he loves me and wants what will make me happy. I'm sure when you can come next we can post the bans.*

*Take care of your heart while we are apart – remember that it belongs now to me.*

*Lovingly,*
*Marian*

\*\*\*\*\*

*19 April 1836*
*My darling James,*
*Spring is finally in full bloom – the crocus and hyacinths gone, the tulips fading and the iris spreading its colors about the countryside. I went to my favorite place today – as much as I can favor any place that doesn't have you in it – and sat on a log, enjoying the many shades and hues of green springing into life throughout the ravine my log overlooks. How amazing nature is.*

*As the trees come alive in spring, your love has brought me alive. I am so eager for your next coming and for the formalization of our union that I am breathless with anticipation.*
*Yours in love always,*
*Marian*

\*\*\*\*\*

*21 May 1836*
*Beloved,*
*I have been somewhat under the weather for a week or two. Just a not quite feeling the best – somewhat lacking in energy and sleepy and a bit queasy at times. Spring fever, I suppose, although spring is past and summer is here.*
*Yours until I find the energy to write more –*
*Your loving*
*Marian*

Catherine surmised that the sag in Marian's energy was the first suggestion of her pregnancy. How she wished she might have written even just *one* more letter, the sharing of the joy with her father that her mother must have experienced when she was knowing of the child to come, but there was nothing more.

It could, of course, have been the overture of some malady that might deprive a young woman of her vitality and then her life – James had so regarded it from the time he'd been told of her death. He'd only suggested the countless nights of agonizing regret he'd spent mourning her loss, castigating himself for not being there for her in her final hours and moments. How he'd blamed himself, as if had he been with her he could have prevented

179

the sickness, the death.

He should have known, when her letters ceased, that he was needed. He should have left his work and hastened north. He should have... At last, there had been if not an end to the 'shoulds,' a pause in the agony, a numbing of the turmoil of his being, and finally an acceptance of his aloneness if not of his innocence. So Catherine had discerned from the twist of his face and the faraway focus of his gaze when the pain, still vital despite its suppression, was masked.

"Papa," she said. "Papa. It wasn't your fault. It's obvious that Mother underestimated the depth of their insecurity, that they could deny their daughter her joy to protect their social status. She who had known them for a lifetime misjudged them. There was no possibility that you could have guessed; you had never even met them. You could do nothing but believe what they chose for you to hear. It wasn't your fault, Papa." And so saying, she softly kissed his cheek where she had wiped the tears away, and at last the pain was a bit weaker.

# Chapter 19

The furniture-building part of the factory was essentially closed down for the duration, but the upholstery section hummed with activity twelve hours a day. No one wanted furniture right now, what with most families having at least one member away, in either a Union camp or a Confederate, or the husband or son or brother might be dead or missing or lying in a backwashed city of festering wounds that both sides struggled to support and heal.

The upholstery section of the factory had been quite easy to convert to the production of sturdy canvas tents, packs, and tarpaulins, paraffined against rain and dew and shipped out in a steady stream of freight wagons. It had been necessary for Joel to journey clear to Washington, D.C., to secure funding for the project, but the tales of mud, cold and misery that filtered back with the return of men too damaged to fight again were persuasive. President Lincoln himself had seen him, with Charles Balsom, a one-legged veteran after less than a month in the war, and had seen immediately that tarps and tents to protect the troops would result in soldiers that were more effective and in more likely recoveries of the wounded.

Only the dogged insistence of Miss Emily had kept Joel from joining the fracas himself. "You will *not* leave her alone again!" she thundered. "This war began without you and it will continue nicely without you. You will find a task here that you can do to support the cause, but you will not take my granddaughter's fiancé into anyone's line of fire. Do you understand me?"

"Ma'am," he began.

"Mr. Benson! I will not tolerate you leaving to join the war. Should you slip off of a midnight to do so, understand that I will withdraw my consent to your marriage and you shall inhabit your big house alone, if you survive the war. There will be no wife; there will be no children. Not of *my* lineage. Do I make myself entirely clear?"

"But Miss Emily – my friend Charles has already gone and all the other young men are gone or leaving. I can't remain here in comfort while others fight for me..."

"For you? What is it of yours that's being brought to the question? What belief? What property? Just what is it for which you would fight?"

"Ma'am, my loyalty to my comrades – "

She cut him off mid-declaration. "Your loyalty to your comrades. Indeed. To whom? To your wife? To the sons and daughters for whom you have planned? You remember well our discussions about the war when Catherine's father, Captain Mason, was here, do you not? He travels half the country and back and reads arguments from around the world, and you think *you*, sitting here in Piddletown, America, have a better grasp of the conflict than he? Better than the international observers of the *London Times*? Better than the citizens of New Orleans, and St. Louis, and every other town and city up and down the Mississippi?

"*Boys* go to war, to seek excitement and glory, unless the war is to defend their homes and families or their sacred beliefs. It appears that in the South that condition may apply. But it does not apply here. Nothing applies here except the pocketbooks of others. And mark my word, if those persons were to be identified, you'd find them nowhere near any battlefield. No. They're the men with cold eyes, looking at each other over their ill-gotten gains, and laughing cynically at those naive enough to fight or die to make them wealthier and more powerful."

When he had finally been defeated and was gone away, Miss Emily sat by the window, looking out at the river far below, and wept.

~ ~ ~

The arrival of the *Marian Dee* and the *Genevieve* was timely. The tent manufactory was just gaining momentum, and Catherine and Genevieve insisted on taking part in the work. Other young women and a few older ones joined them, taking places that might have been filled with men at other times.

With her need to keep 'Toinette in check and her love for small children, Genevieve established in a large airy room that had been a display area, a place for the children of the workers. Anna became her assistant, scrounging rugs and cots, slates and chalk, and a few books. Sarah used a corner of the room in the mornings to tutor a few advanced students in mathematics or languages, when all but the littlest children had lessons, while in the afternoons the children rested and played.

And even the wee ones absorbed the stories and learned to count "one, two, three" or *"un, du, trois"* and to greet the teachers with such things as

*"Guten Tag, Fraulein Anna."* In their eagerness to grasp language the tots were entirely careless of *which* language it might be, and thus they arrived at foundations for later, more formal learning, that would be the envy of less fortunate students.

James, unwilling to leave his finally-found family, made short trips to Cincinnati or St. Louis, as did Will. The crews, however, gradually slipped away to serve one side or the other. When finally there were too few to man both boats, James made arrangements to dock the *Marian Dee* in the surge basin at the Lock and Dam #41.

He took pains to make her unusable, taking down both engines as if for rebuilding, and stowing the carefully greased pistons, valves, and connecting rods in the Westmont stable, high above the river. He couldn't bear the thought of anyone commandeering the boat that had borne Marian's name and his heart for all these years, to risk a careless engineer to blow up the boilers, as happened too often, especially with new boats run by poorly trained crews, or to steam her into the war to be destroyed by cannon. The first mate, still able, but too old to be tempted or conscripted into the war, was kept on to protect the boat from rust and mildew and to guard against thieves and vandals.

Will, who had been born into the relatively large and largely skilled cadre of cultured, Catholic, New Orleans blacks known as *personnes de coleur libres*, was appalled when he heard Samuel's story of Martha's journey to freedom and of the lash marks on her back. He shuddered at the thought that chance had given him freedom with no charge but his own honest work, while it might as easily have sent him away from his family forever and left the lash marks on the beautiful, fine skin of Genevieve.

He then began to accept loads of supplies for the Union troops ranging down the Mississippi through Confederate lands. On one journey south, he carried a contingent of black troops, newly freed and bent on winning freedom for every other enslaved soul in the South. The *Genevieve* was holed twice by cannon, but both times above the water line, and she was patched and continued her float for freedom.

Will sent letters north by upstream-bound steamers when he was south, and stayed a day or two each time he passed New Albany. He was torn either way, leaving Genevieve and the children, or leaving the cause in which he'd come to believe, but somehow it seemed that his struggle to aid others to find and keep freedom was a part of the price of his own freedom, his wife's and children's, and his mother's and hers.

He didn't risk floating clear to New Orleans, knowing the *Genevieve* would likely become a prize of war should he enter those crowded and muddy waters, but he clung to a belief in the good sense of his mother and her companion; they would, they must, survive. They'd summered there for a decade, since Will and the brothers he'd kept and educated could afford the house with its several acres.

The neighbors were friends, the area away from any highway and a day up a stream too shallow for anything but a poled pirogue or flatboat. Land was cheaper there, and once they'd found it, they thought it well also that it would be unlikely for others in fear of the summer storms and plagues of the lower delta to find the comfortable house and appropriate it as their own shelter. It was most likely peaceful there in such a backwater.

While the *Genevieve* skimmed briskly through the waters above St. Louis, reasonably fleet in the less crowded waters of the upper Mississippi and the Ohio, Miss Emily was indeed delighted to shelter Genevieve and the children. Antoinette, as Catherine had predicted, had stolen her heart almost before Emily was aware that the child – with her family – had arrived.

Emily espied the hack turning into the lane and saw the flame and the strawberry of James' and Catherine's hair. She took no note of any other in the carriage. She had come to live with herself again, enriched by the friendships she'd never sought nor accepted during Edward's life or in the years of blind ritual after, when she tried to maintain through the old motions the old beliefs about life. Several of the ladies of the town came to Westmont now on three afternoons weekly, to roll bandages and collect other materials useful for the troops, and to lend support to each other in the absence of family members.

It was with a warmly comfortable feeling of anticipation that Emily hastened through the kitchen – to the door most convenient to the stable and most likely to be used by Catherine. She had made only a step and a half past that door before she was set upon by the small, pink-garbed bundle of energy that was Antoinette.

"You are Miss Grandmother Emily," the child announced imperiously, once she'd been untangled from Emily's skirt. "You must be; you *are*, aren't you?" Not waiting for reaction or confirmation, she continued confidently "I know all about you! You're Miss Catherine's Miss Grandmother Emily and you live in this wonderful house where you can see the river away down the hill.

"You have a cook named Angel who makes cookies for good little girls, and you have big girls who come to school here so you can teach them to be proper young ladies. I expect you'll teach me so also, won't you?" looking up with a cherubic smile. "I shall be delighted to teach you French, if you'd like. I believe you would like that, wouldn't you, Miss Grandmother Emily? I believe we're going to have a great deal of pleasure here, don't you? You will be *my* Miss Grandmother Emily also, won't you, since I had to leave my other grandmothers in New Orleans? I would be very lonely without a grandmother, Miss Grandmother Emily. Have you been lonely without a grandchild while Miss Catherine was with us? I'll help make it up to you since I'm here, now..."

Genevieve, laughing and shaking her head at the child's flood of rhetoric, took her hand and said firmly "Antoinette! How do you greet ladies properly?"

Antoinette collected herself and spread her skirts wide, dropping a reasonably graceful curtsy for a four-year-old, and said, "How do you do? I'm very pleased to meet you, Miss Grandmother Emily. I'm Antoinette, and I've come to play with you so you won't be lonely."

Catherine, also laughing at the child's cheeky assurance, so like her own meeting with Antoinette, reached across the child and collected Emily in a hug. "I've missed you, Grandmother. It's good to be home again." Taking a step back she continued, "Please meet my friends, Will and Genevieve Isaacs and their son, Lawrence. You've already met their daughter, Antoinette. We've kidnapped them from New Orleans to keep them safe from the war."

Emily, warmed by the little child's trust in her and by the love of her granddaughter, captured Antoinette's hand with her left as she reached her right out to Genevieve and Will, and in a move guaranteed to win the heart of a boy, shook hands then also with Lawrence. "I'm happy to meet you. This is your home as long as you need it. Please come in.

"Let's see if there might be any cookies here for this young man," she said, smiling at Lawrence. "Oh, my! Would you like a cookie also?" she asked 'Toinette, as if she had just become aware of the little girl's presence.

"Yes, Ma'am, Miss Grandmother Emily. And I would surely like a glass of milk with my cookie, if you please."

"It doesn't get much better than that," Catherine laughed. "Enjoy her while you see her. Inevitably there will be many moments of *seeking* her in the days to come."

And so it was that Emily was a bit relieved that Genevieve took the child with her to the factory, but she found herself glancing often toward the lane as afternoon shadows lengthened, waiting for the small breath of joy who persisted in addressing her by the entire title 'Miss Grandmother Emily,' and who sang Creole French *chansones* for her and found Emily every evening as she was being led away to bath and bed, to bestow on her the treasure of a child's moist kiss.

~ ~ ~

The war didn't reach the monastery directly, of course, but on two different occasions, Father O'Maine came of an afternoon, conferred briefly with Mother Clare, who then called in on one occasion Sister Frieda and on the other Sister Emelda. When each had been apprised of the death of her brother, Wollaf for Sister Frieda and Edmond for Sister Emelda, they were given time to grieve, and the sisters joined together in Masses said for the souls of the dead. It was of no importance that Wollaf had fought on the Union side while Edmond died in Confederate gray. They were the same to God, it was certain.

Not all of the nuns had family left outside the convent, and some who'd had no contact with the outside world for the years they'd been cloistered, had no way of knowing what family they might have left or who among those families might be threatened by the war.

As it was a task of the convent to pray for those in the world without, Father O'Maine brought news as it was available of the state of the conflict, and each day after Mass there were now moments of prayer for all who suffered from the war, and for the souls and families of those who'd died for their beliefs.

Traffic on the river had changed as the conflict wore on, Mother Clare noted. There were countless boats in the beginning, going up and down stream. A few who frequented Stevens Landing, below the monastery, had become familiar to her. Some of these vanished, including the trim blue and white sidewheeler she'd often noted at the landing.

It had always seemed lovely to her that some captains or owners memorialized the women in their lives by naming their boats for them. She wondered if the women who had shared their identities with the boats grieved those boats now sunk or only the men now absent, perhaps slaughtered. Surely, it was so.

~ ~ ~

186

The wedding was small and lovely. Garlands of fresh ivy and garden flowers decorated the church. They'd discussed options, and chose to keep to their original plan to wed in the spring, even though the wedding would have to be simple because of the war. Catherine was radiant in ivory satin and yards of hand-tatted ivory lace, purchased during Marian's adolescence and left undisturbed in its protective tissue after her departure, brought now to frothy perfection for her daughter by seamstress Nell Harmony, one of Emily's bandage-rolling friends.

Genevieve dressed Catherine's mass of strawberry blond curls into an upswept profusion of ringlets, banded near her head with tea roses stitched to satin and cascading down to her neck and shoulders. She carried a bouquet of the same tea roses, cut fresh that morning from the bush by Emily's front door, swathed in satin to protect her hands from the thorns.

Anna had been softened by the love shown her by Catherine, her friends and family, and consented to attend Catherine at the wedding. She looked up at the cross-topped steeple for several moments before she was able to enter the church building for the first time, two nights before the wedding, to rehearse for the celebration. She stood now, however, in the vestibule, unafraid in this alien place inhabited by friends.

As the organ began a proclamation of joy, the door at the rear of the church was opened and Catherine gazed at Joel, beside the aisle at the front of the church with Charles at his side, waiting for her to come to him, to join with him. Gratefully taking James' arm, she led the procession to the altar, where Father O'Malley, flanked by altar boys in scarlet cassocks and white lace-trimmed surplices, stood, smiling as she floated toward the altar.

A beaming James raised a teasing finger as if in warning to Joel, bent and kissed Catherine gently on a flushed cheek, and placed her hand in Joel's, holding both for a moment. The couple, with their attendants, knelt on satin cushions for the high Mass, as James, unchurched but reverent in his love and gratitude, knelt beside Emily, holding her hand secure in his.

Then it was finished, Catherine the wife of Joel, and her life, which had begun anew twice before, with her liberation into the care of Sarah and Samuel, and with the finding of the young woman by her father, began yet again.

Chapter 20

Joel and Catherine stood at the baptismal font, James Christopher, in the long, white, lace and eyelet christening gown worn now by four generations of his father's family, held ready in Catherine's arms. "James and Christopher. Two saints, two grandfathers. What better start could an infant ask?" Father O'Malley murmured.

He'd fussed a bit at first about Will and Genevieve being godparents for the tiny boy with red-gold hair, asserting that godparents who lived in New Orleans – where Will and Genevieve were certain to return soon, with the dreadful conflict at last ended and General Butler forever evicted from the city – could be of no value to a child in Indiana.

They'd reminded him that Will was 'Captain Isaacs' of the steamboat *Genevieve*, who'd plied the rivers between New Orleans and Cincinnati and St. Louis and Sioux City for all of his adult life. The mothers of Will and Genevieve, brought away from the carpetbaggers and the homeless, drifting shells of men ruined by the war on that riverboat, testified to the speed and comfort of the journey.

Father O'Malley knew Will, and knew Genevieve, who'd lived here for nearly three years now, very well and knew they could be trusted with the *soul* of the babe. Convinced at last of their actual physical availability to the boy, he consented to their sponsorship.

Young James Christopher, already called 'Jamie' to distinguish him from his maternal grandfather, was presented by his godparents, and Father O'Malley raised the cup, pouring thrice the holy water over the infant's head, as he said, "James Christopher, I baptize thee in the name of the Father, and of the Son, and of the Holy Ghost."

The tall pillar of wax, impressed with the sacred signs of his eternal adoption, was snuffed and given to Catherine after Jamie's formal welcome into the church, to be a symbol of his spiritual inheritance, perhaps lighted at birthdays or used to mark his passage through other sacred moments, such as his first communion, confirmation or marriage.

"My hair is white and I've led no one to follow the Lord into the priesthood, laddie," the Father spoke gently to the boy he'd appropriated to warm his arms at the small family celebration after the christening. "Perhaps you'll be he." He held the infant up facing him, and as he spoke, the blue eyes gazed at him, unblinking, and then the infant smiled.

~ ~ ~

It was a scramble of feelings when Will and Genevieve, with handsome young Lawrence and the still irrepressible scamp Antoinette, left Westmont. Genevieve was glad to be going home, anxious about their home in New Orleans, empty these long months, but sorry to be leaving Miss Emily and the family here.

Miss Emily had no mix of feelings at all. She had come to love the young family without reserve, and while she understood their need to go home, their departure came as a sharp loss for her.

"Miss Grandmother Emily, I am so sorry to leave you like this. I'm afraid you will be lonely again after I'm gone. I shall write you letters, Miss Grandmother Emily. Indeed, I shall. That will help, I'm sure, until I can come again." 'Toinette tugged Miss Emily down to her level so she could plant a wet, smacking kiss on her cheek. "There. That should help keep you while I'm gone," she announced.

"Indeed, it will help while you're gone," Miss Emily assured her, with a suspicious hint of moisture in her eyes.

"Remember, Will will pick you up early in December, and you're spending the holidays with us in New Orleans," Genevieve said.

"But that's really too much, when you don't even know what condition your house may be in— "

"Early December. Absolutely. The house will be fine by then, even if it's gone and we have to rebuild it," Genevieve insisted with a smile. "We will not be able to have a satisfactory Christmas without Miss Grandmother Emily, you know!"

And so with smiles and hugs they boarded the *Genevieve*, and then they were gone.

~ ~ ~

"Grandmother, I'm making an office for myself at the factory, so I can more conveniently do the bookwork for the business. We're finally getting back to full production and we need to remain financially conservative for a while yet. I've located an extra crib where Jamie can nap while I work there, and I wonder if I might beg a favor from you?"

"What is it, child? If I have it, it is as surely yours as it is mine," Emily responded in a firm tone.

"But this is rather special, I believe— "

"What ever is it, Catherine?"

"I've given a great deal of thought to it, Grandmother..." There was a pause, during which Emily only waited. "I've meditated on it over several years and it seems quite clear to me that my grandfather simply lost control and his sense of reason when both of his children forsook him, as it were."

Emily looked up sharply, but remained silent.

"I would like to have something which I believe my grandfather used daily, or nearly daily, during his life here with you."

Catherine again hesitated, but Emily again prompted "And this thing that you would like is—?"

"May I have my grandfather's desk, Grandmother? It was, in effect, his place of business, and if you consent, I would like to use it for my place of business."

Emily vacillated. Is that true? she pondered. I've prayed and done penance for our actions, both my way and then Father O'Malley's way, since that evil time. God knows I didn't actively want to hurt my children, or my grandchild – surely Edward was overwhelmed by circumstances beyond his power to meet with reason also, was he not? Edward, is it so? Are the healing words our grandchild offers truly the way it was for you also? A feeling of peace came upon Emily. "Of course you may, my dear child. I'm sure your grandfather would wish it so also."

Joel came as Catherine struggled with the last drawer. When neither she nor Emily could find a key, she'd tried tugging and wiggling, but the well-made piece of furniture defeated her every effort. "Would you like me to try?" he asked. "Sometimes we furniture makers hide secrets within our work. Perhaps the maker of this fine piece did something similar."

Catherine gladly moved aside, and Joel knelt in front of the desk, slipping each drawer in and out a time or two. One drawer – the second down on the left side – did feel a bit different. Joel slipped it entirely out of the desk, glanced at the back of it, and reached a hand into the space the drawer had occupied. Snugly compartmented against dust, Joel's questing fingers found a small pocket glued against the rear dust cover of the desk. Within that pocket was secreted the missing key for the last drawer on the right side of the desk.

~ ~ ~

James and his engineers had just finished rebuilding the engine of the *Marian Dee* and inspecting her boilers. The crew had holystoned the decks and polished every piece of brass and of mahogany to a fine gloss.

When Samuel came with a spare horse to fetch him, James ordered the engineer to run up a trial head of steam to verify the condition of fittings and gauges, and assuming such would be found to be in safe running condition, ordered the mate to proceed with a trial run up a few miles and back, with the boat and crew to stand by at the downtown docks, where she was to be immediately stocked with food and fuel and the cabins made up for passengers, while they awaited his return.

He came back aboard about midnight. The mate, Joe, verified the condition of the boat and its stores, and James ordered steam to be built in the dark before dawn; their passengers were expected at first light and they would leave immediately. James retired to his cabin to rest, but found his boggled mind unable to quiet itself, and giving up, he spent the night at the stern rail, gazing downstream and awaiting the dawn, filled with hope and dread that left him grateful he'd hired an experienced Ohio pilot; it was certain he'd be unfit to guide the boat on the morrow.

~ ~ ~

*Miss Marian Durrant*, the envelope read. Beneath it another, and another, and... A few envelopes down lay one addressed to *Mr. Edward Durrant, Esq.,* and beneath that several more for Marian. All were still sealed with red wax. They were neatly stacked in a box in the front of that – now unlocked – bottom drawer.

Miss Emily was as shocked as the others. After consideration, she said, "I believe we must open them. Too much has been hidden in this family for too long." It was she who had sent in haste for James, surmising that those letters to Marian, while addressed in the long unseen hand of Anson, were most likely sent through Anson by James.

The letter for Mr. Durrant, in an unknown hand, Miss Emily opened with shaky hands. Perusing it rapidly, she then read aloud, tears falling the while:

191

*31 January 1837*
*My dear Mr. Durrant,*
*This is to inform you, in deep grief, that your son Anson was killed in an accident yesterday. The foredeck was wet from rain and his foot slipped as he leapt to carry the line to the cleat to make fast the boat. The boat was still moving, and as he fell, he was caught between the leading edge of the deck and the dock. His chest was crushed. He died instantly; he did not suffer, indeed, there was not even time for him to fear death or injury.*

*Anson had become the closest friend of my life. I will miss him always, although I realize my grief is slight compared to that which you and his mother will suffer. I do commend him to you with pride, however. He was a man of honor in all things, a man of his word always and a hard and cheerful worker who will be missed by every member of the crew.*

*As this occurred in New Orleans, it is not possible to return his remains to his home for burial. It is a mark of the respect with which Anson was regarded by all, that Captain Louis T. Marat, owner and chief pilot of the Daisy Lee, has made provision for the body of our fallen comrade to be interred in his family tomb, in Layfeyette No. 2, here in New Orleans.*

*Please find enclosed a map of the city streets and the plat of the cemetery, with the tomb of the Marat family marked. The tomb itself, which is of course above ground, as are all such here in this watery city, is clearly marked with the Marat family name, so you will have no difficulty finding it when you visit.*

*The name and address of Capt. Marat's solicitor is also forwarded, should there be any matter with which he might be able to assist you.*
*I remain your grieving and obedient servant,*
*James Algonquin Mason*

James and Samuel arrived and came directly into the family gathering, leaving a stable boy to walk out the hot horses. James confirmed that the letters to Marian were from both him and Anson, and gave them to Catherine. "I would like to read them again when you've had a chance to see your mother from this perspective, but I believe they should be yours to keep."

It was only then that Catherine, who had spent the time waiting for her father fingering and caressing the envelopes addressed to her mother, explored the balance of the articles in the drawer. The primary item was a bound ledger, unlabeled and wound with red string, dipped in sealing wax. The book had obviously not been opened since last sealed by Mr. Durrant.

Catherine handed the ledger to her grandmother, who held it a moment, the expression on her face suggesting a fear of the contents. At last, she popped the seal and opened the book, laying it flat on the desk in front of her.

12 November 1839
*Expended the sum of $3000 on this date, to pay a dowry for Marian Jeannette Durrant to the Carmelite Monastery of Indian Butte, Indiana.*

*19 December 1839*
*Expended the sum of $7.85 as expenses for self and driver to take Marian Durrant to the Carmelite Monastery of Indian Butte, Indiana.*
*Expended the sum of $40 to Absolom Hinder, as retirement as head groom from the Westmont Estate of rural New Albany, Indiana.*
*Expended on the same date the sum of $30, along with a good reference, as severance for Rosemary, former head cook of the Westmont Estate.*
*On the same date, the sum of $20 and reference as severance for Ella, former upstairs girl of the main house at Westmont Estate.*

*1 December 1840*
*Expended the sum of $500 as Christmas donation to the Carmelite Abbey of Indian Butte, Indiana.*

*1 December 1841*
*Expended the sum of $500 as Christmas donation to the Carmelite Abbey of Indian Butte, Indiana.*

*2 February 1842*
*Expended the sum of $200 bridal gift to the Carmelite Abbey of Indian Butte, Indiana, on the occasion of the profession of Marian Jeannette Durrant to the Carmelite vocation.*

*1 December 1842*
*Expended the sum of $500 as Christmas donation to the Carmelite Abbey of Indian Butte, Indiana.*

*2 December 1843*
*The sum of $500 as a Christmas donation to the Carmelite Abbey of Indian Butte, Indiana.*

*1 December 1844*
*The sum of $500 expended as a Christmas donation to the Carmelite Abbey of Indian Butte, Indiana.*

The donations abruptly ceased without explanation, or at least the record of such was abruptly terminated, and Mr. Durrant had been a man careful with records.

The silence grew and lingered as each person in the room considered the information thus revealed. It was Sarah, finally, who had the courage to put the question: "Is it possible that Miss Marian still lives?"

The others simply looked at each other dumbly, tears running silent down more than one pair of cheeks. Finally Catherine asked "Does anyone here know where Indian Butte is?"

"I believe I do," Samuel responded slowly. "If it's where I think it is, it's not a real town, it's just a rural area that I guess someone maybe hoped would someday become a town. If it's as I think, it's downriver maybe 40 or 45 miles. There's a bend in the river there, and oak and cedars rising up above the river. I've only been there once, but I believe that's what someone called it. There was a farm there then, a log house and barn, with a landing built out into the river. I think there was a road somewhere up the hill, but I never saw it."

"I think I know the place you're describing, although I'm not familiar with that name," James offered, his cheeks wet and his color high. "If you like, the *Marian Dee* is ready to travel again. We can go there tomorrow and see. It will take only a few hours to get there by boat, and the ride is comfortable. Do you think..." he queried Miss Emily.

"Please. Please take us. Take us as quickly as you can. If my Marian is alive I must know, please!"

"Of course, Miss Emily. I'll go now and make final preparations. Samuel, if you can bring them down at first light? I believe you and Sarah should accompany us, if you'll bring someone to return the carriage and team— "

Samuel looked at Miss Emily, who gazed back steadfastly. "Of course you and Sarah must go. It's you who saved Marian's child, whom she loved so well." Her voice broke at last, and Catherine and Sarah moved to either side of her, rubbing her shoulders and comforting her with a low murmur.

"And Joel and Jamie must come so Marian can meet them. If she's still there – if we find the monastery and she's still there– " Emily broke down again, but grittily raised her head and finished "If she's still there she may have become accustomed to the place and its ways now, and she may not choose to come home with us, so everyone must go now, so– "

She finally lost control utterly and sobbed. Catherine and Sarah helped her up and took her to her room, where Catherine bathed her face with a soft, cool cloth, and Sarah helped her into a nightgown and tucked her up under a light comforter. Sarah held out a dress, simply cut of a rich blue fabric. "If I remember, blue was Miss Marian's favorite color. This dress should travel well, would you like to wear it tomorrow?"

Emily simply nodded.

"I'll come early in the morning and help you get ready to go," Sarah promised.

"Catherine will be busy with her own kit and Jamie's."

"I've talked with Anna," said Catherine, "and she's agreed to remain here and be in charge tomorrow." Emily nodded again, and Catherine kissed her brow, then turned and blew out the lamp, walking with Sarah to the door.

"Sarah!" Emily called. "Will you please have Samuel send someone to notify Father O'Malley of this and ask if he can accompany us tomorrow? If we're going to a monastery it may be helpful to bring a priest to translate for us, as it were."

"Of course, Miss Emily." And so it was done.

"It's agreed then. Everyone will meet at the pier at first light. Samuel and Sarah will bring Grandmother, and Joel and I will come with Jamie. The boat is very comfortable," she assured Sarah. "We can rest aboard. It certain no one will get much rest tonight."

# Chapter 21

The refurbished engines softly *chuffed* in the predawn chill, but the pilot reached up and pulled the cord to sound the great three-tone chimed whistle to signal to any traffic on the river that the *Marian Dee* was reversing its engines and leaving the dock. No one had been able to rest and they had gathered a good two hours before dawn to begin the journey. As they floated free and turned with the current, the chime sounded again, to tell any sister river vessels that they were now advancing toward the channel, all ahead full.

Dawn chased off the wisps of vapor hanging about the fringe of willows overhanging the river, and brought the bright summer greens of the wooded shores into focus. Samuel lingered with the engineer, learning about the propulsion of the boat, and James fled to the pilothouse, where he watched ahead anxiously, but left the control of the boat in the competent hands of the hired pilot.

Sarah and Catherine encouraged Emily to rest in her cabin, but she also was too anxious to be closed away from the river of hope they traveled, and finally the women settled in comfortable chairs on the bow of the Texas deck, shaded by the pilothouse above. Joel took Jamie, who was wide-awake and unwilling to be held quietly, and sought out the company of Samuel and the engineer.

Father O'Malley looked to be sure that Miss Emily was as comfortable as she might be under the circumstances, and then quietly made his way down and back, finding the company of the other men.

The crew moved about quietly and efficiently. The hawser that had made her fast to the dock was coiled about the capstan, each coil perfectly aligned with the coils above and below it. The spotless decks were swabbed, and the cook brought forth a simple breakfast, suspecting that no one of the tense passengers would tolerate anything heavy.

The galley was scrubbed spotless and a simple lunch was planned, although the cook was new to this boat and its travels, so he was unsure if they'd lunch aboard or ashore. He was ready in either case, and no matter what the disposition of the passengers he was prepared to feed the crew.

~ ~ ~

Father O'Maine intoned "*Ite missa est*," and the Mass was finished. He'd just left the enclosure when he stopped short, staring down toward the river.

"Mother Clare, I believe you should see this," he suggested, frowning. He'd hastened to the refectory, where the nuns would be sharing their breakfast in silence, and motioned for her to come away into the hall. He led her outside the enclosure, toward the bench she favored for meditation in good weather, and she was stopped short, as the priest had been.

Clare counted them again, nine people, seven white and two black. Five men and four women. She easily recognized Martha and Robert Stevens, whom she saw from time to time, both in the abbey and below, in their farmyard.

One old-looking woman walked up the slope with them, a white woman, and one young white woman, she with strawberry blond hair. The young woman carried an infant, an infant with red-gold hair. A mature-looking white man had hair that had faded somewhat and receded a bit, but it was still clearly red. Hauntingly familiar red hair.

The younger white man had dark hair and nothing to remind her of anything – of anyone – familiar, and the fourth man wore the cassock and collar of a priest.

The black man and black woman walked hand in hand, both helping the older white woman from time to time. The black couple looked familiar, they looked like – like both grayed somewhat, but they were, they certainly were, Sarah and her Samuel.

The tall, red-haired man – had she forgotten him – could she ever forget him? No, never! It could not be, but it was, it was James! The young woman then, she realized as the group reached the clearing where the priest and the nun waited, was Catherine. Her own–

"Catherine? Is it truly you? Oh, my darling Catherine!"

Hitching her robe, she ran across the separation and met Catherine, who was suddenly sobbing "Momma! Momma! It is you, after so long, it is truly you!" They held the embrace and then separated again to arms' lengths, to take in every feature, each of the other.

Clare then became fully aware of her mother, standing silent and afraid, and folded her into her embrace, holding the dear cheek against hers for a lingering moment, shifting her attention at last to the red-haired man, who stood awash in tears, seeing again the beloved at last.

197

"James. Beloved, beloved James." She stood on tiptoe and kissed his cheek lightly, caressing his other cheek with her palm. "How did you finally find me?" she asked, shaken finally by her own sobs.

"Your father died sixteen years ago," Emily said. "His secret was kept until Catherine unlocked it yesterday. Well, strictly speaking, Joel unlocked it for us— "

"Mother, may I present my husband, Joel Archibald Benson, and our son, James Christopher Benson, called Jamie." The sturdy baby looked quizzically at the nun and then, without warning, dived into her arms.

"Oh, Catherine! This feels so like holding you when you were a baby. You were such a treasure! I was so broken-hearted when I lost you!"

Father O'Malley moved quietly to the side of the baffled Father O'Maine, and quietly explained the circumstances of the family rift and the astonishing discovery yesterday of the fate of Marian and the likely location of the Abbey.

"Shall we go inside?" Father O'Maine asked. "That might be somewhat more comfortable than standing here in the woods— "

"Please, yes, come inside where we can be comfortable." The sisters had finished their breakfast during the reunion outside, and had separated to their various tasks for the morning, so the group was led into the refectory. "Please find seats and make yourselves comfortable," Mother Clare requested. "May we offer you refreshment?"

Catherine assured her mother that they had breakfasted on the riverboat. Clare suddenly became aware of the boat. "It is the boat with blue trim, isn't it? The *Marian Dee?*"

"Yes," James responded. "It's the *Marian Dee*. I bought her not long after I was told you'd died. I couldn't bear the loss. She's always kept me in mind of you and of the love we shared," James continued.

"I've noticed her many times over the years, put into the Stevens' landing to load wood. I thought it nice that it was trimmed in my favorite color and wore the name I'd borne in family life, but I never considered that it might have been so called for *me*. I just found it a pleasant facet of life here, to have the beauty of the woods and the foreverness of the river below, and then an attractive riverboat with a lovely chime whistle and a name that recalled warm memories of being well-loved in childhood," she finished, laying a warm hand on her mother's cheek and bending to caress her again, cheek-to-cheek.

"And I was drawn to this place the first time I put in below, and each time since then. I think in the beginning that is primarily why I always stopped here for wood. Then I got acquainted with the Stevens and came then to visit with them and know I'd always get everything I paid for, as well as to experience the peace that emanates from the monastery here."

Robert and Martha had held back, but Mother Clare noticed and brought them into the gathering. "Surely you are family now also," she said. "I believe you played an important role in helping us find one another again. Had James not come often to your landing so many times over the years he would have been less likely to recognize the location so you could come so quickly."

When the family had talked and renewed their relationships for an hour or two or three, Mother Clare realized there was other family in the precincts who had not yet been introduced and included. Leaving for a moment, she rang the bell by the front gate that was used to call together the community for prayer and meals. As they gathered in the foyer, she led them to the refectory.

"My dear sisters," she introduced them, "please meet the family that gave me life so I might share it with you. My dear mother, Emily Durrant. The loves of my life, James Mason and our daughter, Catherine. Our most dearly beloved daughter– " she said tenderly, loving the young woman again with her moist eyes.

"Sarah, my companion and the foster mother of Catherine when I could no longer care for her, her husband and Catherine's foster father, Samuel. Catherine's husband, Joel Benson and their son, James Christopher, called Jamie to distinguish him from his grandfather here. The family pastor, Father O'Malley, whom I understand has played a large role in the healing of a great deal of pain in the family. The Stevens you know, of course."

"Of course," smiled Sister Martha. "My own sister in name," she explained. Martha Stevens agreed with a smile of her own and the two joined hands.

Mother Clare lovingly introduced each of the other nuns, saying a few words about each to help memorialize them to her family.

"I believe some explanation is due the good sisters," Miss Emily interjected. As the group grew quiet, sensing the pain in the woman, she began to tell the story so familiar to most of them.

"Our son Anson and Marian, our daughter," gesturing toward Mother Clare, "met James while visiting the riverfront one day..." She told the tale gently, making no excuse for herself or Edward, and giving large credit to Sarah, Samuel and Father O'Malley.

"Had Father not intervened," she said, "I was ready to send Catherine back into the terrible isolation where she'd spent most of her childhood." Not even James had been aware of the room with the slit of a window until then. His expression was beginning to change from shock to anger, when she said simply how she'd tried to do penance for her sin, spending long hours kneeling in that same room, until forbidden to do so by Father O'Malley.

Emily had James tell Marian and the others of the death of Anson. He added, "I'd believed for years that Marian also had died," and told the story of his discovery of Catherine. He spoke particular gratitude to Samuel, who had fathered the child he had not known of until past her need for a childhood father.

Sister Naomi, who cooked for the community, slipped away to prepare lunch for everyone and Martha Stevens, divining her purpose, joined her in the kitchen. They quickly assembled a simple repast. Sarah, seeing that Martha also had slipped from the group, joined them in time to help carry the trays of food to the refectory, where everyone was quickly served.

James spoke quietly to Father O'Maine, who quickly agreed with the suggestion. "Since this has become a feast day for the Carmelite community and newfound – or newly rediscovered – friends and family, Captain Mason has invited everyone to be his guest on the riverboat the *Marian Dee*. Is that agreeable?"

The nuns acceded eagerly. The community then repaired down the hill to the landing, with James assisting Sister Margaret, an older woman who had difficulty clambering down the path. She clasped his hand easily and was warmed by his sheltering arm around her shoulder. Looking mischievous, she announced to the group, "Look! I've found a beau at last!" They were still giggling as James led them up the stage.

They put out into the channel and beat upstream until midafternoon, when James signaled the pilot to come about. James stood silent behind the community of sisters as they shared Vespers with the family.

Father O'Malley in particular was touched by his inclusion into the monastic activity. He prayed the Liturgy of the Hours each day as his holy Office, but he'd not shared such with a community since he'd left seminary years before, and even then, the Office was often a solitary meeting with his Lord. The power vibrant in the communal Office was amazing and humbling.

Sister Mary Joseph asked for a few moments after the completion of Vespers. "When I came to the monastery I was lost and terrified and certain that my real life was over. I had given birth to a child, a wonderful, beautiful little one whom I called Erin Regina." Here she stopped briefly, choked by the pain of her loss.

"My parents believed the man with whom I'd shared the intimacy which brought into being that lovely babe was unworthy of our family. They forced him to leave town and confined me until after the birth of Erin. After only two brief months with her– " a sob escaped "– my mother announced that they had found a couple in a distant city to adopt Erin. I protested, and they took her from me. My mother locked my in my room while my father took my little one away forever.

"My father then brought me here, believing I should do a lifetime of penance for my carnal sin. I came at night – my father rang the bell and then walked away from me, back into the darkness.

"Mother Clare gave me back my sanity. Now I understand how she recognized and honored my agony: she'd experienced her own. I believed I was spoiled and worthless, as my parents had led me to believe. It was Mother Clare who encouraged me, who lent me strength, who taught me of the loving care for us that God gives so freely to all who can accept. Because she led me gently – but *persistantly!*" With a quick smile at Mother Clare, "I am here today, a woman of joy and serenity.

"My Erin – if her parents chose to keep that name for her – will now be coming into her own young womanhood, wherever she may be. I pray that her parents have had the wisdom to lead her into a knowledge of God's love. I could not have done so had I kept her, for I lacked that understanding myself.

"I would like to thank the family of Mother Clare for sharing so deeply their pain and love with us today. While I have of course shared this in confession," nodding at Father O'Maine, "only the gifts of this day have given me the freedom to share myself with my sisters, and to be able to finally thank Mother Clare, my guardian and benefactor."

Sister Mary Joseph walked to Mother Clare and clasped her hands, tears rolling freely now down her cheeks. Mother Clare accepted the silent tribute and then, reaching out, gently gathered Mary Joseph into an embrace, kissing both of her cheeks.

As Sister Mary Joseph returned to her place among the other sisters, Mother Mary Clare moved to the front of the group. "Beloved," she said. "All of you are so beloved of me. I will forever be grateful for each of you, and for the matchless gift of this day. Mother, James, Catherine," she touched each of them with a loving look, going to each among the family group in spirit and loving them tenderly.

"I will treasure forever each of you, as I will treasure forever this day.

When I was brought to the abbey, I believed I'd been torn from the life I was meant to live. Only when I'd been here a while and came to acquaintance with the Silence, did I realize that the events of my life that had seemed so tragic were in truth God's way of bringing me home.

"This is my home," gesturing toward the woods and the monastery. "You are all my family," motioning toward her mother, Sarah and the others. "These also," signifying the community of nuns, "are my sisters, my family. I have been unusually blessed throughout my life. Few nuns," with a special, warm smile for Sister Mary Joseph, "know the joy of giving birth and holding in our arms that wonderful infant," sending a loving glance at Catherine.

"Few families have the treasure within of belonging with a community of those so specially chosen by God as Carmelites. This is forever your treasure," to Emily and the others. "You will be a part of every Office of prayer, of every Mass, of many silent, personal moments that those of this community spend daily with our Lord. This will always be also your home, to carry back into your worlds within your hearts."

Mother Clare reached out and claimed Jamie from his father. "A special blessing here for this beautiful grandson and his father. You carry a matchless name," glancing at James, "and heritage. You, little one, will be blessed in all your ways, in all your days. When I am privileged to go and meet my Lord in person, you will be the treasure I bring Him in my heart. My full mother's, my grandmother's heart.

"You," taking James' hand, "are the love of my life. No Lover or Groom less than the Son of God Himself, could supplant you in my heart. And even He has not taken your place; He has only given me room in my heart to take His own place, while leaving yours reserved for you alone.

"I suggest that we share freely our supper together. I ask each and all that we may enter the Silence together with the evening Vigil. Still in silence then, we sisters will take our leave of you, beloved family. Perhaps you would like to share with us as we return to our enclosure by keeping a silence yourselves. As you choose, of course.

"We offer our gratitude to the crew of the *Marian Dee*. You keep the boat so beautifully clean and trim, and you have given us your respectful attention on this most unusual cruise today. I'm sure we're the first nuns some of you have seen," with an impish grin, "so perhaps we've been able to dispatch some of the old crow or old witch myths– "

This sally was received with a few abashed grins and sideways looks at each other, as the men shuffled their feet. "You, of course, have abolished the myth of the dirty sailor for us," she added, unable to resist teasing the willing. "To the cook, our thanks for what we know will be a memorable meal. Some of us may be too busy to pay much attention to the food, but we want you to know we appreciate your work and care."

Supper was subdued by anticipation of the separation to come. The two groups blended into one, with nuns sitting among family and vice versa, as if they were daily companions. There were many gentle touches among the individuals seated at tables made festive by the crew on the Texas deck. There were moments already of silence as the meal was finished, before the final prayers in common.

Mother Clare rose from her table and addressed the group. "My love and my blessing to each of you. Father O'Malley and Father O'Maine, will you close our supper with your blessings?"

The two priests rose and faced the group. "We offer our joy and our sorrow to the Lord," said Father O'Malley. "And we bring to you the special blessing of the Lord, in the name of the Father, the Son, and the Holy Ghost," as both men signed the cross over the group. Father O'Malley noticed that the first mate and a few others of the crew had knelt beside the starboard rail to receive the blessing also.

When the community had been blessed, Father O'Maine turned to his companion. "My blessing and the Kiss of Peace for you, my dear brother," embracing him cheek to cheek. They shared a long look and handclasp and retired to the rear of the group.

Sister Margaret, the elder of the Carmelite community, rose and approached Emily. "My special blessing to you, my dear. Your pain is washed away and your joy is complete. May you have always, peace and all good things for you and yours," and she leaned forward, pressing her dry cheeks to one and then the other of Emily's damp ones.

The Office of Vigil – sacred, confident, joyful readings – was shared and the community again became two groups, the nuns moving together toward the ladder to reach the boiler deck and the landing stage. Mother Clare paused and kissed again the forehead of Jamie, and gazed a final time at the family assembled. While many shed tears, all felt the peace of the moment.

Mother Clare rejoined her community, and they left the steamer, climbing again the hill toward the enclosure of the abbey. The family, who had followed them to the open bow of the boiler deck, where the gangway had been winched down to meet the Stevens' pier, watched the procession. And to all came, softly, the Silence.

Printed in the United States
868700005B